MW01611482

Novels by Annabelle Lewis

The Carrows Family Chronicles

Charlotte McGee, Book 1

Titan Takedown, Book 2

Carrows Justice, Book 3

The Bad Penny, Book 4

Fisher of Men, Book 5

Mr. Hyde, Book 6

Short Story

Caliburnus

DEAD CAT, RUN

ANNABELLE LEWIS

Publisher's Note

This book is a work of fiction. People, characters, places, events, and situations are the product of the author's imagination. Some historical names, celebrity names, and actual venues appear in the novel in order to place the story in a historic or modern cultural perspective, but these names are used in an imaginary context and do not suggest that any of the incidents ever happened, or the celebrities endorse the work, or participated in any way.

Contact Annabelle at annabellelewisauthor@gmail.com

Text Copyright ©2021 Annabelle Lewis
All rights reserved.
ISBN-13: 978-1-7343757-1-8

First Edition
Publisher: PePe Press
Cover Design: JD&J Design LLC
Interior Design: Manon Lavoie

Dedication

For Boozer, Max, and Gemma.
Your purpose is no mystery.

Prologue

Clotho and her sisters, Lachesis and Atropos, looked down from the heavens unto the ancient city of Cumae near the Tyrrhenian Sea, and into the long trapezoidal passage and the Cave of the Cumaean Sybil. The spacious cavern with its one hundred openings of light was at last silent.

The sisters considered the chamber from their perch on Mount Olympus and watched Clotho weave life from her distaff. Lachesis said, "Our father, Apollo, sought the Sybil's virginity in exchange for a wish. Foolish, she gathered up the sand, wishing for a life with as many years as the grains in her hand."

Clotho finished the tale. "But when she ultimately refused his request, he granted her life without eternal youth. His vengeance has made her suffer enough. A thousand years she lived, wasting to nothing but dust." Clotho weaved the *Book of Fate* as she pondered the sad and twisted life of the Cumaean Sybil. "It is time for this child, with the gift of prophecy and seeing, to finally live again. Always. The gods have willed it. She was meant to help man. She is beyond us. She is the destiny of goodness. It was written."

Lachesis nodded in agreement as she measured the long thread of this destiny's life. She frowned at the globe of the heavens as she measured. "Apollo will know she lives. He will seek his vengeance again."

Clotho's back bent with the heavy burden of that truth. Finishing her task, she stopped weaving. "Then let the games begin."

Atropos, the eldest of the three sisters of fate, the sister of inevitable death, stepped forward with her shears and snipped the thread in her sister's hand. "Fate has spoken."

Present Day

BOSTON

Chapter 1

Sidrah Keeling shook her head with impatience and reluctantly closed her eyes. She immediately regretted it. Visions of her dream—no, *nightmare*—from the evening before flashed once again, fresh and unbidden. A sickly sweat broke out on her neck, and her eyes popped open. She'd spent all morning trying to erase the powerful episode. She'd even instructed Marta to remove the sweat-stained sheets on her bed before she left the house.

"That's all I have, Detective. I'm sorry," she said.

Sitting in station D-4 of the Boston Police Department serving the South End, Detective Bodine challenged her. His mouth pressed into a hard line, and he shook his head. "It's not enough. Do you realize how many men named Brian are out there?"

Sidrah's stomach roiled; she *would not* lose her composure. "I gave you more than that." She tapped her finger on his desk, emphasizing her contribution. "Truck. Black truck. Old black truck. Ford. White guy with a wedding ring. He was casing a Pride Convenience store, looking at cameras. He drinks coffee. Eats donuts."

"Donuts!" the detective said, then glanced behind him at the smirking face of a cop in a nearby cubicle.

Sidrah caught the look as well and gave the cop a large fake smile. Aware that her presence was viewed with contempt by doubters, she turned back to Bodine. "Screw you. I also gave you a fucking name and the tat. That's definitely worth something."

Detective Bodine sat back. At length, he nodded. "It's helpful. But not until we catch him."

Sidrah grabbed her bag off the floor, ready to leave. She'd tried. That's all anyone should ever ask of her. They had no idea how painful it was to crawl into the headspace of a twisted person. She hadn't seen the guy's face, but she'd felt his desires. He was burning up with them. He was searching for a victim. Stalking one. He wouldn't stop until he found her. She knew it, and so did the police. They were desperate, which was the only reason Bodine had reached out to her.

She put her hand in her large tote and extracted a baggie containing a button. She placed it on his desk. "Here's your evidence back. All I can say is that you've got the right guy here. He's dangerous. He's sick. He's going to rape again. He's violent."

"Which is exactly why you have to try again, Sidrah." He leaned forward and whispered, "Someone out there is going to get hurt."

Sidrah felt a pressure behind her eyes as she reluctantly closed them to try again. She'd attempt one last time to remember details from the dream. Tears, unbidden, formed behind her lids, most likely bent on ruining her makeup. *Damn it. Damn it.* She forced herself to keep them closed— searching, searching. Her eyes snapped open, the back of her fingers automatically going to her eyes to blot the mascara before it ran. "He's got a ball cap. I could see it in the mirror. Blue cap. Says *Wembley.* And a logo."

She jumped up. "I'm sorry. That's all I have."

Detective Bodine grabbed her hand. "Thank you, Sidrah. If you think of anything more, you'll call, right?"

She gave him a tight nod, grabbed her discarded jacket off the back of the chair, and walked out. Many eyes followed her. She felt them all. *Dammit.* She hated the stares—the you're-a-freak ones. For one reason or another, she'd dealt with them all of her life.

Sidrah burst out of the police station and took a big breath of the cold, clear air, then shrugged on her jacket. She walked with purpose toward her car, the tallness of her heels giving her a moment of worry as she avoided a lingering patch of ice. Thankfully, winter was almost over. Reaching her new Mercedes, she felt a moment of solid comfort, safe almost, as she unlocked the door with her key fob and got inside. The engine started, and she breathed deeply and pulled down the visor to inspect her face.

"Dammit, Sidrah. You did the best you could. You did," she counseled herself and shoved a shaky hand into her bag. She yanked a clean tissue from a pack and placed it between her lashes, adjusting them back into position and soaking up the last of the tears. "Come on, girl. Pull it together. You gave them some good stuff. They'll find him. In the mean- time, you've got a man to meet."

She snapped the visor mirror back into position and put

on her sunglasses. After a quick look around, she backed out of her parking spot, then tore out of the police lot. Some dick in uniform gave her a look. *Jump in the car and follow me, cop. I dare you.*

With a laugh, she visualized the chase, brightening as she sped off down the Boston street. Once again, she'd used her gift to pay it forward, laying a metaphorical wreath on the altar of whatever power had bestowed it, but now it was her turn. She had a luncheon with her investment broker, and the man was worth impressing. It was a shame he was so damned nerdy.

Chapter 2

———

Jenny sat on the uncomfortable stool in the Pride Convenience and flipped through the gossip rag, ogling all the celebrity side-by-side before-and-after lip-filler treatments. It gave her the willies to think about having needles injected into her lips, or anywhere else, for that matter.

Jenny knew reading the magazines from the racks was a small mutiny that bothered Mr. Thompson, the owner, but she didn't care. He needed her as much as she needed him. She smiled at the security camera in the corner—no one around to see her—and blew a big bubble from the wad of gum in her mouth—another infraction—and then waved at the camera.

Giggling, she flipped through the pages of the magazine as she did a mental checklist of the tasks she was supposed to accomplish before the next shift came in to relieve her. All done. Fresh coffee was percolating at the brewing station.

She yawned and chewed her gum. Five a.m. couldn't get here fast enough. She'd have enough time for a few hours' sleep before afternoon classes. Being a senior in high school had a few nominal good points. The school administration, apparently weary of enforcement by the time students were seniors, allowed some of them to phone in their assignments and only attend class in the afternoons. Thankfully, she was all caught up on her homework; the work came easy for her.

She ran a hand down her long ponytail, realizing she'd feel better if she took a quick shower before hitting the sack. Her thick blond hair had a natural wave to it when it air-dried and didn't require styling. She *could*, maybe she even *should*, but she didn't feel the need to bother too much with her appearance. The more invisible she was, the better. It was safer that way, especially when walking down the hormone-infused, hyper-scrutinized hallways of Palmer High School. She couldn't wait to see the last of that place. But she had yet to decide where she was going when the ordeal was over.

She glanced up as the door opened, and a guy wearing a hat came in. He didn't look at her; he just kept his head down as he walked toward the restrooms. That was odd. Most people at least glanced at her, especially in the middle of the night, when they were usually the only two humans inside the small convenience store. She looked at the clock. Five minutes before Harry arrived. Hopefully, he wouldn't be late for his shift.

As if on cue, the door opened again. This time, it was Harry. The older man looked tired, but he waved as he walked through the gap and behind the long counter. "Good morning, Jenny," he said.

"Mornin', Harry," she said as she hopped off her stool. She reached under the counter and tapped her employee number into a small machine to clock out. Then, she spit her gum into the trash. "You good?" she asked as she watched him stow his jacket and lunchbox under the counter. "I got everything going."

Harry gave her a warm smile. He was a nice man, mostly retired, but he worked part-time for some extra cash.

"I'm sure you did, young lady. Thank you for that."

Jenny smiled at him as she grabbed her jacket and walked toward the door. "See you around, Harry." She waved as she left.

Once outside, she walked briskly to her car in the chilly air. Parked around the corner in the area Mr. Thompson had officially designated as out of the way from customer traffic, her small beat-up Mazda was sandwiched between Harry's car and an old black pickup. It was strange that the customer inside had parked back there. Her keys were already out and ready as her dad had often instructed, but just as she reached the car door, she froze. A strong hand clamped down on her mouth, and a large body seized her.

"Get in the truck," the man said, manipulating her with a force she couldn't fight. Before she could do anything, she was inside his pickup, a knife to her throat. "Fucking scream, and you die," he said.

With her heart hammering in her chest, she complied as he pulled his hand from her mouth. He slammed the truck door shut. Her hands leaped to it, but the door was locked. She fumbled with the buttons, unable to get anything going as the guy opened the driver's door and got in. Once more, he pushed the knife to her face, then shoved her down toward the floorboard. "Get down there. Stay down, or you die. You fucking die! You hear me?"

She could barely see his face through her tears, and even though she did what she was told, he forced her head down further. The truck roared to life, its rumble running through her body as she huddled on the floorboard, her head on the truck's seat. She glanced at him but came away with an eyeful of knife as the guy focused on driving one-handed, the knife positioned near her head.

No time to process all the details as they drove. She couldn't believe this was happening. It was a zig she hadn't seen coming.

Chapter 3

Max humped his way through the Wellesley College campus center, yanking his backpack onto his shoulder when it began to slide. Hungry—no, scratch that, ravenous—he snarled in frustration that he couldn't jump in line at the pizza stand and grab a slice. He'd need to wait until he got home. He frowned, remembering he had no ready food there either. As he rounded past the heavenly smells from the greasy Chinese buffet, someone called his name, and he slowed.

"Professor Dyer," a girl said.

Inwardly, he rolled his eyes but stopped, forcing a look of tolerance onto his face. He didn't recognize the student, but then, he usually didn't. It was better to avoid eye contact with the nubile freshmen. Many young girls throughout his career had presumed there was something other than scholarly interest lurking there. He tried everything he could to discourage them.

Now, though, forced to a standstill in their territory, he could have almost predicted what would happen next.

Once he stopped, not one, but several young, eager smiling faces peered up at him with their batting lashes and flirty looks. It was exhausting.

"What is it?" he practically barked.

"Oh, sorry," the one who'd spoken said.

"Office hours are posted online," he said roughly. Regrettably, he only saw looming interest and blushing cheeks. The heat rising around the group was practically tangible. He had to get out of there. He began walking away, but out of guilt, he turned his head back. "Make an appointment. I'll speak to you then."

Did he hear giggles? *For God's sake. Don't look back again.* He wondered for the thousandth time if working at a women's liberal arts college was a bad idea.

He cleared the union without further intrusions and got out into the street. He put his head down as he walked across campus, then grabbed a beanie out of his coat pocket and shoved it on. No need to bother with the gloves. He wouldn't be touching anyone.

Looking forward to getting home, he rounded the corner of a busy street near his parking lot and ran into a group of men in suits. His backpack fell to the ground, which caused some of his items to spill out. He cursed softly as one of the men knelt to help him retrieve his gear. But then, out of nowhere, a large reddish dog shot between them, grabbed a pair of his gloves, and took off.

"Hey!" Max stood and then ran after the dog. Not more than a few long strides later, the game of chase stopped. He stared with horror as the dog ran into the street, mindless of the oncoming traffic.

"No!" He threw up his hand and yelled. His heart in his mouth, he watched in slow motion as a car slammed into the dog. He dropped his pack on the sidewalk, ran into the street, and screamed at the traffic. Everywhere cars came to a screeching halt.

His pulse raced, tears choking him as he reached the dog, hesitating only a second before he laid his hands—uncovered—without thinking, onto the soft fur. The gloves the dog had been carrying lay near her front leg, which was bent at an odd angle. Blood, too, was coming from somewhere.

"My God," Max cried. His hands, *his uncovered hands,* ran down the dog's body—without receiving a vision. Marveling at the empty sensation, he gently touched the dog's face. The beautiful beast looked at him and released a small, pitiful whimper. She licked Max's hand softly and closed her eyes.

Max closed his eyes, and momentarily dropped his head back with the wonder of the moment before he regained his senses and began to scream at the driver, who had been hovering nearby. He gently stroked the dog, cooing to her with tender words. *Where are her tags? Where had she come from?*

The only answer he had was that no one nearby came running to claim her for their own. From that moment on, Max took charge, yelling instructions. He'd see that the dog got help. Nothing in the world was more important.

MAX DYER SAT in the vet's office, his head in his hands, safely gloved now, and waited. The dog had been in x-ray and examination for what seemed a long time, but at least she wasn't dead. The man who'd hit her had helped Max put the dog into Max's car, and he'd driven her to the vet. With his large frame, he'd barged in the front door, the dog in his arms—whether unconscious or dead he didn't yet know. He'd yelled once again for help.

He'd never felt panic, or any intense emotion, over an animal before, never having had pets of his own. Most of them, he only feared. Because canines, humans, or whatever the fuck kind of creature that roamed the planet, all of them had a history. And they shared themselves freely, without invitation, to Max whenever he touched them.

Until this dog. He'd felt nothing when he'd touched her. It was almost as if the dog had no history. As if she'd newly arrived, whooshed into the world, and lit on his doorstep without previous thought or feeling. He realized the dog had feelings, but the miracle of not sharing them with him was new.

Some people might consider his wretched powers a gift. They were assholes. They didn't know what they were talking about. His life had been anchored to his abilities, which formed him, hurt him, and prevented him from being normal. He'd encountered no one on earth with a similar predicament, and the thoughts of *why him* and *what the fuck happened to him* were his big damn secretive burdens to carry.

He hung his head with guilt, realizing that he'd never been able to use his gift to help those who needed answers—unsolved crimes, missing persons. The ability to see the past could be valuable to others, but it was hard to wrangle his visions, and he'd never tried. It might be time to change that, but he didn't know who he could trust or how to begin.

But now this dog. The blessing! The relief of not being shocked, of just touching another being, overwhelmed him. But a dog couldn't speak.

She couldn't die. She just couldn't.

"Mr. Dyer," the vet said, walking into the room.

Max shot out of his chair. "How is she?"

The vet nodded. "Alive. Fairly good, considering. Her internal organs seem intact; her pressure is steady. We've got her sedated."

"Her leg . . ." Max interrupted.

"Yes. I'm afraid that will require surgery. It's a significant break. I understand you brought her here, but she's not your dog?"

"No. Does she have a chip?"

The vet shook his head. "No. So we're at a juncture. At this moment, someone needs to make a decision. Do you want us to proceed with the surgical repair? Are you willing to take responsibility? I'm afraid the healing may be difficult. Depending on their temperament, some dogs don't do well in the recovery phase for an injury like this. She'll need quite a lot of care and treatment."

Max inhaled with relief. "I'll pay for it. She's mine."

The vet cocked his head. "I see you've formed an emotional attachment. Have you considered that someone else might claim her? May argue that point? They may claim her but not reimburse you. The costs will be substantial."

Max gave him a forceful look. "She's mine. I'll take good care of her."

The vet glanced at his nurse, who had followed him out. She was staring up at Max with what looked like adoration. *God.*

"All right then, Mr. Dyer. We'll get her into surgery. She'll be with us through the night. Leave your information at the desk, and we'll be in touch."

Max shook his head. "I'm staying. How long do you think she'll be?"

The vet shrugged. "I don't know. A few hours. It depends on what happens when I get in there. She's a young dog. Maybe one year old. Her health, otherwise, seems to be good." He paused for a moment. "What name would you like to give her, Mr. Dyer?"

Max blinked. He'd never named a dog before. He couldn't think of anything special on the spot. "How about Bones."

"Bones," said the vet. He put out his hand to shake.

Max looked down at it, his own hand gloved. He safely embraced it and swallowed hard, giving the doctor a firm shake.

The vet nodded. "She'll be okay, Mr. Dyer. Bones. She's made of sturdy stuff."

Chapter 4

J*enny, Jeeennny . . .* She pulled back from the sickening need to vomit and reminded herself to focus on her predicament. The man was going to hurt her. No question. Rape, kill, maybe both. She had to figure this out. She took inventory of her assets. Feeling her name badge pressed into her chest while sandwiched on the floorboard, she thought with regret that Mr. Thompson had chosen to go with nametags connected by two magnets. One that closed with a pin could have been useful. When the big moment came, maybe she could have shoved it into his carotid. But no. Other than her useless magnet, she had no weapons other than her mind.

The guy had ripped her purse out of her hands and thrown it behind him into the truck's roomy back seat. If there was anything else she could recall from her one-second glance around the truck, it was negligible.

She had to focus. Her life depended on it, but it was incredibly hard. In the past, every time a zig had been thrown at her, a zag always presented itself soon after. It was what she was used to. It's what made her "oddly" optimistic. *Odd* was her mother's word. Funny how one word, spoken so few times in her life by a woman she'd spent so little time with, had made such an impression.

She was still the "odd" girl in her mind, and the word had done its damage. Or maybe not. There were a zig and zag to that too. The zig—or the bad part, was her mother calling her odd. The zag—or the good part—was that the impression, the sheer weight of that word on her small soul, had given her social caution. People looked at her like she was a freak. It was a step away from odd, but not in a good direction.

Now she'd been given a terrible zig. Where was the zag? How would it be delivered? She knew it was coming. *Knew it.* Down in her bones. She only had to focus on finding it. Hone in on her déjà vu. Concentrate on her premonitions. Her very own déjà vu on crack. She knew how to purposefully use it, but most of the time, she tried hard not to. Things mostly came to her, unbidden. Now, though, she needed it badly. It was the only big gun in her arsenal.

The man was practically panting. His acrid smell filled the truck, repulsing her. How much time did she have before he stopped driving? Where was he taking her?

She tried to tune him out—his energy and his stink—to *focus on the situation.* But then she stopped. What would she see? Her death? Her rape? No! There was a zag coming! She needed to believe that. Don't fear the gift. *Use it, Jenny.*

She squeezed her eyes closed as tightly as they would go and let her arms fall, one hand slipping between the seat and the door. And zag. Just like that, her left hand by the door felt something metal. And loose. And long. A knife. Where the eff that knife had come from or where the eff it had been, who knew. But she now had it. A small smile came to her lips as she grasped it. When she did, she saw the future. Her gift, her crack baby, working. Mr. Badass Rapist wouldn't be getting a simple name badge pin in the carotid. He had something much better coming his way, aimed directly at his balls.

The only problem was, she also caught a glimpse of herself when it happened. She had no pants on.

The truck shook, the ride turning rough as they left a paved road and drove onto some kind of gravel. The guy came to an abrupt stop, forcing her head to be jerked back from the seat. He got out, came to her side, and wrenched open the door.

"Get out," he barked.

Her face was wet with tears as a melon-sized lump strangled her breathing. She got out of the truck and discovered that he'd brought her to an old barn. The enormity of her problem hit her.

There was no one around. Not a single person in sight. Wherever they were, the place had long ago been abandoned. He pushed her inside the barn-like structure.

"Get on the blanket," he ordered.

A nubby wool blanket waited on the ground, and he pushed her toward it.

She stumbled, her eyes looking up to a broken window, its jagged glass like snarling fangs. A cold wind blew through the deadly spikes, the barn, a creepy funhouse of evil. She turned to stare at him in mock defiance, the long blade shoved up the sleeve of her coat, held in place by the elastic cuffs. Her opponent was large; she was small. He outweighed her by at least a hundred pounds. And now they were face-to-face. She could see him, his face greasy and grotesque, as he flung his blue hat in the corner and yelled at her.

"Take it off. Everything. Now!"

He held the knife in front of him like a character in an Indiana Jones movie, tossing it side to side like he was playing a terrifying game of catch while his prey squirmed before him.

She leaned over and pulled off a shoe, trembling as she grasped the second one, then pushed them both to the side. She had to do something!

"What's your name?" She almost peed her pants, her voice quivering as she spoke. Her entire body trembled, working from a different set of instructions than what she was giving to her brain. She was losing control.

He sneered. "Now, why would I tell you that?"

Her teeth chattered, not only from emotion, but from the chill in the barn, and she noticed that he had strange teeth. Something about them seemed unnatural, like they were too big for his mouth. He licked his lips as he stared, and glistening drool lingered on them. He reached up and swiped it with the back of his sleeve.

Gesturing with the knife, he said, "Your pants, little whore."

Little whore? Maybe he had the wrong girl. "I'm not a whore," she said.

"Your fucking pants!" he roared. He began touching himself.

Jenny slid her jeans off. Her trembles grew. Would she die by freezing to death or from shock? She had to calm herself. She had to.

How was she going to stab him? She'd seen it! She knew it was coming. She'd seen him lying on the ground, blood pooling. She'd heard his screams. She'd seen him trying to pull the knife out! She must have stuck it in far. Hard. Really hard. With force. The only way that was going to happen was for him to be close to her. The thought of it made her sick, and she gagged on a bit of vomit.

She kneeled and crossed her arms over her chest. Her right hand slid inside the arm of the other sleeve, and she moved the knife, unseen, to her right hand—her dominant. With her left, she helped push it up into place.

The guy was having a field day in front of her, going to town with his hand down his pants. He practically didn't need her. She swallowed again, realizing how stupid that was. For all she knew, he had plans to kill her when he finished.

She had to get him close. "You drop your pants now," she chattered out.

He smiled. His mouthful of crooked teeth seemed to grow like descending fangs. He slowly bent over and took off his shoes. "We going to play doctor, little girl? Am I going to examine you?"

She nodded, her head bobbing over and over with fright and cold, like she was having a small seizure. She almost couldn't stop it.

He dropped his pants. Stripped bare from the waist down, he walked toward her. Between the knife and his penis, she now had two items pointing directly at her. As he came close, closer, she searched desperately within herself, focusing all her strength on giving him a big smile. God knew how it actually looked, but it stopped him. Pretty damn close. From her position, she was able to whip out the knife and plunge it into him. It crunched like it was going into a head of cabbage.

Zag. It was done. He screamed as if the world had just exploded. She picked up his knife, the one he'd dropped, and grabbed her shoes and pants. She then took his pants from the puddle on the floor and ran like hell. Once outside, she ran to the truck and threw his pants on the ground. Searching for the keys, she cried, snot running down her nose and over her mouth as she realized they weren't there. She looked over her shoulder. Not seeing him, she opened the truck and looked inside. The keys were in the ignition.

She leaped in. The truck started, and like that, she was off, screaming with hysteria all the way to the Palmer Police Station.

———————

Now what's happening? Jenny lay staring at the ceiling in the hospital emergency bay. After she'd presented herself, hysterical, at the police station and told them where to go, they'd brought her to the hospital. Now, people came in and out of her small space, and all she wanted to do was go home and crawl under a rock.

She wanted to see her dad. *Daddy!* He was on his way. How was he going to react when he found out what had happened? She worried about how he was going to take it. At least they'd be in a hospital for that scene.

The curtains of her bay were mercifully closed now, and she rolled onto her side. A kind nurse had given her several heated blankets, and she threw one of them over her head as she squeezed her body into the fetal position and thought about the past few hours.

But she didn't want to think about it. She'd never been so afraid in her life. The cops told her she'd been brave. At least, some of them had. One or two had been reluctant when she'd first appeared. She'd seen it in their eyes. Who were they? Why were they judging her, questioning her like she'd done something wrong for stabbing the guy in the balls? What was wrong with them?

She'd almost been raped. Almost. Under the blankets, she covered her face with her hands and began to sob, wishing it all away. She jerked her hands back when she realized something sticky still clung to them. *God!* It wasn't a dream. The sickening *crunching* sound of the knife as it entered the man's body would be with her forever. She threw back the blankets and jumped off the table. She had to wash her hands and face before her dad got there. Her legs buckled as she hit the floor.

Chapter 5

Sidrah Keeling, having just double-checked that she'd properly set the staunch security system on her home, walked upstairs to run a hot bath. It had been a good day.

She climbed the carpeted hardwood stairwell, bypassing the elevator that ran through all five floors of her large Victorian home in Boston's South End, and made her way to her sanctuary—her master bed and bath. Redesigned after she'd purchased the place, the bedroom itself was gorgeous, with soft track lighting around the ceiling, tastefully designed color elements, and plush furniture. Her California King was a ridiculous size for someone who lived alone. But one never knew, did one?

She also loved nothing more than throwing small parties for herself on that bed. Food, beverage, laptops, she'd spend an entire day, rolling from one station to another—the quadrants of entertainment in various corners.

Walking past the bed, she entered her closet, flipping on the center chandelier lights. She'd had the room converted from a large bedroom. Now it was complete, with a three-way mirror and a center island for her unmentionables and jewelry. She kicked out of her heels and lovingly stroked them. "Good boys," she said as she placed them on one of the many racks. Stripping with careless abandon, she knew Marta would pick up her garments from the floor in the morning and deal with their upkeep and cleaning. It was almost indecent to live in such a slovenly manner, having a housekeeper clean up after her, but then again, it was her life. Her castle. *Her* money. Her prerogative to do whatever she liked.

As she walked through to the master bath, she used her cell phone to set the proper ambiance lighting and sat on the side of the tub. She pulled the drain closed and turned the tap, letting the hot water begin to fill the mini spa. After selecting a glass jar filled with lavender oil, she poured some into the water and then added a purple bubble bomb.

It was a beautiful sight.

She went over to the little fridge and extracted a split of champagne, already thoughtfully opened by Marta earlier that day in preparation, and poured some of the sparkling liquid into a crystal flute. She turned on the towel warmer and laid her face against a soft fluffy robe hanging near it.

Sidrah couldn't wait to get back to her novel about Empress Josephine Bonaparte. Reading relaxed her. It educated her, transported her into other worlds, cultures, and families from the safety of her own fiefdom. The characters, real and imagined, surrounded her as family and gave her comfort.

She returned to the tub and got in, adjusted the temperature, and pulled over a caddy. She propped up the book, opening it to the last ticked-back page and placed it next to a plate of imported cheese and fruit. With the split on the ledge beside her, she lay back, deeply inhaling the delightful, relaxing lavender. Just as she began to read, her phone rang.

She scowled, hesitant to break the spell of her practiced respite. But then, she reluctantly pressed the screen to answer the call.

"Detective Bodine," she said, splashing her legs a bit. She wouldn't allow him to wreck her mood. "Whatever can I do for you?"

"I thought you'd like to know that we caught the guy."

The splashes were for real now as she pushed the cart out of the way and sat up straight. "You did?"

"Yes. The guy attacked a young girl. He picked her up at Pride Convenience early this morning."

Sidrah's hand flew to her throat. "What happened? Is she okay?"

"She's in the hospital. But yeah. Brave little thing. She's okay. Defended herself. Got clean away, but not before she stabbed him in the balls."

Sidrah's eyes flew open. "You're kidding me."

"Anyway, I thought you'd want to know."

"Yes. No. Thank you, Detective. I appreciate it."

"We didn't have a whole lot of time to do a thorough job with your tips since we only met a couple of days ago, but the guy's name is Brian. He drives an old black Ford. Married. No record. No prints in the system."

She closed her eyes, feeling the sting of tears well up behind them. "Yeah. Well. I'm glad the girl's going to be okay."

There was a pause before he answered. "Thanks, Sidrah. I know this is hard for you."

This time, she let her tears fall. "Goodnight, Detective."

She hung up and slid farther into the water. She hated being right about the guy. She hated knowing who he was, but she did. The animal had spent a night in her beautiful bed. Maybe not literally, but certainly in her dreams. Her gift had allowed him inside, and it was these times that scared the shit out of her. She knew her precious sheets had been changed, but there wasn't enough lavender in the world to get him out of her head. She could feel in her bones that she and the poor little victim had that in common.

Chapter 6

Jenny opened her eyes, immediately flooded with gratitude that she was alive and safe. The familiarity of her bedroom, the feel and smell of her blankets, the light streaming in through a window over her cluttered desk filled with books and schoolwork—this was her safe spot.

Judging from the amount of sunlight, she'd slept way past midmorning. She turned and picked up her phone, checking the time. Almost noon. They'd given her drugs to help her sleep last night, and she was glad she'd taken them. She hoped her poor dad had gotten some sleep too.

Hearing voices, she turned her head to the door, wondering who was in the living room downstairs. No doubt, people were coming by to see how Jenny-the-Freak was doing. *God.* What were the kids at school going to think when they found out she'd stabbed some guy in the balls? That was going to go over. The guys would probably huddle, holding their privates when she got close to them in the hallway. She'd be more ostracized than ever now.

"But how could you let her!"

Jenny's eyes flew wide. It was her mother's voice. Jenny threw back the covers and crawled slowly, careful not to make any familiar creaking noises, and pressed herself against her bedroom door so she could listen.

Her father was speaking. "It was her choice. She wanted the extra money for her college fund. You know how independent she is."

"At a convenience store," her mother said dryly. "In the middle of the night while you're home, sleeping soundly, and our daughter is out working."

"Don't start, Kate. We've been through enough."

Jenny had heard enough too. Her parents, probably only together for a short time this morning, were already at it. They'd divorced when Jenny was in kindergarten, and although she knew it was for the best—them being oil and water—it was still upsetting that they fought so much when they were together.

She crawled slowly over to her closet and then stood before it. She peeled off her favorite stained hoodie, which her dad had given to her, and replaced it with the one her mom had sent her the Christmas before. Yale, emblazoned on the heavy blue sweatshirt, was a pipe dream on everyone's part for various reasons. Her mother should have known it was crazy ridiculous to get into that school.

Her mom, Kate, had always had high goals for her. Most of them were unattainable. Some of them were based on her disapproval of how Jenny saw the world, and some of them were based on what she would have liked to accomplish in her youth. All that said, her mother's primary beefs were kept superficial. It was an unspoken pact between them not to delve too deep. Going there was a grossly uncomfortable journey, primarily for Kate.

Jenny grabbed a ponytail holder off her desk and did a quick finger brush through her wild hair before banding it up and off her face the way her mom liked it. She glanced in a desk mirror and inspected her face before walking across the room and opening the door.

Her mom and dad both looked up at her with expectant, almost horrified faces as she came down the stairs. In that instant, Jenny realized it was a reaction she would probably have to get used to.

They both stood, and Kate opened her arms, then immediately dropped them out of habit. The infinitesimal moment of confusion wasn't lost on any of them, but to her credit, Kate reextended her arms and walked over to her. "Jenny."

Jenny held her mom. And maybe because it was such a rare event, it felt all the more powerful. Jenny couldn't help it. She began crying.

"There, there, baby," her mom cooed. "I'm so sorry. I'm so sorry."

More kind words passed between them until Jenny finally released her mom and pasted on what she hoped was a brave smile as she walked to her dad. His arms were fully extended, and she walked into them like an old familiar blanket. "It's okay, honey," he said.

Following Jenny's lead, the three of them sat at the small kitchen table. "Are you hungry? Ready for breakfast?" her dad asked.

His face looked so lost that she knew it would help to give him something to do. "Sure."

He smiled lovingly at her and got up. He'd know what to bring her.

Kate reached a hand across the table toward Jenny's but

then retracted it. Her long, pointy nails glistened with pink polish. Her wedding ring, as always, jumped out as something exceptional, even to Jenny. The sheer weight of the rock must have been heavy for her mom's thin fingers.

"How are you, baby? Did you sleep last night?"

Jenny nodded. She pulled her legs up onto the chair and tugged the collar of her hoodie up, covering her lips. "Yeah. When did you get here?" she mumbled.

Kate sat up straight. "I would have come last night, but your father said not to, that you were sleeping. No one called me until last evening. Simon and I drove up from Manhattan this morning. I was traveling with him for business. We left at the crack of dawn, and he dropped me off. We weren't sure you'd be ready to see him yet, so we thought, maybe just me."

Jenny nodded. Simon was not a comforting soul. Talk about awkward. Her dad brought her a cup of coffee and placed a bottle of vanilla creamer next to it.

"Thanks, Dad." She gave him another encouraging smile.

Kate crossed her arms. "Your father and I have been talking. You are most definitely not going back to your job."

Jenny rolled her eyes as she poured in the creamer. "I know that, Mom. I don't want to go back either."

"Good. It's ridiculous that you were working at a dirty convenience store to begin with. In the middle of the night, in this remote, backwater town. It's no wonder something like this happened, working at a place like that . . ." She trailed off as Jenny shot her a look filled with daggers.

"It wasn't my fault, Mom!"

Kate reached out a hand, then pulled it back. "No. That's not what I meant. Your father . . ."

Jenny balled her fists. "It wasn't Dad's fucking fault either!"

"Jenny! Don't raise your voice and use profanity at me. It's not ladylike."

"Come on," her dad said. "Let's not argue. Jenny, we only want what's best for you. But I'm afraid you're going to have to tell us what's next. I just want to help you, baby, but I haven't got a clue how."

"I want to help her too!" said Kate. She glared daggers at her ex. "In fact, Simon and I were talking, and we have a few ideas. First of all, it's past time that you owned a weapon. We thought a nice 9mm Glock 43 would be right for you! We'd pay for the lessons, naturally. You could undoubtedly get a conceal and carry. Simon thinks the gun would be perfect for you."

Jenny looked wide-eyed at her father. His mouth was set in an uncharacteristically tight, angry line.

"What is wrong with you both?" said Kate. "It's a reliable, no-nonsense gun."

"Mom. I don't think I want to carry a gun."

"But, Jenny, if you'd had a—a gun," she stammered.

"I took care of it. It worked out. It usually does for me. Remember?"

Kate blinked rapidly and licked her lips. Jenny stared at the beautiful, well-put-together woman in front of her, recognizing her mother's discomfort with the topic. Her mom had always reminded Jenny of a Stepford Wife. It was a joke she shared with her dad from time to time, though he didn't encourage it.

The three of them, their small family, were fractured. And, the fact was, there should have been one more at the table. Jenny often blamed herself for that too.

Her earliest memory of her crazy gift was seeing a friend's brother shoot a squirrel from a tree. She saw the event and what would happen before it actually unfolded. She'd told her mother about it, not having a word yet for premonition, but Kate had counseled it away as a logical prediction. Then there was the time Jenny had seen a knife slip and cut her mother's hand. In her own simple, three-year-old way, she'd told her to be careful and to put the knife away, but Kate hadn't. Predictably, the knife slipped. This time her mother blamed her. The distraction and worry had caused it.

Then, the events picked up. Her déjà vu crack baby grew. Her parents knew something was different, but their feelings about the odd occurrences weren't cemented, and all hell didn't break loose until the day of the big accident. Jenny had been four years old, strapped in the back seat of the car next to her infant sister, Cassie. Jenny had seen the accident before it happened and screamed at her mother to stop. Kate, in a hurry, hadn't listened.

If they'd had problems before that day, things went into free fall after that. With everyone in pain and chaos, unable to manage their feelings, her mom and dad had separated, then divorced. Her mom gave almost no fight in the custody arrangements, leaving Jenny to live with her father.

Maybe Jenny was a painful reminder, but her mom definitely could have made more of an effort to be in her life. Instead, she'd married a wealthy square-headed, buzzed-cut Republican and member of the NRA, who loved that Kate always looked put-together and carried a gun. Jenny had once argued that just because she had money, good hair, and a gun, didn't mean bad things couldn't still happen. Her mom had not appreciated the counsel.

Jenny knew her mom worked hard to believe that she could stay in control, but the veneer cracked whenever she was with her. In fact, all of them felt raw when they were together. Maybe because Jenny was alive, and Cassie wasn't. Maybe because Jenny was a living reminder that Kate had been given a warning. And maybe because she thought Jenny's gift was something out of this world— uncontrollable—it was something to be feared.

Over time, Jenny's parents acknowledged that her gift somehow detoured bad things from happening, but then, none of them understood the meaning behind it, or if or when it might wear off. Those were her mom's words. Jenny had overheard them arguing. Her dad had retorted that Jenny was born an angel, and who were they to question it? She liked her dad's sweet pronouncement better, but she didn't think that was true either.

Sitting at the kitchen table, each of them recognized the juncture and were, in their own ways, reconciling their asses off. Jenny was too, since thoughts of how her gift had betrayed her by not warning her about the attack, pressed on her mind. Jenny crossed her arms on the table and laid her head down, heavy with the depression and confusion and all that had happened.

Her mom jumped up, startling Jenny, and grabbed the empty glass in front of her, then walked a few short steps to the kitchen. She placed her glass in the sink and sunk her head, then turned around and brightened.

With a broad pageant smile plastered on her face, her mom said, "Simon and I would also like to see to your college expenses. Naturally, we've been discussing it forever, but we were waiting to see if that's what you really wanted. Assuming you go to college, Jenny, we'd like to pay your tuition."

Jenny blinked. The offer had come out of nowhere. Simon—absent-of-any-depth-of-feeling Simon—had never been close to Jenny. But he had great feeling for his money. The generosity he'd displayed over the years included items that Kate had had on her agenda. Braces. Hair appointments. Clothing boutiques. All good stuff, but still, there'd never been mention of Jenny's future. Nor of funding it.

Jenny had had too much pride to ask for the obvious. But at this moment, she didn't want to miss her chance to lock this down. Simon, the keeper of the purse, was making an offer, which she assumed had come out of guilt.

She'd be a fool to refuse. "I've applied to a bunch of schools, Mom. You know that."

Kate came back and sat at the table. She folded her hands and smiled. "Of course, I know that, darling. Of course, I do."

Jenny gave her a deadpan look. "I got into *every one* I applied to."

Kate's eyes flew open. "Did you! Well, isn't that wonderful!"

Jenny glanced at her dad, who seemed to be mulling over the situation himself. She'd miss him, but she was more than ready to fly the nest. Until this moment, there'd been obstacles on how to afford the wings.

"Wellesley, Mom. I'd like to go there. It's a private college. With room and board, it's about seventy-five thousand dollars a year."

Even saying the number out loud sounded ridiculous. Not in a million years had she considered that doable. But Kate and Simon were talking big, and Jenny thought it was a good idea to match them. They could always negotiate their way down from that.

Kate put a hand to her throat. Her diamond ring, sagging from the gravity of that simple motion, was most likely worth at least one year's tuition. "That's nearby. The Boston area?"

Jenny smiled and nodded.

Kate looked at her ex. "Well, I suppose it's the least we can do. Given your current circumstances, I don't see how you can afford that."

Jenny saw the look of disappointment and sadness in her father's eyes. Kate was working to shame him. Jenny reached out and grabbed her mom's hand, startling them all. "You're wonderful to do this for me, Mom. I'll do my very best to make you proud. I promise."

Her mom began to extract her hand, but Jenny continued to hold it firmly. Was she doing this as punishment for trying to shame her dad? Maybe. But then it shouldn't feel like a punishment to hold your own kid's hand. Maybe that was why Jenny pushed it.

She finally released it and saw her mom's mind working. Kate wanted to ask Jenny if she'd seen something but didn't dare. Magic. The devil. Something un-Godly. Jenny had heard her mom use all those words in heated behind-closed-doors arguments with her father. *Odd.* That word too. *Oddly,* it was the one that hurt most, the one that lingered.

Jenny didn't worry that the devil was involved in what she could see. No worries about that part at all. It always felt . . . untainted was the best way she could describe it.

"Thank you, Katie," said John.

Jenny looked at her wonderful dad. She saw resignation, possibly relief, but there was happiness in there too. He was glad for her. Just as a parent should be.

Chapter 7

Jenny focused hard on the screen images before her rather than on the other distractions of her college classroom. The smallish lecture room at her dream school, Wellesley, had four lengths of risers in an oval arc facing the front of the room. There was a wide work area or desk in front of each chair, and her classmates were busy with their laptops or books or lecture. Her space held her new precious MacBook, provided by a contribution from the victims' support fund that her social worker had insisted she participate in.

After the incident, she'd received help from various individuals and groups to counsel her through her feelings. Truth be told, after the shock of the attack wore off, she didn't feel all that bad. There had been nightmares and some initial anxiety about strange places, but her innate optimism was apparently stronger than her fear. She knew she might be underestimating the long-lasting damage, but in the short term, she thought she'd rallied.

The knowledge that her attacker had been an actively

sought serial rapist also helped her recovery. She had stopped him. It was a good feeling to know that he was currently sitting in some jail cell, awaiting a trial, and his new life without his balls.

The whole damn event was something Jenny actively worked to push down. It wasn't easy. The memories popped into her thoughts every single day, but she used the tools of recovery, determined not to let it affect her happiness. She was at Wellesley! She was surrounding herself with positive experiences! She hadn't been raped! She was practicing self-care and living the dream!

All that said, she also believed her special gift had put her on the man's path. That part had rocked her.

Why had it done that? Why had it put her in front of him as his victim? Sure, the outcome was that bastard's arrest, but if it had gone wrong, she'd be dead by now. Why would her gift put her in that kind of danger? For that matter, why did she have the gift at all? *And for God's sake, why was it changing?* The visions had increased tenfold since the accident. She blinked back the hamster wheel of lifelong questions. None of the answers had ever been forthcoming and probably never would be. She had to get a grip.

She sat up straight, furiously reminding herself to focus and to absorb the wonder of her new life. She was out of high school! Out of Palmer. Away from the prying, curious, empathetic, and often frightened eyes of those who knew her past, her tragedies, and her oddness. She was free! And the freedom and anonymity felt good.

She glanced at the girl next to her and made a fast lunge to stop the girl's beverage from toppling onto her laptop. She'd seen it before it had happened.

"Oh my God! Thanks!" the girl whispered.

Jenny smiled at her and resumed her focus on the professor, who was currently reviewing the syllabus for his freshman course in European History. It was difficult to concentrate, however, because, in addition to her daydreams, she'd been engaged in a staring contest with the beautiful dog lying near him.

"Isn't he fucking gorgeous?" her classmate whispered, indicating the professor, not the dog, with her eyes. "We're so lucky to be in his class."

Jenny looked at the man, really paying attention to his features for the first time since she'd walked into the classroom. His hair was dark, and there was lots of it. He had a broad face with deep-set dark eyes. What was also impressive was his height. He was tall, maybe six-four, and except for one foot in a walking boot, his body appeared quite toned.

Jenny lowered her head and asked, "What happened to his leg? Why is he wearing gloves?"

The girl shrugged. "I don't know. But I heard he runs. People text alerts when he's out."

Jenny looked back; Professor Dyer was looking directly at her. She pulled her head back with worry that she was being rude, but then her eyes dropped again to his dog, who continued to calmly stare directly at her.

Professor Dyer glanced down at the dog and trailed the look from it back to her. He did a double-take of the situation, and Jenny's face reddened as they communicated an acknowledgment of that focus. But then, he got back to teaching.

After class was over and the students began to file out, she gathered her things in a small hurry to get back to her dorm and meet her roommate for lunch. Instead, she found herself walking down the risers toward the dog. The animal looked squarely at her as she approached.

Professor Dyer looked at the dog also. "My office hours are posted for questions," he said.

Jenny glanced at her teacher but was drawn to the dog. Her heart rate picked up a little; she was nervous that she was overstepping, but her hands had a mind of their own. She leaned over as both of them met on either side of the dog's head, and her fingers slid into the thick fur. The gentle dog whimpered at her touch.

"I'm sorry. She's so sweet. I just had to say hi."

Professor Dyer didn't say anything for a few moments, just watched them. "That's Bones," he said.

She looked into the dog's eyes, and her head bent without fear, resting on the dog's forehead as their eyes met in close quarters. She repeated the name softly. "Bones. Hello, baby."

The dog whimpered and rolled over onto its back, exposing her belly. Jenny rubbed her. "You like to run, don't you, girl?"

"She does," said Professor Dyer.

"But you can't right now, can you," she continued to speak with Bones. "Those ducks miss you, girl."

Professor Dyer cleared his throat, and Jenny stood up.

"I'm sorry." Jenny adjusted her gear in her arms. "Thanks for the great class." She began walking away.

His voice stopped her. "How do you know about the ducks?"

Her eyes popped open before she turned back. In her vision, Bones had been running toward them. She shrugged. "I run around the lake. Just figured she'd have fun with them too."

"You run?" he asked.

She nodded with enthusiasm and brightened. "Yeah. I love it. I'll take her out with me if you can't." She gestured toward his walking boot.

"I got a bad sprain chasing after her. I'm rehabbing, but I'm almost done with the boot."

"Oh, sorry," she said, glancing at his gloves. She wasn't going to ask about them.

He turned toward his desk and picked up a piece of paper. As he wrote on it, he said, "If you're serious about the run, here's my cell and office number. It's downstairs. She could use the exercise."

Jenny grabbed a pen off his desk and wrote her name and number next to it. "I could change and pick her up later today from your office. Does that work?"

He nodded. "How about four o'clock?"

She and the professor stared into one another's eyes for a moment. She felt him assessing her but didn't flinch. "Four works. Do I get extra credit for this?" She smiled.

He broke eye contact and began to gather his things. "No. But I can pay you."

"No need to pay me," she said. "I was just kidding about the extra credit." She reached down and kissed Bones on the head. "See you at four!"

Taking the risers two at a time, she ran out of the classroom and the building. She'd made another friend. This one was a dog. *One day at a time,* she reminded herself of the mantra she'd learned in therapy. Today felt good.

Chapter 8

Max Dyer watched the young girl bound out of the classroom. He appreciated her youthful enthusiasm but felt out of sorts from the conversation and the hasty deal he'd struck. He didn't sense a romantic interest from the girl. *Thank God.* He thought that for the moment, he was safe from unwanted attention, but he'd have to make himself remote and keep those guardrails up around her. It was tedious, and some might think him vain, but experience told him to be careful around his students.

He looked down at Bones, who stared up at him, smiling. "What are you looking at? Why were you staring at her? Did you know she'd offer to take you for a run?"

The dog licked her lips. Since her accident some months before, they'd become dependent on one another. First she, physically. Then he, emotionally. She was emotionally dependent on him, too, though. They were now constant companions. Her presence on campus had become known, and since Bones was the model of good behavior—at least when others were around—he saw no harm in keeping her with him all day. No one on the faculty had made noise about it. The only problem was the female attention the dog received. Youthful students, easily excitable by the dog's cuteness, would often wave and coo in her direction. It was the last thing he needed, but Bones ate it up. She almost taunted them, daring them to come forward, then pranced about afterward like a dressage horse.

Max had put up a few flyers in the location Bones had first appeared, though he hoped no one would come forward to claim her. It was incredible that no one had. Where had she come from that day? After getting to know her, Max realized she must have been somebody's pet. She was housebroken. She'd lived with people before, but they hadn't chipped her. And as far as he could tell, no one was searching.

Bones took to her new name immediately and clearly understood many words and rules. Not that she always complied. Not when the two of them were alone anyway. She'd let her freak flag fly when the doors closed at their house—creating trouble, stealing his meals, pouncing on him when he didn't expect it. She was a fireball of playfulness when they were alone and also insisted on sharing his bed. Another battle she'd won by sheer stubbornness and sneakery.

But when he took her out in public, she put on her manners like a show pony. "You're ridiculous," Max said. He took off a glove and scratched her behind the ear.

The anomaly that he could touch the dog freely without being bombarded by images of the creature's past was still shocking. Logically, he'd known how much he'd missed, but he hadn't accurately predicted the enormity of the experience. The bonding, the intimacy of just being with another soul without fear, was a gift he'd be forever grateful for. The relief he felt touching her was immense. The pain he'd suffered in distancing himself, if only through a layer of gloves, fell away when he was with the dog. But the mystery of her appearance remained. He didn't know what to make of it.

He put his laptop in his backpack and was about to pick up the piece of paper his student had left on the table, then stopped. He stared at the note with Jenny Gallagher's name and number. There was something about her. Had he seen her before? Bones had stared at her. Why? The dog had practically compelled her to come down after class. Why that particular student? There were questions here, and he needed some answers.

Max took one last look around, making sure he was alone before taking a deep breath and picking up the note with his gloveless hand. In a flash, Jenny, her life, or at least portions of it, burst before him. He saw the attack. He saw her tears, the screaming as she pulled into a police station. A man was crying, standing before her in a hospital setting, kids sneering at her, whispering. There was something else too, but he wasn't sure what. A light somehow surrounded her as she gazed into the sky. A lightness to her quality. Her person. Her soul.

He dropped the paper, and his hand tingled painfully like it was coming awake. "Who are you?" he said, releasing the connection.

He'd do some research on her. He needed to find out.

Max, with Bones on her leash, walked swiftly to his office in the basement of the old history building and unlocked his private sanctuary. Once inside, he shut the door and flipped the bolt. Student office hours weren't until the next day, and his slave and grad student was not due that day either. He felt confident he'd be alone for at least a few hours.

Off the leash, Bones gave him a dramatic sigh and walked past him to her chair. It was a large, comfortable leather club chair—the only nice item in the room—that used to sit behind his desk. He'd moved it when the dog was recovering and gave it to her. Back then, he'd put it to the side of the room and began using a standard-issued office chair. After Bones recovered, though, he had tried moving the chair back so she could lie on the floor, but they tussled over it. Bones had won.

"Spoiled beast," he said out the side of his mouth as he sat at his desk. She yawned at him and laid her red head on her long front legs.

Max had never owned a dog, or any pet, for that matter. He didn't know much about how other dogs acted besides what he had gleaned from movies and his real-life observations. But he sensed that the creature who had hurled herself into traffic for a game of chase was one of a kind. Even though he'd been used to abnormal occurrences his entire life, he wasn't sure how to take this one. What he did firmly believe was that there was a reason behind everything. When he wasn't busy trying to eke out a living, he spent his time in search of the answers. So far, the universe had been silent.

Now safely in his office, he pulled off the other glove and laid it on his desk. He took the laptop out of his backpack, sure it was safe to touch since he never allowed anyone near it. Most of his office was "safe" territory, free of others' cosmic energy and detritus, but occasionally he'd be surprised by visions. It almost felt like a friction shock when that happened—a bit unsettling. Still, once the infinitesimal moment passed, his focus moved inward, either trying to shoo the images away or focusing intently to remember them. If he held the connection purposefully longer, as he had with Jenny's slip of paper, the sensation was usually more painful.

The laptop fired up, and he used his credentials to open up Jenny Gallagher's student file. "Something bad happened to her."

Bones whimpered and looked at him, her head still resting on her paws. He'd become accustomed to the dog joining his conversations, and now he had a habit of speaking out loud whenever they were alone. Along with all the other changes the dog had brought to his life, she'd changed the silence of his previous world as well.

It didn't take Max long to understand why Jenny Gallagher had been given entrance to Wellesley. Her life circumstances, her entrance essay, her grades, everything about her showed her potential to excel and make Wellesley a proud alumnus. But the file didn't answer the questions about what had happened to her. He'd seen the carnage of trauma and went to the Google machine. It was a simple find. He read the story.

"I wonder if she's going to be called for trial. Poor kid," he said.

Bones picked up her head.

He scrolled through the machine, searching for more. "Where have I seen her before? Maybe on the news?"

Bones laid her head down.

He sat back in the chair and closed his eyes. No. Somewhere else. He'd been on many adventures—too many lives. So much history was at his disposal. It's what made him good at his job. He could find something that belonged to a historical figure, and once he laid his hand on it, he'd see the visions. Sometimes, he'd been surprised just by touching their names in newsprint—almost like Wikipedia. He'd hover over a name, touch it, and images would flash. Sometimes he'd see many, sometimes only a few, but most of the time, the visions were scattered and random. If he didn't know the written history of the person, it was often impossible to put the images in context.

His phone vibrated in his pocket, interrupting him. He extracted it and saw that it was his mother, Tracey. He put the phone face down on his desk. He'd call her later. No doubt she was just calling to check in.

He loved his mother, though she could be a bit much. Both his parents had been supportive throughout his life, but they were a strange pair. His father, an executive in the bustling insurance mecca of Hartford, Connecticut, had married a free spirit. Scott and Tracey balanced one another out, and they needed that, especially after having a son like Max.

The visions had begun early, but it took time for Max to understand that others didn't have the same experiences that he did, and by the time they'd sorted that out, his mother celebrated Max like she'd hit the karmic jackpot. She used him and his gift kindly and judiciously, coaching him on how to respect it. His father taught him how to hide it.

Maximus, or Max for short, was their only child, and he was fully doted on by both parents. They were, as a trio, fully compartmentalized, each understanding who dealt with what. He could count on his mother to understand the supernatural stuff; his father had roots firmly entrenched in terra firma. Somehow, it all worked.

They had supported him financially too. His schooling had been costly. He'd spent a few semesters abroad, twice in Italy, and he had also traveled extensively in Greece, researching for his doctorate. His thesis on the Sibylline Books had finally given him his PhD, but his parents had made all the financial sacrifices. They'd paid for his health insurance for an indecent amount of time. His car payments, his rent. It was mildly horrifying, but they'd had a condition. Max could never, ever move far away. His mother, and by the trickle-down effect, his father, had suffered from his absence when he was abroad.

The neighboring state of Massachusetts had been middle ground for them. Once he obtained the job at Wellesley, they'd rejoiced. Yes, Max was reluctant to teach at the private all-girls' school, but they'd offered him a job in his desired profession, in the history department.

His parents were relieved when he got the teaching job. They were convinced that he'd be nearby for the long term—a short hour and a half away. They'd locked it down by giving him a huge down payment on a home—a horrible, million-dollar fixer-upper, but one they could all afford in the high-priced retail area around the college and nearby Boston.

Max got up and hobbled over to his beloved single window. Since his office was on the backside of the building, it was one of the least desirable spaces due to its proximity to the storage rooms. But Max loved it for another reason. It had a secluded, private window, and no one gave a shit if he smoked. Well, they did, but then they looked away.

He cranked the window wide and pulled a piece of foil off a roll he kept near it. He'd use that for ashing and disposal. He then reached into a decorative box, a souvenir from his time in Italy, and opened it. He'd filled it with cigarettes already sprung free of their grubby, cosmic-littered boxes. A lighter also lay on top of the pile. Max grabbed it and lit one.

Bones gave him a small bark. Max squinted through the smoke at the dog, recognizing the yap of disapproval. "You've got your nasty, saliva covered chew toys, I've got mine." He smiled at the dog and took another long drag.

He looked out the window; the air wafting inside was warm for the September day, but not in the least un-pleasant. Smoking settled his mind. He knew it was a bad habit, but it was an effective tool to ease his anxiety. That had been an ongoing issue his entire life. His mother feared the drugs prescribed by the doctor. She didn't want his gift to morph, either tamped down into the underwater dregs where Max would feel nothing or somehow freakily enhanced. Smoking, running, drinking, reading, studying, it all helped him, though. He didn't give a shit about the health ramifications. The money, however, that bothered him. Between the booze, the cigarettes, the many loans from his parents, the mortgage, the renovations, it was all expensive.

"And vet bills," he grumbled to Bones.

She licked her leg where it had been broken, looking pitiful, then barked at the office door.

The knob rattled, and then a knock came along with a friendly greeting. "I can smell the smoke. Open the door, Max."

Max smiled as he opened the door for Elias, one of his closest friends and colleagues. "Get in here," he said, closing it again and relocking the bolt.

Elias waved his hand in the air and reached down to pet Bones. "You're not fooling anyone. Someone's going to complain, and then you'll be forced to stop."

"Until that day," Max said. He relaxed and smiled.

Elias plopped in the visitor chair. "Sharon and I are having a few people over for the game on Sunday. You want to join us?"

Max nodded and put out his cigarette. He waved some of the smoke outside. Even he realized it wasn't that effective in disguising his habit. "Maybe. Is it the regular crowd? Who's going to be there?" As much as he enjoyed Elias and his wife Sharon's company, she had a habit of setting him up with her friends. So far, it hadn't worked out.

Elias smiled. "She's got a line on a kindergarten teacher."

Max walked behind his desk, dropped into his chair, and put his hands behind his head. The last woman had been a hairdresser. They'd gone on a few dates, but things soured for him after they'd met in the park with Bones. Admittedly, the dog's behavior had been terrible that day; Bones even uncharacteristically humped the girl's leg. The end came right after when the woman told him she was more of a cat person.

He looked at the dog, who'd put her head down and didn't seem interested. "Can I let you know?" Max asked. His friends were great, but he wasn't sure he was in the mood for another scene where all eyes were on him and the setup rather than just watching the game.

"Sure." Elias got up. "I was given orders to sell the invitation. She feels pretty confident about this one." He gave Max a broad, fake smile.

Max rocked in his chair. "Why is she so determined to match me up?"

"I dunno." Elias shrugged. "She thinks everyone should be married. She worries about you being surrounded by drooling single women. The irony of Adonis and the untouchables, she calls you."

Max dropped his hands below the desk. He'd hit a nerve, and Elias caught the unease.

"Hey, sorry, man. I didn't mean anything…" Elias trailed off, gesturing toward the desk.

As close a friend as Elias was, Max hadn't shared his secrets with him. What he did have was a few ready-made lies about his gloves and his condition. The easiest was a nerve disorder.

Max gave him a relaxed smile to make him feel at ease. "The irony hasn't been lost on me."

Elias walked to the door. "The price you pay for being you, big guy. Let me know if you can make it."

His friend left, shutting the door behind him. He'd think about the game, but he wasn't sure about another one of Sharon's setups. He clicked his computer screen open, and Jenny Gallagher's face popped back up. He frowned, thinking about her. "I know I've seen her before. Some-where. I need to figure this one out."

Bones perked up her head and barked.

Chapter 9

Sidrah Keeling hated being called a whale. The optics were awful, and the moniker almost made her feel like an irredeemable whore.

Lounging in a private, Mediterranean-style cabana near the Bellagio Hotel's elegant pool in Las Vegas, she heard a staff person nearby call her a whale under his breath, referring to her status as a high roller. She didn't glance at the two inappropriately chatty waitstaff, just picked up her margarita and took a small sip. She felt reassured as she ran her free hand down the side of her long, toned leg, flexing it, appreciating the satisfying cut of muscle she'd earned through her daily regime. Yoga, Pilates, running, weight training, and a disciplined diet kept her slim and fit.

She inhaled and closed her eyes in satisfaction, thinking of the crazy good ensemble she'd purchased that day, which would cause men and women alike to drool. She'd turn heads on the floor tonight—for several reasons—while she searched for him.

She lowered her shades and looked around the busy

pool area. Where was he? Why was this man, this effing gorgeous man coming to her in her dreams, but not in real life? The situation was a tiny bit new to her. Her visions usually came when she slept holding an image in her hand, but he had appeared without a prompt.

Not only that, but the face had come to her now more than once. If there was one thing Sidrah believed in, it was her dreams. They'd made her a fortune. She listened when they spoke, but so far, they hadn't given her a clue about where to find him. Why was he in her dreams? She'd be sure to ask if she ever found him.

Sidrah sighed, putting her glasses back into place, and resumed reading about Josephine and her little pug named Fortuné. After she'd married Bonaparte, she'd refused to kick the dog out of her bed, and Napoleon caved to her wishes. The little dog's sway was so strong that the man who'd murdered millions without care cuddled at night with his wife and a dog.

Looking out at the pool, Sidrah tried visualizing this scene, an innocent dog humanizing a monster. She knew the power of dogs, the devotion they gave, and she loved them too, but from a distance. For many years, she'd wanted a dog of her own. So far, though, she hadn't dared to get one. The pain of her last moment with a young dog named Argo was still too fresh when she touched it. Maybe it would forever be.

She pushed away the sad memories and took another sip of the cool, citrusy cocktail, then placed it beside her, counseling herself to be happy about the rest of the dream. Last night, in her sumptuous, complimentary hotel suite at the Bellagio, she'd slept soundly in her king-size bed, cocooned in the satiny smooth Egyptian cotton sheets, and worked her magic. She held a collection of coins and chips in her hands while she skedaddled off to la-la land to encourage the visions.

Not every dream she had in Vegas produced a winner, but last night she'd seen herself winning the jackpot at a megabucks slot machine. She'd woken in a peppy mood, sitting straight up in bed, running through her time-honed process for making sure every detail remained clear. She captured the images from the dream before she lost them.

She'd been to Vegas often enough to visualize that the winning coin slot machine was conveniently housed at the Bellagio. She'd recognized the carpet and the walls. Jumping out of bed, she ran to the Google machine and verified that the current megabucks jackpot stood close to thirteen million dollars.

Now poolside, she closed her eyes and visualized the scene to come. She smiled, recognizing the area where the winning machine stood, too. Near a pillar and striped awning across from a familiar exit, she saw herself replacing a woman seated at the fated machine. The woman was distinctly dressed in a long red satin dress. She would be approached by a man who would helpfully announce the precise time and that they were late for dinner.

Assuming the night was tonight, Sidrah would be there, ready to watch the innocent couple toddle off, unknowingly leaving a fortune behind. Sidrah would claim the seat, win big, and voila! Another pot of gold would fall her way.

She shrugged, contemplating the luck of the win from the purview of the casino. Someone had to win; it might as well be her. After she won, the jackpot would turn back over to begin again at ten million, waiting on average for one or two players to win each year.

She supposed the casinos would be curious about why she continued to be so incredibly lucky, and she thought it might earn her a black mark, but she didn't care, not for this one. She'd lost enough money gambling to hopefully muddle their suspicions, though she wasn't going to pass on a jackpot. Her gambling days—at least in Las Vegas—would temporarily come to a halt after the big win.

She'd add to her fortune and continue to play at investments with the insider information she obtained through her dreams, given to her for some unknown purpose.

She'd begun her vast accumulation of wealth in stinking Florida. After winning the lottery there, she immediately moved upon accepting her millions and set herself up in Boston. Now, she left Boston from time to time, following her dreams, and always, always coming up lucky.

A ruckus had started nearby, and Sidrah glanced over to see what was going on. A gaggle of women—no, girls—most likely a bachelorette party, was in full swing. Sidrah's lips tightened as she recognized her jealousy. It saddened her that she had few friends. No one really knew who she was. The friendships she did have had to be kept superficial. It was the downside of having a secretive, somewhat supernatural life. She hid her authentic self, possibly to her detriment, but she counseled herself to focus on the positive. For now, she'd ride her wave of luck as long as it lasted. God knew she'd had enough hard knocks in her life. She deserved the good fortunes that came her way—sort of.

She'd helped many other people, though. But that had only begun once she'd had enough money to protect herself. When she had enough resources to make sure she could bolt, or hide, if necessary, she'd reached out to law enforcement to assist in cases. She'd been doing it successfully for years. Her friend Detective Bodine was almost her personal pimp. He'd loan her out to various other cities, to vetted detectives who promised to have her back and keep her reputation private. They'd use her to delve into criminals' minds and help solve crimes. Perhaps even more importantly, she was also helping victims.

Her money protected her. And sometimes, sometimes, she contemplated personal payback to those who'd abandoned and hurt her in her youth. But it was too risky. She'd rather live her life, her beautiful life, until the day came when the jig was up. Because she believed it was coming. The man behind the curtain would appear to tell her why she had been given the gift. Then, he'd determine whether she'd used it for good or bad.

She felt she'd been good, but one never knew, did one?

Sidrah picked up her phone and glanced at the time. Sitting up, she shoved her beautifully tanned, pedicured feet into her sandals. Time to leave. She'd need to shower and dress in her ravishing new Naeem Khan dress, ready to sit down at the slot machine for her big win. An early flight out of Vegas was waiting for her in the morning. Time to go home.

The only loose end was the guy. Where was he? How did that handsome man with the head full of black hair and brooding brown eyes come into play? Would she meet him this evening after her big win? Would they celebrate together? That thought cheered her further. Thirteen million bucks and a new handsome lover. Life was most certainly good.

She gathered her things and left the cabana, her head on a slight swivel as she scanned the faces around her. Where was he?

Chapter 10

Jenny felt like she could fly as she and Bones ran along the shoreline of Lake Waban, the private lake on the beautiful Wellesley Campus. They'd made their way through the winding paths of the wooded hills and then to the lake. The freedom of running, the wind on her face, in her hair, always refreshed her spirit. She'd let Bones off the leash to chase a few ducks. That had been in her vision. There was a leash policy, but Jenny knew that Bones would behave. The two of them had their clandestine moment before she put the dog back on the leash, and they took off again at a clip toward a meadow, then the campus.

The old oak trees surrounded them, and they passed many other women also running, biking, and partaking in outdoor activities on the glorious September day. Jenny couldn't have been happier. With the sun on her face and her wonderful new friend beside her, she knew she'd chosen the right school to attend.

She'd visited the liberal arts campus once on a field trip when she was in junior high. The idyllic campus setting, the successful, gifted, driven women, receiving a world-class education so that they could one day make a difference, had left an impression on her. Never in a million years had she thought her dreams of attending such an excellent school could come true, and yet here she was, running through the campus. Her new home.

As determined as she was to make a fresh start, her visions had increased since the attack, and it was making her head swim. It felt like they were trying to take over sometimes, screaming at her to pay attention, to manage them. Every time she felt overwhelmed by the demands of her visions and painful memories, she'd been able to pull herself up, to breathe. But it was getting harder. Maybe she hadn't rebounded from the kidnapping as easily as she tried to convince herself. Would she ever be normal? In her opinion, the word *normal* was vastly unappreciated. It felt like an elusive, luxurious dream.

If only she had some answers, she might find her path. To a degree, she supposed that was true for everyone. *Stop being such a baby, and be grateful*, she scolded herself.

She came to a stop outside the historic ivy-covered brick building of Founders Hall, where her history lectures took place. She and Bones lay down in the soft grass. Jenny did some stretches while Bones panted and watched her. The dog's beautiful amber eyes filled her with peace. Love and life could be so simple, too. She'd try to remember that.

"Come on, girl," Jenny said as they entered the building, heading toward the basement. A few students and teachers passed her on the way. One older woman squinted, giving her and the dog a second glance before they rounded the corner to the basement level. Along the path, she stopped to look at a bulletin board with a poster announcing a first-year seminar on American Hauntings. She noted the information, thinking it might be something to check out. The supernatural had always interested her.

When they reached the closed door, Jenny was about to knock, but Bones gave a soft bark. She waited until Professor Dyer opened the door.

"Hey, welcome back. Did she do okay for you?" he asked.

Jenny dropped the leash as Bones walked past the professor at a leisurely pace and made her way over to a bowl filled with water. "She was really well behaved. We had a good run," said Jenny.

Professor Dyer went over to the dog and unclipped her leash. "Thanks for that. I'm sure she enjoyed it."

Jenny smiled, uncertain of what to do next. "Okay, then! I'll see you later." She turned to leave.

"Hey. Do you have a minute?" he said. "Can we talk?"

Jenny glanced at Bones, who put her ears back and came her way. The dog put a paw up and patted the air. Jenny leaned over to pet her. "Sure."

"Can I get you something to drink?" he said, depositing the leash on a cabinet and walking to a small fridge.

"No, thanks."

Professor Dyer wandered to the back of his desk. "Take a seat. Not there," he said, pointing to a big leather chair. "You'll have to fight her for that."

Jenny smiled and took one of the office chairs in front of the desk and sat on her hands while Bones took the leather chair. Instead of curling in, the dog sat at attention.

Professor Dyer cleared his throat. "So, how is campus life? I understand you've declared in journalism. Is that right?"

Jenny nodded, warming to the topic of her scholastics. "Yes. I think so. I was on the school paper in high school. I mostly phoned the stuff in. Kind of special interest articles. Events. They'd plug them in."

"I read one of them. You have excellent insights. Nice clean writing."

Jenny brightened. She hadn't expected him to say that. She appreciated the compliment.

He crossed his arms and continued. "Have you joined any societies, any special interest groups on campus?"

She looked at Bones, who had cocked her head and seemed to be waiting for an answer, too. Jenny drew her brows together. "Uh, not officially. I'm taking my time. The Clio Club—history." She waved her hand around. "That seems interesting. Maybe the Agora Society."

The professor's eyes widened. "So, you're interested in politics?"

She nodded. "Yes, I am. Sometimes."

There came an awkward pause, and she sensed Professor Dyer was looking at her like he wanted a more detailed answer—both he and the dog. As she was gathering her thoughts and about to ramble, a vision flash interrupted her. She, Professor Dyer, and Bones, were eating somewhere, and he appeared agitated. Had she done something wrong with the dog? Why were they eating together?

"Ahh," she began, but then had another flash. A woman, a beautiful one, joined the argument.

Jenny blinked rapidly, snapped to, and smiled. "I watch the news. The country's in trouble. Sometimes I think I can help."

He nodded in a friendly manner like he was genuinely interested, so she continued. "I used to have this fantasy about working for the UN. Although God knows what I was doing there."

Professor Dyer frowned at the dog, who was still perking to her every utterance. He said, "Have you traveled much? Are you planning to study abroad?"

"I think about Italy sometimes," she replied without thinking. "Sometimes I see myself there, looking out at the sea, walking through passageways. Talking to people. But that's probably stupid. I can't speak Italian. Languages are not my strong suit."

"You don't have to know Italian to speak with people," he said encouragingly.

She felt frustrated that she'd shared that last bit. *Walking through passageways?* What the hell? Where had that come from? *He must think I'm an idiot.*

He picked up a pencil and tapped it on the cluttered desk. "Do you have any brothers or sisters? Relatives, maybe, that are over there?"

She smoothed back her ponytail and tucked a few strands of hair behind her ears. She didn't like talking about her family. But so far, the professor seemed like a safe bet.

"No. On all counts."

He nodded. "I'm an only child, too. But I took the time to travel. You should meet with your guidance counselor and get that worked out. It's important to see the world, Jenny. Especially while you're young."

She thought about that. How would her mom and Simon feel about shelling out the bucks for more? For travel? She couldn't believe she'd gotten away with what she had. No way she wanted to press her luck. She flashed on Professor Dyer standing near the mouth of a cave. A rough tunnel, carved out of rock, with light beaming inside at intervals that made it seem alive, purposeful, tantalizing.

"You've probably traveled the world," she said, working hard to focus. The visions were so distracting. And they were definitely escalating.

He shrugged. "Some. What other subjects are you interested in?"

Jenny was beginning to feel nervous with the distractions and her inability to focus much. She wanted to leave, but the dog cocked her head again. There was no doubt she was listening.

She looked at Bones. "Does she do that often? It's like she's listening to me."

Professor Dyer shook his head. "Not all the time. But she certainly has taken a keen interest in you."

Jenny stared into the dog's eyes and flashed on the accident. Before she could stop herself, she reached over, grabbed the dog's leg, and petted it. "You poor baby. You're all better now, though, aren't you?"

"How did you know about the accident?" said the professor.

Jenny's eyes opened. *Dammit.* She had to get control of what she shared. She continued to pet the dog, who was licking her hand. She didn't answer immediately, distracted by another flash. This one was of the professor, his head in his hands, sitting in what looked like a vet's office. The big man now sitting in front of her had been crying. She recognized that he was a sensitive person.

"I dunno. From somewhere. A car accident, right?" She continued to flash through the scene.

"Yes."

"Where did you come from, girl?" she asked Bones, petting her head.

Professor Dyer inhaled, and Jenny turned to look at him. His eyes were wide. "Do you know something about her previous owners?"

She released the dog and swallowed hard, her throat dry. "No. Did you say you had some water?"

He got up and bent over the fridge, then extracted a cold bottle of water and handed it to her. He wasn't wearing his gloves. His hands didn't appear to be pox-ridden or deformed. Why did he cover them? As their hands momentarily touched, in a flash, she knew why.

Her heart tripped over itself as he looked down at her. Their eyes connected, hers growing large, seeking his for mutual recognition. He released the gaze and quickly walked behind his desk. He stood, rubbing his forehead, and stammered, "Jenny, ah . . ."

A sweat broke out as she looked at her hand where they'd touched. A warmth was spreading through her. Because she knew in that instantaneous touch that he had some kind of gift, just like she did. Fear gripped her. Excitement, too. *Jump up and leave. No! Ask him! Does he see things, too?*

She raised her eyes and nervously looked at his face, then over at Bones as the dog whimpered, patting the air with a paw in her direction.

She turned back to the professor, who'd sat, his elbows on the desk. He touched the sides of his head. "Ah, so . . ." he began, hesitating again.

Jenny inhaled. If she had it right, it was a miracle. She couldn't help plowing forward and saying it for both of them. "You see things, don't you?" she practically cried, her voice unrecognizable in its high pitch.

Professor Dyer froze. His jaw dropped. He looked as though he was about to shake his head but stopped midway, his eyes darting to the door and back to her. "I don't understand. What are you asking?" he said.

Jenny swallowed hard. Had she gotten it right? Professor Dyer's fists were balled, his skin slightly pale. He probably thought she was crazy. She wanted to cry with relief and fear, but instead, she bit her bottom lip. She hadn't wanted to tell *anyone* at Wellesley. She didn't want to be judged and regarded as a freak. She didn't want her beautiful new life to change by admitting—to a teacher, no less—that she was odd. But she'd seen him in her vision. And he was testing things with his gloves off. She saw the shocks and the closed-eyed processing on his face. She'd seen him shed tears over the dog. She saw, she saw, she saw . . .

She jumped up. "You see things in visions. With your hands, don't you?"

He stood, looking upset.

He had to admit it. He had to! Hot tears sprang to her eyes as he put his hands up in front of him, warding her off.

"Stay calm," he said.

"Admit that you do?" she pleaded. "I see things too!"

Bones leaped out of her chair and came to her, whimpering as Professor Dyer went to the door and shut it.

He nodded and said quietly, "I do."

Her knees wobbled, and she sat back in the chair. The dog put a paw on Jenny's leg and her head in her lap.

Professor Dyer went back around his desk and sat as she gushed. "I'm sorry. *Please* don't tell anyone about me. I just want my life to be normal. I'm so sorry."

His face wore a worried look as he rubbed a trail down the side. "It's okay, Jenny. I promise I won't say anything.

You can trust me. If anyone in the world knows what you're going through, it's me."

He gave her a pointed look. "Did you see something when we touched?"

Bones was moving her head back and forth while the two of them spoke. "Yes. I saw you touching things, reacting. I could feel it."

He sat back in his chair and exhaled. "Yes," he whispered.

"I feel like a freak sometimes," she said, her face reddening as she brushed back some tears. Bones whimpered.

He sat up rigidly and made strong eye contact. "No. You're not a freak. Don't say that. You're, you're special," he stammered.

"Well, if I am, then you are, too. What do you see? Visions? Premonitions?"

He shook his head. "In a way. I can see the past."

They let the weight of their confessions sit between them for a few moments. Jenny's heart thumped away in her chest, though it was beginning to calm. She couldn't believe she was sitting in front of someone who understood. He was probably the only person on the planet who could understand what it felt like. *Oh, God.* What was he going to do with the information?

"Don't tell anyone!" she insisted again.

"I won't," he said, clasping his hands and rocking them. He squeezed his mouth into a tight line and spoke quietly. "It's just . . . I saw something today about your past. I was concerned for you, is all. I wanted to check in to see how you were adjusting."

Her stomach flipped. *Oh, no.* "You saw the attack?"

His eyes softened. "No. Parts. Yes. Maybe. I'm so sorry that happened."

Jenny looked into the dog's eyes, which seemed to implore her to understand. "She's special, too. Isn't she?"

"I dunno. She's intuitive. Dogs sense things. It's hard to say."

Jenny opened her water bottle, her hand shaking as she, at last, took a sip.

"I'd like to continue the conversation, Jenny, but maybe not on campus. God, I can't believe I said that." He shot another worried look toward the closed door.

Jenny stood, realizing he seemed almost more nervous than she was. Bones thumped her tail and pulled her ears back again. The dog's eyes grew large and watery as they looked at her. Jenny caught another flash and smiled at the professor. "You're going to make frozen lasagna later. I'm telling you now it will be awful."

Professor Dyer's jaw clenched, but then he seemed to make a decision. He grabbed a piece of paper and wrote on it. "Here's my address. Can you get there without a bunch of females knowing where you're going?"

Jenny wiped her forehead with the back of her hand, still on shaky ground. "Yes. I have a bike."

He ripped off the sheet of paper and handed it to her. She looked down at it. "That's close. I guess I can be there in an hour."

"Jenny." He stood, cautioning her with a serious tone. "I think it wise that neither of us tells anyone about this."

She breathed out hard. "I couldn't agree more."

Chapter 11

Jenny flew out of the Founders Building and across campus, not far from her dorm—Tower Court. She crossed Severance Green, the courtyard of Tower Court, and ran through the space to the six-story castle-like structure she called home. Then she rushed into the main lobby with its old-school chandeliers, to the nearest stairwell. After running up to the third floor, she pushed the stairwell door open, then ran down the hall toward her room. Most of the doors were open, this being a Friday, and there were girls everywhere, enjoying the party atmosphere.

Her door was shut. She unlocked it and pushed inside. She lived in a double suite—she and her roommate, Lisa, on one side of the Jack-and-Jill style bath, and two other girls in the next room.

"Hey, Lisa," she said, a bit breathless, as her roommate, wrapped in a towel, was just getting out of the single shower.

"Hey!" Lisa smiled. "You going with us tonight?"

Jenny put her hands on her knees and bent over, breathing deeply before dropping onto her bed and removing her shoes. She couldn't believe the day she'd had. Still restless from the run and the monumental conversation, she jumped up and poked her head into the bathroom door. "Is anyone else using the shower? Can I be next?"

Lisa waved a hand as she leaned into the mirror. "Help yourself. They're out," she said, referring to their suitemates.

Jenny ditched her clothes and got in the shower. The hot water felt good, calming, as the salt of her sweat rinsed away.

"You coming tonight?" Lisa repeated through the curtain.

Jenny thought about it. There'd been talk about a party at someone's house in Boston where the parents were out of town. She'd been somewhat interested before, but now she had this thing with Professor Dyer. "Uh, I don't think so."

"Oh, come on, Jenny. You never go anywhere," Lisa whined.

It was true. It was only September, but Jenny was already getting a reputation for being a homebody. The thing was, it was safer that way. There was always so much noise in her head when she was around others now. The visions could pop and bounce. It was annoying. Not always, of course, but she had almost no control over them. She had to push herself to be social.

"Um, I don't know," she finally said, not wanting to commit.

When she finished with her shower, she wrapped herself in a towel, and Lisa made room for her at the sink. Jenny grabbed her comb and began the process of detangling her hair, fresh from washing.

"There's going to be guys there, thank God," said Lisa. "I can't believe how much I miss all those smelly juveniles."

Jenny smiled as Lisa applied her makeup. "When are you leaving?"

"In an hour." Lisa rolled her eyes. "I know. It's ridiculous for it to start so early, but we thought we'd get a bite somewhere before we head to the party."

Jenny didn't know the girl who was hosting it, but she'd seen her around the dorm. She was a sophomore, and she always seemed to be surrounded by pretty girls. Margo, that was her name. Jenny considered her roommate, Lisa. She, too, was a pretty girl. From Hong Kong. It was beyond cool to think about Lisa's exotic life. From the pictures she'd seen and the stories she'd heard, Lisa had lived a life of real high-rise privilege. Seriously chaperoned from an early age, Lisa was now wild to enjoy every aspect of her American college experience.

Lisa stopped applying mascara midstroke, her eyes darting in the mirror to Jenny. "Tell me you're coming."

Jenny gritted her teeth, about to opt out, but then stopped—and flashed. She saw Lisa passed out on a bed somewhere with someone above her crying, trying to shake her awake.

Jenny grabbed Lisa's arm. "You can't go."

Lisa pulled her head back. "What are you talking about?"

She felt sick. Now what? These fucking junctures! She'd seen Lisa clearly in trouble, and it would most likely be tonight. But she often wondered what her role was in these situations. Was a *warning* to Lisa good enough? Was she supposed to intervene? Was the person supposed to experience something so that they'd do their own zig or zag, zag, zag? God, the decisions wore on her! Sometimes, the visions were so much responsibility. Her mind raced as she tried to determine what to do.

Jenny shrugged. "I mean, how much do you even know about Margo? Is she, like, a *safe* person?"

Lisa continued to get ready. "Of course, she's safe. You've met her friends."

It was true. She had met them in the dining hall, but she'd never partied with them. Not to mention she'd never really partied in Boston at all. And she didn't have any extra spending money for restaurants, bars, Uber, or whatever was coming their way tonight.

As if reading her mind, Lisa said, "If you can't pay, don't worry about it. I'll take care of you."

Jenny put her comb down and walked out of the bathroom. She dove into her drawer and found some clean underwear. Thank God for that. She tugged them on, then sat on her bed and looked over at Lisa's space. Stuffed animals, a few at least, had been lugged all the way from China for her American adventure. Jenny looked into the button eyes of one, a somewhat pitiful elephant, its fur almost worn off.

Lisa was a friendly, sweet, and welcoming girl. Jenny had gotten lucky to get her as a roommate. She knew that. But now, well, there might be trouble. Scratch that. Lisa was definitely going in the wrong direction. At least tonight.

Just then, Lisa poked her head around the corner. "If you come out, I'll loan you some jewelry. Your pick!" She popped back out of view.

"What are you going to wear?" Jenny asked, biting her lip. She closed her eyes, remembering exactly what she'd seen Lisa wearing in her vision. Maybe it wasn't tonight.

"Something to show off the curves. My dark skinny jeans, a tank, maybe some long necklaces."

Jenny sighed. Same outfit. She couldn't go to Professor Dyer's tonight. She needed to play wingman for Lisa instead. She dug her cell phone out of her shorts' pocket, then looked through her backpack for his cell number. She found it and texted.

Can't come. Got a zig I need to follow. Raincheck?

Chapter 12

Max glanced with irritation at his phone. "Man, " he said. He frowned and shook his head. Why had she canceled their meeting? He'd never before been able to speak with someone about his gift, especially someone who shared a similar phenomenon. The adrenaline rush he'd had over the thought of finding another person like him was now replaced with disappointment.

He looked at the text again. What did she mean by a zig? Was that some new slang? Was she for real? He'd seen flashes of her past, but he wasn't as sure now. Was she screwing with him? Had she been lying to him? He sat down on a small barstool near his kitchen counter and thought about the encounter.

Unless she was really, really good at reading his mind, she had to be the real thing. Right? He picked up his phone and was about to text back but then stopped himself. How was he going to manage this? She was his student. He'd been hasty about inviting her over in the first place. He could lose his job if things got misinterpreted by her or if people found out he'd invited her to his home. Should he trust her? Maybe she didn't trust *him*.

He looked at Bones lying nearby and watched her glance swivel between the oven with the lasagna inside and back to him. It was incredible that when he'd pulled open the freezer door, there was a Stouffer's inside. He'd scraped the frost off the top of the old box and tossed it on the counter. He'd long forgotten it was even there.

Did Jenny think he was interested in her romantically? Had he scared her? He was her teacher, but he was also a man—an *old* man compared to her. It was exhausting to always worry about misrepresenting himself to young women, but that was the gig.

He'd entered her name and number into his phone after she'd left him the information earlier that day. He could text her back. Or not. Eventually, he typed . . .

No problem.

It was noncommittal.

"Shit," he said as he laid the phone down. Bones looked at him. "Looks like it's lasagna for you and me, kid."

Max sighed loudly, a knot in his stomach as he walked to the counter and picked up a box of red wine. He gave it a shake, encouraged that it seemed fairly full, and opened a cabinet in search of a glass. Finding it empty of wine glasses, he chose a coffee cup and rubbed a finger on the rim, getting rid of some dust before he filled the mug. He reached back inside the cabinet and retrieved a cigarette from a bowl, then extracted the large crystal lighter next to it. He lit the cigarette and took a long drag. Leaning back against the counter, he picked up a coffee cup and surveyed his house. It was a mess.

Dirty dishes filled the counters—the sink too. There was a bowl on the counter still filled with crusted milk from breakfast some days past. Wads of dog hair had piled up on the nicely finished oak floors, bundled in the corners like tumbleweeds. Clothes, clean piles and dirty alike, were strewn on the one good couch and a couple of chairs. Empty glasses, overflowing ashtrays, food, books, papers, magazines, dog toys—the place needed a lot of work. And he wasn't even looking at the construction issues. One wall was still entirely unpainted drywall. His mother had painted some sample colors on it in streaks, but he had yet to make a decision.

"Maybe she made the right choice," he said thoughtfully, thinking of Jenny and the mess he'd invited her to witness. He took another long drag off his cigarette, placed it in a mostly full ashtray, and then opened the dishwasher. It was full of dirty, funky smelling dishes and not yet run. He reached into a cabinet under the sink without his gloves, confident that he'd wiped the karmic grime off the miscellaneous household items under the counter, and grabbed the Cascade. He filled the dispenser with the last dregs of the dish soap, the bottle burping at him, protesting its status as empty. "Put that on the list," he said to Bones.

She shook her head and walked out of the room.

Max decided he might as well spend some time cleaning. Jenny might still be coming over. Somehow, destiny had brought them together. Maybe he shouldn't scare her off by being such a pig.

Chapter 13

Sidrah dragged a fingertip over the top of the large, square, built-in dresser in the middle of her closet. Everything was perfectly clean, as usual, and wonderfully organized. Marta was a dream. She kept the house in tip-top shape, all packages, maintenance, cleaning, and cooking, neatly dealt with. The trash cans always clean, the countertops sparkly. Fresh food and delicious meals were on hand at all times, easily accessible to sate Sidrah's every whim.

Having arrived home from Vegas some hours before, Sidrah was finally alone and back upstairs in her bedroom, her beautiful sanctuary. Marta had seen to her luggage. Her dirty clothes, including the luxurious cocktail dress she'd worn the evening before, were either tucked away or in the laundry room, ready to be professionally taken care of.

Sidrah kicked off her shoes and began to remove her jewelry. She smiled at the bauble she'd gifted herself after her big win. A new emerald. Her favorite. She extended her hand and looked at the dazzling gemstone, thinking it was worth every penny. Her seatmate in first class had commented on it too. She'd been pleased with the admiration, but she occasionally worried that she was displaying too much wealth in public. It might be time for her to check out other options when she flew. NetJets, a private aviation service, would probably have travelers accustomed to gemstones like hers. She frowned at the thought, realizing that was a bit sad. She never ever wanted to become complacent or unappreciative of the glorious gifts and lifestyle that surrounded her. She loved them. Every. Single. One. Like an artist, she sometimes marveled at things to the point of distraction.

She popped the large buttons of her designer jacket and dropped it on the floor, then ran her fingers over the delicate lace of her bra. Gorgeous. Perfect. And she wasn't talking about her breasts. She ran her fingers over them too. The flowered, delicate lace of the push-up La Perla bra cost nearly four hundred dollars. Those designers were doing God's work. The lingerie was worth every penny.

She released her breasts and dropped the bra to the floor, continuing to disrobe and toss off garments with abandon, like throwing peanut shells on a barroom floor. She enjoyed her bath time ritual like nothing else on earth. Tonight, she would celebrate. She was home. Safe. And much, much wealthier than she'd been only two days before when she'd left Boston.

She decided to watch a bit of television tonight while bathing. She pulled up the options on the menu, working hard to set the perfect mood and landed on *Ocean's Eleven*. She smiled. George and Brad. *Yes.* She'd bathe with them.

She leaned over to run the water and wondered why she hadn't found Mr. Right. It was the only really odd part of her vision. While she was in Vegas, she'd expected him to appear around every corner, but he never had.

"Where are you, *mon amour*?"

She smiled, thinking of his beautiful face. She couldn't wait to meet him, couldn't wait to ravish him. Perhaps tonight. If only in her dreams.

Chapter 14

No problem. Jenny frowned at the recollection that Professor Dyer had texted her something so casual, so brush-off. They'd had an epic conversation, and there was more to have! *No problem. No problem.* She practiced various inflections of the tepid response in her mind, trying to get a feel for his intent as she rode in an Uber with Lisa and a couple of other girls.

The night had been okay so far. They'd had dinner at a sushi place and were now on the way to the big party. What would happen there? Jenny ran a hand nervously through her hair. She was focused now. Lisa would need to zag hard, or Jenny would. Maybe her presence alone was enough to detour the disaster that might come. Or not? *God,* she never knew what to think.

She couldn't wait to have a conversation with someone who actually might understand. Professor Dyer. Professor— *no problem*—Dyer.

She'd text him tomorrow. Or maybe tonight? No. She couldn't let anyone see her doing that. She'd heard talk among her friends when they went over their schedules. Professor Dyer was a thing. A catch. Eye candy. Everyone seemed to love him from a distance. No one went so far as to say there was something creepy going on with his gloves.

She'd be the talk of the party if they knew she'd had a personal conversation with him and run his dog. She was glad she'd only used his initials when she'd logged his number in her cell phone. God knew what would happen, to both of them, if that information fell into the wrong hands.

But you've done nothing wrong—neither of you.

That was cold satisfaction because she realized they were both, quite possibly, freaks. And there was no way anyone could know. She worried a bit that he had somehow deceived her, but no. She truly thought he was on the level. Was he safe? She assured herself that, yes, he felt safe. And if he wasn't, well, God knew she was good with a knife.

The thought of the assault sickened her, and she choked it down. She never wanted to think about it again. Of course, that was impossible. There was probably going to be a trial; she would doubtless have to appear as a witness. She didn't think anyone at Wellesley knew about what had happened. Except now, Professor Dyer did.

Jenny looked out the Uber window at the slow but exciting Boston traffic. It was a cool place to live. Tonight, she just wanted to keep her friend safe and have fun. She'd have to work hard to accomplish both those goals, but she'd sure as hell try.

Chapter 15

The opening notes of Beethoven's *Eroica* registered somewhere in Turner Black's deeply relaxed brain. The powerful music, written about Emperor Napoleon, appealed to Turner as his chosen wake-up call in his private sensory deprivation tank.

His mind, his beautiful mind, was fully relaxed, yet wonderfully alive. The experience in the tank had once again filled him with information about his life and its purpose. He floated naked in the shallow pool of salted water for ten minutes longer, listening to the music before opening the tank's door and embracing the light of the world—his world to conquer. A place to leave his mark. He was doing beautifully.

Fifty-five years he'd lived, possibly only thirty-five of those fully aware of the creature he was. He sighed with a deep peace as he walked to the nearby shower and turned on the hot water. Red LED lights framed the ceiling-mounted shower heads set to pour two feet of waterfall onto him as he walked inside. Beethoven, still playing in the shower while the water streamed through the red lights, filled him with adrenaline as he prepared for the day.

Leaving his special room, he walked to the long stone risers of his modern stairway, running a hand along the iron and glass banister as he made his way upstairs to his bedroom. He walked past a stretch of wall containing a saltwater aquarium filled with a cornucopia of coral. People often thought it was empty of fish and were startled when a small fish or shrimp was introduced to the tank. The fish, exploring their way to the bottom, were instantly devoured when the coral below them came alive. Not coral, of course, but one of the most venomous creatures that lived in the sea. A stonefish.

"Soon," he said to the tank as he walked past and entered his bedroom. He stopped for a moment to sit at his desk and do a quick Google search to confirm his vision. When in his float tank, his mind was a portal, open and receptive to reams of information given to him by the gods. Among other insights today, he'd seen a woman. She was a stranger, but her location on the planet could not have been more convenient.

"Today, 3:00 p.m. Houghton Chapel. Wellesley Campus. She'll be there."

He took some time to scroll through the event—an outdoor rally for the governor's race hosted by the GOP. He gave a crooked smile at the screen, loving the coincidence that his own profoundly dark candidate—Governor Jett Franklin—would be there to make a speech. He'd give his boy a quick hello before he scoped the crowd for the woman from his vision.

She'd be there. Tallish, thin, with creamy light-brown skin. Very pretty. She wore a pair of silly black and white polka dot palazzo pants and a sleeveless white silk shirt. Her lips were painted red. With her large sunglasses in place, she'd be easy to pick out of the crowd among the student body.

The question was, why was she there? Why had she come to him in the tank? Her purpose in his life was unclear. He looked up, stopped by a small, almost imperceptible flutter of anxiety. What was that? When was the last time he'd felt that emotion? Was the woman to blame?

Chapter 16

Another delightful fall day filled with possibilities dawned over Sidrah's Boston home. This one would be major. Because today, by God, she'd finally meet him. She'd seen the strange man again in her dreams. This time, she knew exactly where to find him. She recognized the Wellesley Campus. Not only that, but there was also signage up around a podium on the green. She'd checked out the situation online and discovered what the outdoor event was about.

And while she was *not* happy about attending a rally for her pig of a governor, Jett Franklin, she'd go because he'd be there. Her boy! The one she'd been searching for. Sidrah got ready, having decided to wear a sensible outfit, something practical, so her heels wouldn't sink in the grass. She worked her ensemble around a pair of black and white Stella McCartney platform sneakers.

Now sitting in her lunar-blue metallic E Class Mercedes Cabriolet, she put on her large Gucci sunglasses and pushed the button to retract the roof. The car, parked in her carport near the back alley of her home, purred for twenty seconds while the top vanished into the trunk. Sidrah pressed another control for the gates to glide open and then sped out the alley toward the Wellesley Campus. She thought about what would happen when she met Mr. Right and smiled in anticipation. One thing was certain: she'd capture him and find out what the devil was going on.

Walking toward the venue in her flowing and playful Michael Kors pants, she eventually made her way across the green and into the crowd. She backed up a bit, onto a slight incline, and scanned the heads. The governor was standing near the raised dais, shaking hands and laughing like he had not a care in the world. He took some selfies with what were obviously students, and then took the stage.

Sidrah played with the strap of her purse, frustrated at not seeing her man. So she decided to move to the other side. A male voice, coming from behind, stopped her. She turned around with a bright smile but immediately dropped it. It wasn't him.

"Hello," the gray-haired man said. "Glad you could make it out today." He extended his hand.

Sidrah looked down at his hand and shook it. "Hello," she said as she turned and continued walking.

He followed her. "It's so nice out today. Although a picnic blanket and a bottle of wine would help."

Sidrah stopped and turned back to him. She didn't want to be rude. "Yes. I'm sorry, I'm just looking for my friend."

The distinguished man put his hands in his trouser pockets. She noticed his tailoring. He was very nicely put together and not at all difficult to look at.

"I see," said the man. "My name is Turner Black. Pleased to meet you."

Sidrah's stomach fluttered with nerves, although precisely why, she couldn't say. The anticipation of meeting Mr. Right? Anxious to politely get away from this man? Irritated about listening to the bastard on the podium drone on about making changes he had no intention of making? She adjusted the strap on her purse and nodded. "Hello. I'm Sidrah."

"Sidrah. What an unusual name. Are you a supporter of the governor?"

Sidrah rolled her eyes. Thank goodness she still had on her glasses. She assumed that Turner Black was a supporter, but again, she didn't want to be rude. Out of her periphery, she saw someone who might be her man. She turned and stood on her tiptoes to get a better view. *Bingo.*

She shook her head. "Uh, not really. I'm sorry, I really must run."

Before she could turn, the man extracted his wallet from his pocket and pulled out a business card. He handed it to her. "My card. I don't usually pick up women . . . really ever. But forgive me, this time I couldn't help myself. I don't want to be rude and keep you from your friend. But if you're interested, could I buy you dinner later this evening? Or we could meet for a cocktail. Say, at the Oak Bar? At the Fairmont?"

Sidrah glanced at the card. *Black, Holt & Palmberg. Turner Black, Founding Partner.* It was a law firm in Boston. The guy was the real deal. She wasn't sure about seeing him later, but then again, she didn't want to shut the door completely. One never knew, did one?

She smiled. "Maybe? Can I say that? I'll give you a call later if my plans with my friend don't work out."

"Please call." He smiled.

She walked away, stuffing the card into the pocket of her pants. She shouldered her way toward where she'd last seen the man with the dark hair and finally broke free from a large section of crowd before she came upon him, standing about two bodies away. Her breath caught as she got her first real look at him. Mr. Right was drop-dead gorgeous. Although, his wardrobe might not be. He wore a tight black T-shirt and some cargo shorts. A therapy boot covered his left leg to his knee, and he wore a dirty running shoe on the other foot.

She was leaning around the person next to her, examining him, when he turned and looked at her. His eyes were a piercing brown. She stood up straight, startled, hiding behind the person on her left. She took a deep breath, then moved past the person until she came around Mr. Right from the back, on his left side. Thank goodness there'd been no one else there to maneuver out of the way.

She leaned her head toward him and said in a low voice, "Hello. Wonderful fall day for this event, wouldn't you say?"

He looked at her again. This time, she took off her sunglasses and stared directly up into his eyes. A warmth filled her. She smiled at him.

"Yes." He turned back to look at the stage and crossed his arms.

She looked down and kicked the dirt at her feet. "Is he your guy?"

He tugged at the lobe of one of his ears. "Not exactly. I work here. Faculty. Thought I should make an appearance."

She let out a long breath and put her hands on her knees. "Oh, thank God. I didn't know how we'd manage."

He looked at her, puzzled. She stuck out her hand, and for the first time, noticed he was wearing gloves. *Why?* "I'm Sidrah. Sidrah Keeling. It's nice to meet you."

He looked down at her. Then he uncrossed his arms and accepted the hand. "Max Dyer."

"Max Dyer," she said. "You're wearing gloves. Why is that?"

He pulled his hand back and didn't hide his irritation. "Maybe it's a fashion statement."

She smiled and shook her head. "No. I don't think so."

"How would you know?" he said irritably.

She ran a hand down her ensemble and pulled up the hem of her pants. Wiggling her ankle, she said, "Stella McCartney. They're crazy good. Don't you think?"

"What are you doing here?" he asked.

She dropped the hem and stared into his eyes. "Looking for you."

Max screwed his jaw to the side with a look of impatience. "I see."

She briefly touched his arm. "No. I'm afraid you don't see. In fact, I'd be very surprised if you did. But let's not argue. The fact is, you and I need to talk. Immediately. There's something very important that we need to discuss."

He furrowed his brow. "What?"

She copied his facial gesture and put on her best pleading look. "Max. Max Dyer. If you just give me a few minutes or a little bit of your valuable time, I can explain. But I really, *really* do need to speak with you."

He squinted at her. "Are you a parent?"

"Do I look like I'm old enough to be a parent?" she said, raising her voice. Several people turned to stare at them.

He finally cracked a smile. "Okay. Nutjob," he said.

She rolled her eyes and put her glasses back on. "Follow me then. Let's get the hell out of here."

She began walking. But feeling his hesitation, she turned back and waved him on. He followed, slowly, limping in his boot.

She breathed out a long, slow breath. *Okay, Sidrah, you've found him. Now what in the world are you going to do with him?*

She led him to the parking lot where she'd parked her car. Walking quickly, she hoped he'd continue to follow without conversation because she didn't want to resume speaking until they were alone.

"Where are you going?" he called to her back.

Sidrah grimaced but ignored his question. "I'm just over here." She turned, smiling, and pointed ahead of them at her blue car, the top back in place.

She stopped at the back fender and reached into her bag to retrieve her keys.

Max caught up with her. "Hey. What did you need to talk to me about?"

She pushed her sunglasses on top of her head and gave him a big smile. Once again ignoring his question, she put on her flirt and used her fingertips to play with the blouse on her shoulders, pinching it up as if she were hot. "Oof. All uphill. Must be thirsty work there in that boot. What happened to you anyway? What do you say let's get out of here? I'd love to buy you a drink somewhere. Would you like to drive?"

She gestured to the car and went to the driver's side, unlocking it before he could speak. She hopped inside and started the engine, hitting the button to make the top disappear. Max was still standing near the trunk. She got out and gestured to the driver's seat. "No kidding. It's like a dream. You want to take her for a spin?"

"Nice car," he said, looking it over. "Yours?"

"Of course, it's mine. Who else's would it be?" she said crossly.

He put out his bottom lip. "I dunno. Company car. What are you? A lawyer? Real estate agent?"

"Oh, for goodness' sakes," she said, passing him. She placed a soft hand on his back to encourage him toward the driver's side. Excitement jolted through her. She gulped at the buzz and forced herself to walk to the passenger side, now more determined than ever to spend time with him.

"Just get in, will you?" She got into the passenger seat and shut the door, hoping he'd go for it, that the lure of the car would help him to commit to spending time with her.

She let out a breath as Max took the bait. Once inside the car and behind the wheel, he began looking for the seat controls. "They're just over there," she said, pointing down near his leg, accidentally touching it as he moved.

"I got it," he grumbled slightly as the seat went back. But he did a double-take in her direction.

"Wonderful," she grumbled back, mocking him but feeling heat in his look, their proximity making her heart throb a bit faster. "Where would you like to go for our chat?"

He pulled out of the parking space and, once in Drive, seemed to enjoy the experience. "There's a pub not far. I haven't had lunch."

"Great. Your call."

They drove through the streets, enjoying the autumnal scenes on campus. The trees were just beginning to turn all shades of red and yellow. Max kept the car in careful control, never exceeding the speed limit or going crazy, as Sidrah forced some small banter and talked a bit about the vehicle on their way. Not long after, he pulled into the parking lot of what looked a lot like a Dubliner pub. They made their way inside and were seated in an enclosed landscaped courtyard.

Sidrah looked at the menu. "So, what's good here?"

Max crunched on a handful of complimentary popcorn, some of it missing his mouth and falling to the ground. Birds at their feet scurried over to take care of the debris. "Beer. And they've got a great brat selection. Sauerkraut."

Sidrah blinked back the image of her stuffing a large, messy sausage into her mouth on a first date. She took her sunglasses off and laid them neatly on the table beside her. The waiter came up, and Max did indeed order a sausage meal. She ordered hot tea and an appetizer-sized antipasto platter.

Max stared at her while tossing back more kernels of popcorn. "So. Sidrah Keeling. What's this all about?" he said between bites.

She almost didn't know what to say. She certainly couldn't just blurt out that she'd been dreaming about him. Although, she wasn't entirely sure whether he'd be turned off by that. She took a deep breath. "I'll tell you. But how about we get to know one another a bit first?"

She leaned over and lowered her voice. "I'm definitely not a lawyer, that I can assure you. In fact, I'll be honest. I never went to college."

He arched his brows. "Really? Are you married? What do you do?"

Again, she didn't want to tell him that she had swindled the system with her insider knowledge and amassed a fortune by cashing in on her fortune-telling abilities. "No, I'm not married. I'm ... I've acquired a few investments. You could say I'm pretty good at playing the market."

"Like what?" he said as the server placed Max's pint of beer and her tea on the table.

"Oh, you know, I'd rather not get into the particulars. Now you ... you're on the faculty. You're a professor then?"

Max guzzled a large amount of beer and sat back. "Yes. I teach history, European mostly, to freshmen. I'm working up a few seminars on historical coincidence."

She put her cup on the saucer. "European history, that's interesting. Have you traveled a lot then?"

He shrugged. "Not as much as I'd like. I spent some semesters in Italy and Greece and then some time in Naples working on my dissertation."

"What was that on?" she said, enjoying their proximity but trying hard to stay focused.

"The Sibylline Books."

"I've never heard of them. What are they about?"

"Do you know anything about mythology?" He grabbed some more popcorn and shoveled it into his mouth.

Sidrah blinked back with interest at the unusual topic. They were potentially circling to the metaphysical. As much as she wanted to pretend this was a real date and that Max and she had met naturally, that was not the case. There was a reason he'd been brought to her, and she had to keep digging to find the answer.

"I know a bit." She smiled. "Believe it or not, I did some study on cosmology. I tried reading Carl Sagan. Let me tell you, I should not have tried that alone."

Max smiled. Melting a bit in his gaze, she let her mind fly, imagining how heavenly he would look in a suit, smoldering in some advertisement for men's cologne.

"Tales, fables from the Greeks and Romans. Homer. *The Iliad. The Odyssey.* Have you read them?"

She shook her head. "No. I love to read, though. Are the Sibylline Books in there? What are they about?"

He stopped eating and raised a questioning eyebrow at her. "You want to hear about my dissertation? Is that why we're here?"

"I absolutely want to hear about it! It's a big part of your life, and I do love history." She smiled.

He shrugged. "All right. The Sibylline Books were real enough. Roman history tells us that King Tarquinius Superbus was the final king of Rome before the Roman Republic, from around 535 BC to 509 BC. He was known as Tarquin the Proud—a cognomen of the Superbus. Anyway, a sibyl approaches this king: the Cumaean Sibyl."

"What's a sibyl?" she interrupted.

"A soothsayer, a prophetess. There were quite a few of them around Italy and Greece at the time. They were important to the people and were located in different areas. The Cumaean Sibyl was from Cumae, a Greek colony near Naples."

Sidrah sat spellbound, a bit dizzy even, listening to the story. A prophetess. A soothsayer. Why had she not known of the sibyls or thought to search through history before now? She stared into his eyes, encouraging him for more.

"You really want to hear about this stuff?" he asked again, taking another sip of his beer.

She nodded earnestly. "I absolutely do. Tell me everything about the books and what you've learned."

Max hesitated and played with his glass but then looked into her eyes as he immersed himself in the story. "So, King Tarquinius was approached by the Cumaean Sibyl. She had nine books of prophecies about the future of Rome, but she offered them at a tremendous price. The proud king said no. So, she burned three of the books and offered to sell the remaining six to him at the same price. He refused again. Then, she burned three more and repeated the offer. So now we're down to three. The king, really getting itchy, finally relented and paid the full original asking price for the three."

She leaned forward. "What was in them?"

"Well, they were a collection of oral utterances set in verse. Hexameters. Like the kind used in the *Iliad* and so forth."

A few butterflies flitted around in Sidrah's stomach as she thought about the story. She bit her bottom lip. "They were predictions of the future?"

Max nodded. "Prophecies. Partisans, the ruling class families, originally protected the books, then by priests, who kept them secreted and safe. They used the books quite a lot to help form religious observances to avert the prophesied calamities—earthquakes, plagues, that kind of thing. Only the rites surrounding the expiations, or the sacrifices for making amends, were shared with the public— not the exact words from the oracles. This, of course, led to opportunities for abuse. Officials would wield the words to fit particular needs. Among other things, they led to the construction of Greek temples in Rome and worshiping the gods and goddesses of the Greek culture."

"What happened to them? Are they still around?"

Max took a sip of beer and shook his head. "No. They were lost in a fire. But the Roman senate worked to capture similar oracles. They sent envoys around Italy and Africa and put together a new collection based on sayings from other sibyls along with works that were in private hands. After that, the new oracles were kept in the Temple of Apollo on the Palatine in Rome for about four hundred years. Then, a general burned them, believing the words were being used against him and his government. Dumb ass."

"So, the books were a go-to reference when times got tough? The prophecies were used to support a particular purpose or a remedy for tragedy?"

"Yes. For example, the books may have fueled rumors that Caesar was aspiring for kingship. Only a king could triumph over Parthia." He said the last sentence using air quotes.

"When did Pompeii happen?" she said, referring to the volcanic ruins of the city near Naples.

"79 AD . . ." Max began, but they were interrupted by the server bringing their food.

Sidrah snapped out of the story's trance. A bit unsettled about the topic of prophecies, she busied herself, sampling an olive and a piece of cheese while Max stuffed a massive bite of brat into his mouth and chewed. She observed a bit of sauerkraut dangling from his lips until his tongue came out to retrieve the morsel. He seemed utterly engrossed now on another subject, his food.

What was happening here with this man? Were her gift and his knowledge about a topic near to her heart the reason she'd been drawn to him? She took another sip of tea and cleared her throat. "That's all so interesting. And you teach about this? The sibyls? What was the one's name from the story?"

"Cumaean. Now there's another story. I'm rushing through it, though."

Sidrah watched while he licked his fingers. When the food came, he'd removed one glove and exclusively used that hand to eat. There appeared to be nothing wrong with his hand. She hadn't known what to expect when he removed the glove, but at the minimum, she'd thought there would be some kind of burn or dermatological problem. She considered the situation before asking her question again.

"Why is it you wear gloves, Max?"

He picked up a napkin with his gloved hand and used it to wipe his mouth. "It's personal."

She nodded. "Okay. I was just curious. You can tell me later."

He held up his nearly empty beer and raised it, looking around for their server. Successfully making eye contact with the nubile, attractive waitress, Max swallowed the last of the beer from the mug and set it on the table. "It's your turn, Sidrah. You haven't told me why it was so important for us to talk. Do you have a job for me? Some research?"

She brightened at the idea. It was an excellent ruse. She scrambled to put together a good lie. "Yes! I do. What I need . . . and naturally, I'd heard about you before we met. I'd Googled my way around to you, but I wanted to vet you *personally* before I offered you a job. I need an expert. In some Greek and Roman artifacts that one of my investors has collected."

He gave her a dubious look. "Get an auction house specialist or a curator. I can't price something for its value."

"No. I mean, he's interested in the *stories* surrounding the pieces. He is looking for someone who might be knowledgeable."

Max sat back as the server came and replaced his beer. Sidrah gave the girl a second glance as she waited by the table until Max looked up and smiled at her. Seeming satisfied, she finally walked away.

Sidrah shot a dubious look at the back of the pretty retreating girl, then smiled at Max. "Do you come here often?"

He shrugged as he reached for her platter and extracted a piece of salami. "Sometimes."

She flipped her hands up. "Who said you could take my food?"

"Sorry. You didn't seem to be making much progress. Do you have a dog at home for the rest?"

"No. I don't," she said, putting her head down and stuffing a large block of cheese into her mouth. She chewed with defiance.

He smiled. "I do. If you don't want that, Bones will take care of it."

She softened again at the sight of his smile. The server had not been wrong to wait for one. "Bones? What kind of dog?"

"She's a mix of something. The vet thinks she's got some lab, some golden retriever. I dunno. She's big but more on the red side."

Sidrah caught the look of amusement on his face. "How old is she?"

"One. Or two. We're not sure. She came out of nowhere. I mean, one day, over off College Road, she grabbed a pair of my gloves that had fallen out of my pack and then ran into the street. I think she was playing chase, but she was hit by a car. I paid for her to be fixed up and took her home. I searched for the owners, but she didn't have a chip or a collar, and no one claimed her."

It pleased Sidrah that Max had a dog. "Well, I'm happy to contribute to the food fund. She can have whatever I leave behind."

Max got to work finishing his meal. Sidrah needed to see him again, and now she had an excuse. Not a real one, but that didn't matter.

"So, Max. Will you agree to see the pieces? Tell us what you can about them? I can pay you."

"I'm not sure you've got the right person. You'd be better off with a curator or specialist. I could help you with a few names."

"No, Max. We want you. I tell you what . . ." She reached into her bag and pulled out her phone. "Why don't you give me your information, and I'll text you where to meet me." She pulled up a new contact screen and typed in his name.

"Sure," he said, relenting.

She relaxed as he gave her the number. For the moment, Sidrah was happy. It was a heady and interesting start.

Chapter 17

Max walked into his house, carrying the large take-out container. Bones rushed over to greet him, her jumping and whimpering both endearing and annoyingly aggressive at the same time.

"Okay, okay," he said, going to the kitchen counter and opening the container. He went over to her bowl.

"Sit." He pointed at her for emphasis.

She sat, licking her lips while he dished out a bit of the food. There was a lot left, and he didn't want her to gulp it down and get sick. Once released from the command, she jumped in the air and pounced at the bowl like a cat before devouring her treat.

"I met a girl. A pretty one," he said, smiling at Bones, who seemed interested.

"Her name is Sidrah Keeling. She needs me to provide the history around some antiques. What do you think of that?"

Bones barked at him and ran to the back door, ready to be let out. Max joined her and went out into the backyard, tossing the ball with her for a few minutes. Privacy sections fenced in his good-sized yard, but each section needed replacing. He frowned at the situation as well as his weedy, patchy yard. How the previous owners had gotten away with letting their valuable property go to seed was a mystery. But the fact was, they had. And now his parents were anxious for him to fix it up and make it his home.

He wasn't unhappy with the arrangement. Quite the contrary. It was a relief not to live in an apartment with neighbors, or worse, roommates. He was finished with his education, and now he had a job, a house, and a dog. Things had most decidedly changed for him over the last couple of years.

His phone rang. He looked down at the screen and took off his glove to answer the call from his mother, Tracey.

"Hey, Mom," he said.

"Hi! What are you doing today? What's the weather like up there?"

He took a seat on one of two folding chairs on the concrete patio and settled in for what he knew could be a long conversation. "It's nice. I went to the governor's rally . . ."

"Oh my gosh, Max. You're not supporting that jerk, are you?"

He stretched in the sun, feeling a bit sleepy after his large meal. "No. But it was on campus, and I'm faculty. I thought I should make an appearance."

"What else have you been doing? Have you decided on the paint color? I think the gray is nice."

His eyes closed, his face in the sun, he flashed back on Sidrah and the moment they'd met. Her smile had been beautiful. Pulling himself back to the conversation, he answered, "Uh, no, not yet."

"And how is my grand puppy? What is she up to? Can we Facetime?"

Max smirked and pressed the button. His mom's face popped onto the screen, her smile wide, her love on display. They had a close relationship. She'd accepted his peculiarities the same way she dealt with the air she breathed. Completely normal and a part of them.

"You look good, Maximus. What else have you done today? Have you done the raking yet?"

Max turned the phone around and let his mother get a firsthand view of his messy yard. Leaves and tree debris were everywhere. "Max," she groaned. "I hope you're at least keeping up with the baby's poo-poo."

At that moment, Bones came to his side and sat. She stretched her neck to look at the phone. Tracey waved at her. "There she is, there she is, there's my girl."

Max turned the phone back to his face. "I had lunch with a girl."

She shrieked. "What! I can't wait to tell your father."

Max stretched. "Yes. It was epic, Mom. Love at first sight. I hope you're sitting down; we're getting married."

"Stop it, Max. Don't tease me."

He smirked. "You asked for it."

"Did you really have lunch with someone?" she whispered.

He smiled, recalling Sidrah's forward, but damn alluring pickup. "I did. Her name is Sidrah Keeling. She drives a Mercedes. She has in-vestments."

"How old is she?"

He shrugged and considered. "My age. Maybe thirty."

His mother beamed. "Do you like her?"

He reached down and readjusted the Velcro on his brace. His time with the contraption was up in a couple of days. "Yeah. She was nice. You'd like her. She's very girly."

"How did you meet her?"

"She picked me up at the rally. We went to lunch."

"Oh? Are you going to see her again?"

He nodded, swiftly realizing he was looking forward to it. "I am. She may have some work for me."

"Work? What about dating?"

The thought of what a date with Sidrah might lead to certainly had crossed his mind. She was incredibly pretty, and he liked her energy and the way she looked walking in those goofy pants. And her car. He was definitely attracted to her, but he felt a typical jolt of frustration when thinking about women. "Yeah. We'll see."

They continued their conversation for the next hour as he walked through the house with Bones, showing his mom the cleaning he'd done and some of the projects he'd begun. Eventually placating her with assurances of his love, he got off the phone and began to focus on other issues.

Like Jenny. It worried him that he hadn't heard from her. He thought maybe she'd reach back out today, but so far, no. He moved over to his couch, grabbing his laptop off the coffee table, and stretched out on the sofa, laying the computer on his belly. Bones lay on the floor near him, and he reached down to scratch her head.

He Googled Sidrah first. He came away with the usual paid sites, which offered a full background check, including arrest records, but passed on those. He hesitated, kind of hating himself for it, but checked Facebook too. Not finding her and happy that he hadn't, he then thought about the conversation they'd had at lunch and randomly hacked around the sites he'd been to before on the Cumaean Sibyl.

He scrolled down to a picture of the Sibyl by Domenichino, one he'd seen many times before, and froze. It was as if he was seeing it for the first time. There was something striking there, something new in the innocent look of the Sibyl's upturned eyes. They reminded him of Jenny.

Chapter 18

Jenny, still in pajamas, opened her eyes and looked directly at Lisa's sleeping form, tucked into her bed across from her in their dorm room. She reached down to the floor and pressed the button on her phone. It was three o'clock in the afternoon.

Jenny threw back the covers, padded over to Lisa, and stared down at her. They'd had a long night. She leaned in close to check Lisa's breathing and then left her side, walking over and sliding the door open to the shared bathroom. No one was in there, and the door for her suitemates was closed.

She went back into the bedroom and surveyed the situation from the night before. There were pizza and cookie delivery boxes on the desks as well as a few red go-cups, which still contained the last dregs of rum and Coke.

Yuck. She grabbed the cups and brought them into the bathroom to dump and dispose of. She went back to her desk and flipped open the box for the pizza. There was one piece left, and she picked it up and took a bite, chewing as she thought over the fun evening they'd had. Well, most of it had been fun, but not all.

The fact that Lisa was home and alive was *really good.* Jenny had made sure not to leave her side and monitored her intake of alcohol. There had been some talk that a few people at the party had ecstasy and other drugs, but she made sure they stayed away from that. They'd had a few beers, then piled back into an Uber and took the party back to the dorm. One girl had stayed behind with a boy, but Jenny hadn't seen anything that worried her about that.

Pizza in hand, she retrieved her phone from the floor, sitting cross-legged on her bed while she ate and scrolled through her feed on Instagram from the night before. A lot of what happened was out there, but the images weren't too bad.

What had been bad was the overload of flashes she'd had while she'd been out. Things seemed out of control, and the alcohol *definitely* didn't help clarify what was happening. A big part of her just wanted to blow off steam and have fun, but her visions could be a real spoiler. Several times, she'd steered someone or even a conversation toward or away from something. And sometimes, she hadn't even noticed she was doing it until after it was done. It was a terrible jumble, and it made her anxious.

Jenny sighed and lay down with her laptop. After covering herself with blankets, she opened her assignments. A serious amount of work waited for her. No way was she going to flunk out of college. This place had been her dream, and she needed to get in gear.

What was really on her mind was Professor Dyer and their short text exchange. It still bothered her that he seemed so blasé about her not coming over for a talk. The whole thing was scary, though, too. She felt clammy when she thought back to the weirdness of the developments, but she hadn't had flashes of anything bad when she was around him. But still. When they did talk, what would the conversation lead to?

Maybe she'd text him tomorrow and see about running with Bones. She wouldn't do it today, that was for sure. Her thoughts roamed to the cold Coke in the mini fridge, and she refocused, opened an assignment, and got to work.

Chapter 19

Sidrah went home from lunch, not exactly feeling discouraged that her time with Max had been short, just puzzled by what it all meant.

"Maybe it doesn't mean anything, Sidrah. Maybe he's only another gift from the gods," she said to no one as she slid open the library doors on the main floor. The doors retracted into the walls, revealing another one of her splendid retreats. Since it was Saturday, Marta was not on duty, and Sidrah would have to tend to her own needs.

She flopped down in a chair behind her modern, glass-topped desk and tilted back to look out the wood-framed bay window overlooking her quiet tree-lined street. She put her feet up on the desk and rocked back as her eyes rested with approval upon the space where she conducted a lot of research for her various investments.

Her Victorian home still had the charm of the polished floorboards, but in this room, she'd once horrified an interior designer when she'd asked that the walls be painted over. The woman, unnerved by Sidrah's request to ruin the intricately molded antique woodwork, had insinuated that the young Sidrah was an idiot and flat refused. Sidrah fired her and got herself someone willing to teach her about interior design but who also saw her vision. She'd spent millions purchasing the place for its charm, space, and location, but also for the architecture. It was unique, just like her.

Over the years, she'd spent another fortune bringing it up to date. The bookshelves with the rolling library ladder had been painted a light green. The charming fireplace, with its large surround, was tiled in pastels to complement the touchable light-blue fabrics of her sofas and chairs. A flowery pattern in a large rug, as well as checked accents in the curtains, gave the room further comfort. She liked nothing better than to sink into the soft sofa with a good book, illuminated by one of the many ridiculously expensive but feminine lamps, while a fire burned in the hearth.

Hearth and home. That was what it was all about, right? Sidrah gazed at the shelves filled with mountains of books and other objects that gave her delight, but they held very few pictures. There were no photographs of her family because she had none. Abandoned by her young parents and placed into the foster care system, no one in either family had had the financial and emotional resources to care for her. She'd been moved around the system, and the painful memories of her youth were primarily filled with survival, anger, and powerful urges to rebel. She'd run away from one or two homes, something she felt a bit bad about now. But then, she'd never really felt loved anywhere.

Sidrah had been further traumatized in her youth by her dreams. They were not as clear then as they were now, but she saw things, bits of the future, scattered among her otherwise heavy burdens of teenage angst. The dreams often frightened her. The few times she'd blurted them out, only to later see them come true, had unnerved the people she'd told. So, she kept her thoughts to herself. And dreamed. And dreamed and dreamed.

Of someday having a beautiful home of her own. Of having security. And great clothes. Of someday being able to own beautiful things and use what she knew was an intelligent, albeit unfocused mind, for some purpose. She'd plotted and planned, and wondered if it was possible to use her dreams to help her win the lottery. But she'd had to wait until she was an adult to do it. Working hard and saving every penny she had, she'd moved out of her foster home at eighteen and signed a lease on an apartment. She'd given the last tentacles of her tenuous relationships time to cool and then assured them that she was ready to fly on her own. Then, she'd distanced herself from them as fast as she could. Life had been relatively isolated in her small efficiency apartment. A mattress on the floor had been her bed, a bike her only mode of transportation. But she'd conducted her experiment, sleeping with a lottery ticket and a piece of paper with the date of the next drawing stuck to it.

She'd placed writing utensils nearby, just in case the numbers came to her in the middle of the night. And they did. She was a winner—seventy million dollars, minus tax. She'd chosen the single buyout option, paid her taxes, and got the hell out of Florida. She'd always dreamt of living in New England because it had seemed homey. She moved into a small, secure building in Boston and found herself a realtor. From then on, her path was set. And that path had primarily been about protecting herself, making more money, and maybe discovering the answer to her big whys. Why the gift? Why her? Why her fucked up youth? Why, why, why.

Now thirty years old, she sat in her once dreamed of beautiful home and threw off the stink of negative thinking. She scrolled through the pages of Amazon, looking for antique Greek and Roman relics to show Max when he came to her house. She wanted to be alone with him again, and this time, either figure out how he played into her dreams or go to plan B and just ravish him.

The selection of cheap, obviously fake goods was frustrating. She could easily spend a butt-load of cash on something real, but she didn't want to. Instead, she ordered a bunch of old "certified as real" Roman coins and a mini panini press. They'd be delivered free of charge tomorrow.

She closed her laptop and got up. At the window, she put her hand in her pocket and touched the card the stranger from the rally had given her. Mr. Turner Black. Now there was a man who wanted to see her. But he was so old. At least twenty or thirty years older than she was! He was interested, though.

She walked back to her desk and picked up her phone. With the card in one hand, her phone in the other, she entered his contact information and considered her next move. It was nearly five o'clock now. He'd wanted to meet at the nearby Fairmont, and it was tempting. She was bored and nervous and excited. Lonely even. All good reasons to go out, but her thoughts traveled back to Max.

Not the smoothest character, but her legs had certainly gotten wobbly when their eyes met. She wondered where he lived. What would she wear when he came to her beautiful home? What would they eat? And how long would it take to get him into her bed?

"Get a grip, Sidrah," she said as she put the attorney's card on the desk and left the room. She was hungry. She should have eaten more, but it had been difficult to swallow. She wasn't sure if he knew it, but Maximus Dyer had an undeniable charisma. How long could she hold out before she texted him? Maybe he would text her? The thought lifted her spirits as she made her way into the kitchen.

One never knew, did one?

Chapter 20

Saturday Night

Max woke on the couch late that night, his cell signaling a text. He looked at the coffee table, then past it to where sports highlights and the news played on television. Bones lay on her back on the floor next to him, her four legs in the air. They'd had a nap after he'd graded some papers.

He swung his legs off the couch to sit up and bumped the dog. "Move, would ya?"

Bones yawned at him, rolled over, and began licking herself. Max picked up his phone. It was Sidrah.

I hope this is okay, but is there any way at all that tomorrow would work for you? This is a fast-track deal with my buyer. Sunday? Tomorrow? I'll have food. Pleasseeeeee.

Max didn't think he was right for the assignment. He should turn it down. The job, at least, and the paycheck. But seeing Sidrah again didn't sound bad. He thought about her eyes. Soft brown. Her smile, her face. For all he knew, her body could be a ten under those clothes. He knew perfectly well why he was hesitating, but he fought his trepidations and went for it. He'd take the issues one at a time.

I can do that. Time and place?

"She wants me to help her with a project," he said to Bones. Her ears perked like they were going out for a run. Max pet her until his phone beeped again.

988 West Brookline. Noon?

Max ran a hand through his hair, thinking about his Sunday being ruined by a noon appointment. There was a Sox game he didn't want to miss. And then the Patriots game. Not to mention all the projects around the house and his work.

Yeah. See you then.

He put his phone down. "Shouldn't take more than an hour or two to meet with them, right?"

Bones barked.

Max got up and walked to the fridge, thinking about another beer, then decided he'd had enough for one day. He slammed the fridge shut and pulled down a big jar of pretzels stuffed with peanut butter from the top of his fridge. His mom had brought them from Costco. He would never deny her those small mothering pleasures, especially when they tasted awesome. He twisted open the large cap and stuck his hand in, grabbed a few, and then held one out to Bones. She practically jumped three feet in the air when he tossed it.

"Good catch," he said, screwing the top back on and going back to the couch. He stared at the TV as he crunched on the pretzels, not really seeing it as his thoughts wandered to the events of the last two days and to Sidrah, in particular. He definitely got a sense that she was interested in him. So, what should he do about that?

Girls and women had been a lifelong problem. The main issue was the touching. He wanted to use his hands. He *craved* using his hands. Kissing women, using his lips and other body parts didn't seem to elicit any interruptive thoughts, but when he touched someone with his bare hands, different parts of his brain came alive. His focus was lost. And often, relationships would follow. It was a risk to unglove his hands. The only way he'd been successful at blocking out the images while moaning through the sensory thrill of touching a woman was when he was either drunk or stoned. It helped too if music was playing loudly. And the lights were on. But the combination of all those preventative efforts rarely occurred. Women didn't like them, and he didn't enjoy it as much either.

Sidrah had commented on the gloves within minutes of meeting him. No one did that. It seemed rude. But her directness was refreshing, and so far, she seemed okay with it.

He knew women considered him good looking. Men too. People told him that often enough. He supposed it was true, but dating and real intimacy, even with his friends, had been impossible because he could never tell them the truth. He'd formed no real romantic attachments over time, and it frustrated him. Some relationships were longer than others, but he was notoriously either busy or broke or anxious about the lies and his predicament.

He knew he had a habit of pushing people away, but his parents encouraged him to keep trying. They understood the situation; he'd shared the intimate issues with his mom. He presumed she'd shared the facts with his dad the first chance she got. That was their way. The thing was, he knew he could always count on his mom to play the optimist, and it helped to have his parents in the wings. They'd always been supportive and understanding—the only people in the world he could truthfully talk to.

How would Sidrah feel about the gloves if he made a move? Did she want him? Should he try?

"I'd be fucking stupid not to," he said.

Bones barked.

He texted Elias a hard no to his invite and sat back. What he should be thinking about was Jenny Gallagher. Why hadn't she texted him? They really needed to talk.

Chapter 21

SUNDAY MORNING

S idrah woke at the crack of dawn, almost delirious with excitement. She worked out and showered, then donned some activewear and went online with Door Dash to place an order at one of the best delis in the city. From her experience yesterday, she thought Max might be a sandwich man. She purchased a bunch of pastrami sandwiches, sauerkraut on the side, potato salad, coleslaw, macaroni and cheese, corn muffins, wedge-cut french fries, beans, fruit, and double-chocolate cake. She told them to expect a huge tip if they arrived by 11:30.

She ran downstairs to get things ready. She'd use the center island for the spread and made sure she had the right platters laid out, plates, and flatware. Then she tossed a couple of beer mugs in the freezer. She prepared a bowl with ice to lay the salads in and checked the fridge for beer and wine. Not seeing champagne, she rushed down to the basement to the wine cellar. Finding an appropriate bottle, she turned to leave but then went back for another. She ran up the stairs and placed them in the fridge.

"Chips!"

She opened the pantry, walked inside, and scanned the shelves. There were no chips, but there were nuts and chocolates. They would do.

Finished with the preparation, she placed her hands on her hips, surveying the scene. It was ready. All she had to do now was dress. Last night after he'd confirmed, she'd spent some time going through her options and had had some fun trying on new things, too.

It was cooler today but still warm enough to get away with a short dress and sandals. Regardless, she wasn't going to lose the opportunity to show off her shoulders and legs, which were now smooth as silk and moisturized with an exotic blend from her favorite spa.

She dressed in her messy closet. She'd left things lying everywhere from the evening before, used to Marta cleaning up after her. Her bathroom, too, was a mess, but she'd dried the tub and tried to tidy. It's wasn't that she couldn't do it; she'd just gotten out of the habit.

She looked in the mirror, approving the silhouette of the simple black dress that accentuated all the right parts. Because of her shaking hands, she had to make more than one attempt to insert the classic pair of large silver hoops into her ears.

"Calm down, Sidrah," she scolded herself. She spied her new emerald ring and slipped it on for a boost of confidence. With her armor in place, she felt good. If Max didn't know it before, he'd know soon enough that she was rich. He'd just have to get over it. When the door chimed, she looked at the security monitor. Door Dash was here!

She ran down the stairs and hit the entry area hardwoods, the front door dead ahead. Walking over a gorgeous round rug sitting under a very grand chandelier, she entered the security system code and opened the heavy wooden door.

After tipping the delivery person properly, she ran to the kitchen and got the food out of the containers, placing the contents in the pretty bowls and on the platters. She disposed of the bags and packaging before breathing a big sigh of relief. Then she checked her phone to make sure she hadn't missed a call.

The doorbell rang a few minutes before noon. Smoothing her dress and putting on a confident smile, she walked quickly toward the front door but then came to a crashing halt. Amazon! The coins weren't here yet. She'd completely forgotten about the delivery.

She frowned and slowed her pace, thinking hard about what to do now.

Chapter 22

As he drove into Boston, Max glared into the rearview mirror at the satisfied smile on his dog's face in the back seat. When he'd told her where he was going and explained that she'd be more comfortable at home, she'd gone nuts. The situation was ridiculous, but he'd learned that if he didn't listen to her, she'd make her unhappiness known. On more than one occasion when he didn't acquiesce to her demands, he'd come home to destruction. Once, she'd even taken a purposeful dump in front of him when he walked through the door.

He'd caved to the pressure and put a blanket in his Jeep's back seat for her to lie on. There was a cool breeze today, so with the windows cracked a few inches, she should be comfortable for an hour or so. He didn't like being rushed or worried about her, but he didn't really think he had a choice.

As he neared the destination, driving down the quiet oak-lined street, he peered at the tall, elegant brownstones and did the math. "The richie rich live here, Bones. The super swells."

Max found a shady spot and parallel parked on the street. He got out and leaned his head back inside to say good-bye. "Remember, you asked for it, mutt," he said to the dog. Bones had the audacity to whimper and give him her sad look. "I'll be back," he said with a mixture of annoyance and guilt as he shut the door. Bones stuck her head out the large crack in the backseat window, then pulled her head back inside and curled into a ball on her blanket.

He clicked the lock, then walked down the red-cobblestoned sidewalk to the address. A huge townhouse with a large front walk-up stood before him. Was this Sidrah's place, or did it belong to the guy who wanted his help?

He walked up the stairs, glad he'd worn a clean shirt and shorts, and ran his hands through his hair. At the top step, he rang the bell.

Sidrah opened the door with a wide smile. "Max! Hi," she said.

"Hey," he said, shoving his gloved hands into his pockets.

Their eyes held for a moment before she opened wide the twenty-foot tall door and said, "Come in!"

He stepped gingerly into the richly decorated home and stopped in the attractive atrium area. Directly in front of him lay a winding staircase. To his left was a fancy dining room. The house was tall and deep, and he could see straight back to what must be the kitchen.

Sidrah shut the door. "Thanks so much for coming, Max. We really appreciate it. Follow me!"

Taken again by her beauty, he marveled that they'd only just met yesterday. He felt great being near her. She kind of swayed a bit as she walked down the hall toward the kitchen. He remembered that sway and enjoyed the view as he followed her into the big space. Once there, his eyes left her and widened at seeing the spread of food and the kitchen itself. It looked retro in a way, but the appliances were modern. He recognized some of the superior custom effort that had gone into the design, him being a home-owner himself now.

"Is this your place?" he asked.

She gave him a pretty smile. "It is. I hope that's okay."

"What? No. It's great. I was just wondering where we were."

"Can I get you something to drink?" she asked, walking to the fridge.

"Sure. Beer if you've got it?"

She smiled over her shoulder and did some kind of coquettish dip. "Of course, I do. Domestic, imported. What would you like?"

"Whatever works. Is the guy here?" He looked back toward the front door.

Beer in hand, she said, "No," as she fumbled through a nearby drawer. She began pushing things around, leaned over, then opened another drawer and did the same.

She was obviously searching for an opener and seemed to be having a difficult time.

"Damn, I know there's one in here," she said, banging around.

He glanced at the incredibly large spread of delicious-looking food. As usual, he felt starved and ready to dig in. "How many people are you expecting?"

She held the bottle opener up high. "Found it!"

He reached over and picked up a piece of chocolate. "What's inside this?"

She squinted at it. "Uh, I'm not sure. More chocolate?"

Max popped the whole thing in his mouth as she reached over and handed him the beer. He nodded his thanks while she watched him chew. A pleasant smell lingered around her, and she looked lit up and happy. It reminded him of how he'd found her focused energy amusing.

She suddenly spun around and made a lunge for her phone, sitting on the counter behind her. She frowned at the screen and placed a hand on her chest. "Oh, nooo. Oh, my gosh. I'm afraid he just canceled."

Max opened his eyes large in surprise. There was something overly theatrical about the way she was acting. He finished enjoying his chocolate and said, "I didn't hear it ring."

She blinked at him. "It was a text."

He met her wide-eyed, challenging stare with one of his own. "Text noise then? Special ring tone?" He gave her a suspicious look.

She shook her head. "He texted, Max. I'm very sorry to inconvenience you, but my friend . . . and his colleague won't be able to make it."

He took a sip of his beer, thinking about it now just being the two of them. He pulled out a barstool and sat at the island in front of the food. "I see. So, where's the art? Was he going to bring it with him? Maybe he can send pictures. I could still take a look at it."

She placed her phone face down on the counter and turned back to the fridge. She grabbed a bottle of champagne and set it on the counter. "He was going to bring it."

Max looked over the counter and noticed, among other things, that there were only two plates set out. He picked up a french fry and ate it. "What was it?"

Sidrah fussed with the foil and cork on the bottle, searching again for something, then coming back with a towel. "You know, you might as well stay for lunch. I've got all this food here. Pastrami. Sauerkraut. I know you like that. Did your dog enjoy the antipasto?"

Max nodded, catching on that Sidrah was evading his questions. "Yes, she did. As a matter of fact, she's out front in the car, waiting for me. I wasn't sure how long this was going to take."

Sidrah popped the cork. An explosion of champagne shot out, quite near her face, before she threw a towel over the bottle.

"Whoa," he said as they laughed. Sidrah fussed with cleaning it off her face before she poured herself a glass. Max relaxed a bit. It felt incredibly good to be in her company.

Sidrah toasted him. "I tell you what, Max. If she's house-broken and a good dog, not prone to chewing woodwork or fine things, you could go get her and bring her inside."

"Yeah?" One side of his mouth turned up. She rewarded him with a beautiful smile of her own.

"Yeah."

He lingered a moment in her eyes, then got off the stool. "Okay." He walked down the hall, not at all unhappy that he'd have Sidrah to himself and that he wouldn't have to worry about Bones alone in the car. "Prepare yourself. I'll bring her in. Pastrami is her favorite."

Chapter 23

Sidrah's body swooshed down with relief when the front door closed. "Oh my God." She finished cleaning the spilled champagne off the floor and then got a big plastic bowl out of the cabinet for the dog. She filled it with water and placed it on the floor. With the feast tempting Max and the dog allowed inside, Sidrah was confident she could keep Max around for a least a few hours more.

He was even more impossibly beautiful now that he was in her house. It was like seeing a movie star sitting at her kitchen counter. He smelled right. He filled her home with a magnetic lifeforce, which she was unaware had been lacking until she looked at him like some kind of king sitting on her barstool.

She'd obviously dated before, but this guy was something special. Last night in her dreams, she'd been with him again. The lingering memories from the heat she'd shared with him made her almost swoony now that he was near. What was up with him and her dreams? She had to find out. Did he have a girlfriend?

"Take it easy, Sidrah," she said, as she bent over and did an underfluff to her hair, poofing it a bit more. She bounced back up as the front door beeped and opened. She plastered on a smile and smoothed her hair as Max walked back inside, a big red dog straining against the leash to get to her. The collar was practically strangling her.

"Bones!" said Max. "Calm down, calm down. It's only pastrami, be cool."

Sidrah smiled at the two of them, she too trying to heed the advice he gave to the dog.

"Sit," said Max.

The dog sat politely in front of Sidrah, and with ears dropped, she thumped her tail, waiting for permission to come closer.

"Bones, this is Sidrah Keeling," Max said formally, bending down and unclipping her leash.

Sidrah reached down to pet the dog's head. Receiving a stable response, she knelt in front of her and petted her some more. The dog offered her paw. "Hello," Sidrah said, shaking it. "Nice to meet you."

"She's really well mannered—sometimes," said Max. "Sorry if she scared you. She'll be okay now that she's settled."

"She's sweet," Sidrah said, getting only calm looks from the dog while she dug deeper into her fur and massaged her coat. The dog gave her a soft whimper, and Sidrah felt compelled to hug her. Somehow, she felt Bones return the embrace. She sat back on her heels, and Bones came to her, head down, nuzzling for more.

Sidrah tenderly kissed the dog, then stood and pointed to the nearby bowl. "I have some water for you."

"I think she'd rather have the pastrami," said Max.

Without invitation, Bones leaped up onto a barstool. She sat at the counter, alert, ready to be invited to eat but not touching the mounds of food spread before her.

"Oh!" Sidrah said, surprised.

"What are you doing?" Max scolded. "Get down from there."

Sidrah held up her hand. "No. She's okay. I mean, is she? She's not going to climb on the island and gobble everything down, right?"

Bones shook her head, and Sidrah gasped. "Did she just shake her head at me?"

Max rolled his eyes. "Uh, yeah. She can be . . . I don't know. She's a weird dog."

Bones gave him a dirty look. There was no other way to interpret it. Sidrah watched as the two of them held one another in a staring contest. *Wow.* She got another plate out of the cabinet, her eyes widening as she noticed she'd only placed two on the counter earlier. She put the delicate china plate in front of the dog.

"Would you like a pastrami sandwich, Bones?" she asked.

Bones licked her lips.

"Maybe lose the bread," Max suggested.

Sidrah pulled apart a sandwich and placed the pastrami on the plate, quickly moving her hand out of the way so it wouldn't be bitten. But the dog just sat there, looking at her with big brown eyes. If Sidrah didn't know better, she thought the dog was grateful or ready to cry.

"It's okay, baby, you can eat it," she encouraged, broken a bit by the touching expression.

Bones delicately put her head down and scooped up the meat. She swallowed, then closed her eyes, appearing very satisfied. Sidrah smiled, almost lost in the feeling that she'd just found a new friend. The dog was maybe the most beautiful creature she'd ever seen in her kitchen.

Max cleared his throat. Sidrah snapped out of it, reminded of her other remarkable guest. She picked up her glass of champagne. "All right then. Should we have some lunch, too?"

Max nodded energetically, rubbing his hands together. "Absolutely. It looks like you went to a lot of trouble."

Sidrah handed him a plate. "Oh, no. It was nothing. I cook all the time."

Plate in hand, Max paused to give her a sidelong smile. "You did great, then. Thanks."

She blushed, realizing she wasn't fooling anyone and picked up her plate.

"I had an apple for breakfast. I'm starved," Max said, loading up on an enormous amount of food. "Bones and I were going to hit some fast food on the way home and watch the game, but this is a whole lot better."

"The Sox?" Sidrah said, trying to be polite. She wasn't a huge sports enthusiast, but she wanted this duo to stay with her as long as possible and enjoy themselves.

"Yeah. You like baseball?" He stopped scooping the mac and cheese and brightened.

"I do. Did you want to watch the game while we eat?" She put down her plate and picked up a couple of remotes. Walking toward the round kitchen alcove, she first pointed a remote at the fireplace and started that up, then turned on the large flat-screen overhanging it and scrolled to ESPN. "It's not the same as the ballpark, but champagne and pastrami sandwiches next to a fire aren't too bad, are they?"

Max, with Bones following him, came over. He gaped a bit at the setup and grinned. "I'm glad the other guy didn't show up, Sidrah. The two of us alone is much better."

Bones barked.

Sidrah laughed as she looked down at the sweet dog and petted her. "I think she means the three of us. You're awfully lucky to have her."

She looked back up at Max, and their eyes held again. The chemistry sparked. A real date was most definitely on.

Chapter 24

Turner Black stood in a private box at the Red Sox game, speaking to Governor Jett Franklin. "You're doing well in the polls. It shouldn't be a problem."

Jett grumbled. "That bitch is climbing."

Turner knew he was referring to his closest opponent. A real contender, she'd recently had some good press, and it was pissing his friend off. "She can be managed," Turner said quietly.

Jett turned to him. "Then fucking make it happen. Nothing stands in my way on this one. It's my time, my launchpad to the White House. I don't care who I have to kill to get there."

Turner smiled and checked his periphery. No one was in hearing range. Regardless, he put his hand on the governor's back and leaned into his ear. "Shut the fuck up, you goddammed moron. I'll put you there, but don't you ever, ever not take my calls again. You hear me?"

He pulled away from the governor's ear and emitted a short laugh. Jett Franklin, a stupid, bigoted thug, born with some charisma and without a scintilla of moral fiber, had gotten the message, reacting on cue like the polished turd of a politician he was. He laughed as if Turner had just shared an excellent joke. He guffawed, his head thrown back.

Goddamned idiot. I could stick my hand up your ass, my fingers out your eyes, nose, and mouth and use you like a ventriloquist's dummy. I made you. You're mine. Turner continued to smile, but only at the image of Jett's blood, snot, guts, and brain all over his maw. He looked down at his hand, devouring the image, and licked his lips. One day, perhaps far in his future, he might actually do it. Or maybe not. His visions and dreams were sometimes difficult to interpret. *If this jackweed only knew.*

Once he had moved away from the governor, his presence was immediately replaced by other eager, salivating individuals desperate to be near power. He made his way over to the bar, shaking hands with a few folks on the way, and listened to some innocuous bits of conversation. Eventually, he ordered sparkling water with lime. People often mistook it for an alcoholic beverage. It made him seem like one of the guys.

Not that he disapproved of alcohol or baseball. On the contrary. Both had their useful benefits. He sipped his drink and looked around the packed stadium. People, simple and dark souls alike, were going wild over the sport and their home team. All of them unaware that he could read them, read their auras. He could pick them out for who they were and manipulate them in any manner he chose.

Now that was something to be excited about.

He pulled out his phone and scrolled through his messages. He'd need to reach out to his people soon.

Candidate Mary St. Clair needed to be stopped. And not by fate. Or by Jett, born-to-be-his-puppet, Franklin. No. Turner would see to that work himself.

He sighed. It was how it ever was. Politics needed courtiers. Henchman. Black-baggers. Fixers. Destiny-molding machines. Him.

He closed his eyes and pinched the bridge of his nose, thinking about the woman, Sidrah, who had not called him. It was unusual for people not to reply—his will was very strong. But she hadn't responded. And now he didn't know where to find her. Had he made a mistake by letting her go?

He took a sip of sparkling water and reassured himself not to worry. She'd come to him again one way or another. There was always a dance. Even he had to follow the minuet.

Chapter 25

Trying not to stare at her intriguing guests while they ate, Sidrah marveled at each of them for different reasons. Bones, almost ladylike in her manners, sat in her chair, finished with her smallish meal, but Max was still working on his. It was great that he liked the food and had gone back for seconds, but she found his appetite for large quantities astounding. Still, she felt encouraged by the conversation and the way things were shaping up.

"How in the world do you stay so thin?" she asked.

Max picked up the last trace of pastrami and wrapped it around a pickle. "I run. Usually. Tennis. Handball. I sign up on the faculty list at the university gym, and there's typically a partner to play with."

"That's nice," Sidrah replied. She turned to her other tablemate. It was an odd sight to see a dog sitting there, but Bones was fascinating to observe. At times, it almost seemed as if she was participating in their conversation. Bones's head began drooping, and Sidrah put a gentle hand under the dog's chin and scratched her. "If we're done eating, maybe we should move from the table and encourage her to lie down."

Max got up, went to the kitchen sink, and washed his one, ungloved hand. He wiped it on a paper napkin from the supply on the counter and then put his glove back on.

Sidrah followed with their plates. "Are you going to tell me why you wear gloves all the time?"

His gaze softened. "I'm sorry I can't help with the washing up. I can help you put things away, though."

She shook her head. "That's not an answer. And I don't care about the dishes." She'd genuinely enjoyed the small talk over lunch and the baseball game, but she still didn't know much about him.

He leaned back against the counter, and Bones came to his side. The dog looked up at him, almost as if waiting for an answer too.

"If I told you, there's a chance you might worry about me. I don't like to share my issues with virtual strangers."

"Why would I worry about you?" Did he have some type of mental illness? "Do you have a problem with germs?"

He shook his head. "No."

She registered something, almost pain there, but before she could say more, he took a step and came to her. Her heart jolted as he put his hands on her shoulders, then reached down and mercifully kissed her. His lips were soft, yet firm, and she thought she would die from the electrical spark as he pulled her close. Eager for more, she reached her arms up around his neck and pressed his head to hers.

Max moved with urgency. The two of them molded their bodies to each other, swaying, moving, their hands roaming until he picked her up and sat her on the kitchen island, pushing a few items out of the way to make room.

Oh my God. Heat rushed through her as they explored one another's bodies. The wordless passion intensified, but Sidrah forced herself to break the connection. She needed to regroup and try to understand what was happening.

She pushed him back with one arm. "Max . . ."

He looked into her eyes, questioning but not seeing resistance, and came back for more. She allowed it. She couldn't help herself. She felt out of control, almost as if she could not do anything or say anything, her body taking over as he slid his hand up her skirt and held her backside tight. Her legs had been wide apart, but she wrapped them around him now, her body on fire. She managed to swim up from the depths of passion, using all her strength to push him back.

"Nooo," she breathed. "Not here. Not in the kitchen."

Max stepped back, and she jumped down. She took a deep breath and smiled. "Oh my God, follow me."

Nearly collapsing from anticipation as they walked up the stairs to her bedroom, he grabbed her from behind, turning her body and pressing her against the wall. She kissed him, then once again came up for air and pushed him back, proceeding to take the stairs two at a time. Neither spoke until they reached her bedroom. She went inside and turned around. Maximus Dyer, all gorgeous, all man, stood in the doorway of her sensual salon, like the man of her dreams. Literally.

He turned around to Bones, who had followed them, and shooed her out of the room. "You stay outside," he said before closing the door. He turned back to her, wearing a smile, and approached. If she didn't die from his smoldering look or the excitement of that moment, she could survive anything.

Sidrah breathed, finally relaxed as her naked body, covered in sweat, blessedly entwined with Max. Somewhere along the way, he'd stopped to remove his boot, but he hadn't removed his gloves. The lovemaking had been fairly brutal in its passion at times, each of them swiftly learning about the other's desires.

But her dreams of him hadn't matched the realness of the intensity they had shared. She'd seen some, but not all, of it in her dreams. Thank God for surprises. She smiled and ran her hands through his thick hair—his head, cradled face down in her shoulder, his gorgeous broad shoulders and beautiful neck right there for her to touch, to kiss.

"Max," she said as his breathing quieted.

She listened for a response, her eyes widening when she heard light snoring. *Asleep!* She opened her mouth to protest and shake him awake but then decided she could deal with it for a few minutes. Definitely no longer than five. Or four. She wasn't sure how long she'd last without talking to him again, without kissing him again.

Letting out a small sigh, she was suddenly troubled that he wouldn't feel the same way as she did. Now that they'd slept together, would he want to see her again? So far, she hadn't found the right moment to ask about his dating life. *Was he seeing someone else?*

Their passion couldn't be one-sided. The man couldn't be that good an actor. But what did he think about her? She absolutely knew that she wanted to see him again. Besides his obvious faults—snoring next to her after lovemaking being a prime example—he was an interesting, accomplished, gorgeous, intelligent man with a sense of humor, *finally* in her bed.

She still didn't know why he'd come to her or why she had been led to him, but she hardly cared. *God, life was good!*

Testing the depth of his sleep, she ran a hand down his arm, wondering if the movement would wake him, but received a louder snore. Her hand landed on his glove. It almost matched his light skin tone and was made of very soft calfskin. Without thinking, she inched her finger deep inside the glove through a natural gap in the fabric and touched the palm of his hand. Feeling an erotic impulse and wanting more, she slid a second finger through the gap, making the glove quite tight. She pressed her eager fingertips against the firm skin of his palm, moving them about, and closed her eyes. *Such chemistry!* She could feel something beating between them . . . something nameless but real, pulsing through her fingertips and into his hand. A connection, a responsive vibration. Her fingers dug farther into the glove . . .

"What are you doing?" Max woke and rolled over onto his back. His eyes held a confused look as his forehead wrinkled.

She snapped as if out of a trance. "I'm sorry. What do you mean? I was just touching . . ."

"My hand," he croaked.

He moved back to her swiftly, rolling his body on top of her. His hands came down on either side of her head as he lay resting on his elbows. His face loomed over her, his eyes searching hers. For what? Was there sadness there? Anger? What was he thinking?

"Sidrah," he whispered. "Who are you?"

She blinked, her mouth suddenly dry. "Max, I'm sorry. I didn't know . . ."

He held his hands above her head, then tenderly gathered and stroked a handful of her hair. "No. I know. There's, there's something ... special here. You're different."

He released her hair, and she could feel him doing something above her head. He brought his hand, gloveless, down to her face and then gently placed it on her cheek.

He closed his eyes and groaned out her name. His head dropped near hers. "My God, this can't be happening."

She didn't understand. The world spun as he stroked her face with his soft, perfect ungloved hand. He jerked to a sitting position, removed the other glove, and threw them both off the bed. As he looked down at her naked body and breasts, he gently placed both his hands on her belly, then moved them up in a curve, softly cupping her and feeling her body with a trembling tenderness she didn't understand.

She put a worried hand up to his face. "Max?" she questioned. "Are you okay?"

Relief flooded through her when he smiled and then grinned. He reached down and scooped her up, kissing her over and over as they rolled on the bed. "God, yes. Please don't freak out. I can't believe I'm going to say this, Sidrah, but I've been looking for you all my life."

Her faced flushed, her confidence soaring. That was definitely not the response she had expected, but her eyes and his were locked, as she tried to absorb the firing emotions. They kissed, softer this time, and as they moved entwined, his hands roamed over her body.

She felt something almost close to floating as they coupled, but her confusion broke through the surface. "Max, please tell me about your hands. Your gloves. Why do you wear them, and why did you take them off? I don't understand."

"Sidrah," he said, rolling onto his back, taking her with him. "I don't want to ruin this. It's so wonderful. Isn't it?"

"Yes, of course. But you can trust me. Tell me, so I'll understand."

He pushed the hair back from her face, then pulled her down to kiss her again. "Max," she encouraged, after pushing him gently away.

He stopped moving, searching her face for something, then seemed to come to a decision. "Okay. The thing is, I have visions, sometimes. When I touch things."

What? Sidrah's heart thudded, the blood rushed to her face. "What do you mean? What kind of visions?"

He looked at her thoughtfully, assessing. His jaw tensed. "About the people whose things I touch."

She sat up and straddled him, openly gawking. "All the time? When did this start?"

"Yes, all my life. The intensity of them picked up when I got older. I wear the gloves so I can block out the karmic sludge of other people's lives. But with you, I don't see anything."

This is it. The something, the reason . . . Her hands flew over her mouth, her eyes wide. Max looked almost sickly and panicked when she did, so she quickly removed them. "I see things, too," she whispered.

It was his turn to freeze, his expression wide-eyed. But then it soured, and he pushed her off. "Are you playing me? What do you mean?"

"Playing you? I wouldn't play you. Don't be ridiculous. I mean what I said. I have visions too, but not with my hands. I see things. I see things sometimes . . . in my dreams."

He rubbed his hand over his mouth and gave her a cynical look. "In your dreams."

"Yes."

"Oh my God," she said as she got out of bed and walked into her closet. *What's happening? What's happening?* Her hand trembled with the mantra as she found a silk bathrobe to put on. When she returned, Max had pushed himself up, his arm resting on his forehead, staring at her. She sat on the edge of the bed, shaking a bit. "I-I've only told a few people. It's never gone well. So, I keep it to myself too. I can't believe this, Max. I can't believe this is happening to me. To us."

Max pulled her down. She lay near him, her hands on his chest, and stared. "Tell me more about your dreams," he said.

Her thoughts swirled about being led to him. And now, things seemed to be coming together. She trusted him completely. She had to. Relief that she could speak about it expelled from her lungs before she ran through the story. "I can see the future. Things that are going to happen. The visions are usually accurate, but not all the time. They've been growing in intensity too! Most nights, I'll see something, but I don't always know what it means. Sometimes I do know what it means. They're more focused lately. I've helped the police find people when I see crimes about to happen. I have a friend in the Boston PD. He believes me."

Max moved to sit up, and so did she. "I see the past," he said. "You see the future. What does that make us? Bookends?"

Sidrah expelled a breath and smiled. *My God.* They were meant for each other. Her heart swelled at the thought and that they might indeed have a future together. Just as her eyes filled with tears, the faint notes of the doorbell sounded, quickly followed by Bones barking outside the bedroom door. The dog continued to bark as she ran down the stairs.

Sidrah slid off the bed and went to a security monitor near her nightstand. She ran a finger around the controls. "It's a delivery." She looked up at Max and smiled. "Oh my God! It's Amazon."

Chapter 26

Turner Black controlled his temper as he issued instructions to one of the many moles in his dark army, this one inside the Boston Police Department. "Find her. It's an unusual name. There've been less than two Sidrahs born each year in the last century. She probably has a Massachusetts license. I want her address before you sleep tonight. Do I make myself clear?"

He ended the call with Detective O'Sullivan and put the phone down. Back home after a long day at the ballpark and dinner with the governor, Turner was in no mood. Suffering through polite conversation among nitwit yes-men was often intolerable. But it's how he'd spent most of his days, all his life.

And today, the Sidrah woman had often distracted his superior mind. The more he thought about her, the angrier he became. She'd come to him in the tank. He was given her in a vision as someone to meet. He'd followed the mission, met her, applied his charms, but she hadn't responded. This wouldn't do. He had to know more about her now. It was that simple.

His focus turned to a birdcage in his office. A large parakeet sat inside, barely chirping at him anymore, most likely ready for death. He got up and went to the cage. Her eyes were closed, her small heart still beating, but with effort. "It's time," he said.

He walked to the window of his office and opened it. A dish of bird food and a bowl of water sat on the brick ledge, ready for consumption. He went back to the cage and opened the door. The parakeet's eyes opened as his hand slid inside. He could feel the bones of the starving, dehydrated animal. If he wanted to, he could probably squeeze it to death, and he'd only receive a dry pop.

He walked the bird to the open window and put her beak into the water. The bird responded by taking a drink. Turner put her down gently near it and watched as it perked up, then went to the food. She devoured it. Life literally came back into the creature as he watched.

He shut the window. The bird, trapped outside, was now on its own. Without Turner, without a flock. She stopped eating for a few beats to look at him. He could almost feel her stress and see the fear in her eyes. "Tomorrow," he whispered through the glass. "If you are there in the morning, you may come inside, and I'll be good to you. But you'll prove your loyalty to me first."

He walked away from the window, turned off the light, and walked out. He'd always wanted a pet, but they were never, ever loyal. They bit him. They were disobedient. They ran away. They did not love him. And while he supposed that was okay since love wasn't an emotion he'd ever truly felt or understood, he'd always longed for some creature to be worthy and devoted only to him. Not because they feared him, but because they wanted to stay and worship him.

He'd tried all types of animals; dogs had been the worst. Even the gentler breeds had turned on him. Cats ran and hissed. It was maddening, and he hated them for it. Even Hitler had dogs. Executioners, Roman soldiers, all kinds of dark souls had dogs who worshipped them. It was their way. But none, so far, for him.

People who saw how animals reacted to him were often startled by it. The first time it happened, a person usually chalked it up to being an anomaly. But when they witnessed it again, they realized it had to be Turner himself.

Turner despised the animals for behaving the way they did toward him. He would not be made fun of or mocked or challenged by any simple creature on this earth. It was intolerable.

He went into the kitchen, opened the refrigerator, and pulled out some fresh red veal—reddish because the eighteen-week old calf had been fed milk before it was slaughtered. He got out the Coleman's mustard and placed a dollop on the slice of tender meat, salivating with anticipation, before spreading it onto some Naan bread.

He thought about the next day as he ate the small sandwich. It would be Monday. By tomorrow evening, he'd most likely be meeting once again with Sidrah Keeling. Detective O'Sullivan would find her.

As if on cue, his cell phone showed a text. Turner smiled, tasting a bit of the veal and yellow mustard stuck on his front teeth. He sucked the food from them with his tongue and inhaled with satisfaction as he read the text. He loved it when things worked out. The Fates were on his side. He was one with them.

"Sidrah *Keeling,* 988 West Brookline. A very nice street," he said.

He scrolled through his contacts until he reached the name of his favorite florist. He'd been doing business with the reliable man and his marvelous creations for a decade.

He texted Sidrah's name and address. As well as:

Urgent. ASAP in the morning. Thirty percent tip. $400 arrangement to my card. Make them romantic.

Turner stopped texting and thought about what he should say on the card.

Forgive me for searching for you. Our raincheck tonight, Sidrah? The Oak Bar at the Fairmont at five. Until then, with respect, Turner Black

He liked it. It would do the trick. She'd meet him. "Sidrah Keeling," he said aloud as he went to Google and put in her address. He knew the street. Miss Keeling had money. He cocked his head in thought.

"She could be married," he said.

He thought about that as he put away the tender veal and mustard. He liked his privacy and only had people come to clean once a week—a service. He did not want to bond with a particular housecleaner. It was intrusive and might lead to questions about his various activities and peccadillos.

He walked up the stairs, satisfied at a good day's work. Tomorrow, his plate would be filled with solutions to his problems. Sidrah was one. She was a chess piece on his board, placed there for a particular purpose. She was a weak soul. Her aura was light, not dark, which was as much as he could see. He'd never witnessed colors surrounding people.

Sidrah was not one of his ilk, but he somehow needed to move her, to *turn her.* As usual, the coincidence of his name being almost a pun with the appropriate solution, made him happy. His parents had given him his name, but they were lemmings. As Turner grew up and discovered who he was, he'd been surprised that his parents were both simple and weak. But they'd given birth to him. A dark destiny. The turner of men, to either the dark side—the most likely outcome—or to other consequences. The Fates would take over once he'd done his job.

He'd need to keep placating Jett Franklin too. Jett needed Turner in his corner to keep him steady. The governor's ego was stupidly fragile, and he was given to impulses that could veer him off the presidential track. That could not happen. Once Jett Franklin was in the White House, Turner would have access to the world stage. He became aroused as he imagined the damage he could do there.

Chapter 27

Max reluctantly put his gloves back on after he and Sidrah left her bed. Bones needed some reassuring about being abandoned in a strange house, and she quite possibly needed to go outside. He and Sidrah had been unavailable for a long time, and while the dog had tremendous patience, it wasn't fair to believe her bladder could control itself too.

He put on his shorts, then sat on the bed to strap on his boot. He considered leaving it off since he was so close to being done with it but decided he moved faster with it on. He didn't want to focus on his every step. The three of them trudged down the stairs, the dog running in excited circles around them as they went to the kitchen and out onto the back patio.

Max crossed his arms and looked at the setup outside while Bones relieved herself on a patch of grass. "For such a nice neighborhood, you haven't got a very big yard," he said to Sidrah, who was in the kitchen pouring champagne.

Bones finished, and the two of them went inside, leaving the back door open.

Sidrah approached him, her long midnight-blue satin robe falling loose at her chest as she kissed him and handed him the flute. "I have a rooftop deck for entertaining. Do you want to see it?"

He smiled. "I could be tempted."

She clinked glasses with him. "To us."

Max drank. It was refreshing, and he finished it in one gulp. Out of habit, he put his hand in his pocket and produced a pack of cigarettes.

She turned up her nose. "You smoke? I didn't smell it on you."

He shook one out of the pack and stood near the back door. "My first one today," he said as he lit it. He blew the smoke into the early evening sky and sighed. "So good."

"Gross," she said, replenishing his drink before taking a seat on a barstool. "You've got to quit."

Max was not really listening. Her robe hung open on either side of the chair, plunging deeply in the front. The only thing holding it closed was the small bit of slippery fabric and a belt around the middle. He gave her a lascivious look and sipped the champagne.

She frowned. "You don't think you can lose the gloves while you're in my house?"

He shrugged. "Probably not. Inanimate things often have traces of people. Newsprint sometimes, pictures. I don't have a lot of control over it. It's extremely distracting. Besides, I'm used to them."

"But you have such beautiful hands." She smiled tenderly.

Bones went to Sidrah and sat in front of her. Max looked at the two of them, wondering why his life was changing so radically and quickly. He thought too about Jenny. There'd been a lightness surrounding her. She had premonitions and déjà vu, and she'd stopped that rapist. What were fate and destiny doing to all of them? The thought nagged at him, but he pulled himself back to the incredible present time.

"I think Bones is hungry," he said. "I'm a little surprised she didn't eat the spread on the counter while we were upstairs. Do you have any chicken? Too much pastrami might lead to consequences we don't want to consider."

Sidrah hopped down to pet the dog, cooing at her. Max realized that this might be the most momentous day of his life. He'd longed for this primal, intimate existence but had given up hope it would ever happen. He was able to touch this beautiful, special woman and, at last, experience normal human connection. Her soft skin, her warm body, and the intimacy of touching another human being overwhelmed him. He flicked the cigarette butt onto the cobblestone ground, then closed the door and flipped the deadbolt.

He went to her and nuzzled the back of her neck as she dug in the fridge. Even through his gloves, her silky robe felt soft and exotic, just like her. "I know we need to talk, but maybe we should go back upstairs."

"We do have a lot to talk about." She smiled at him as she walked around the island, tearing pieces of chicken breast onto the plate at the counter where Bones had eaten. The dog jumped up onto her chair and waited until Sidrah gave her the go-ahead to eat.

Sidrah shook her head, amazed. "She's unbelievable."

"You're unbelievable," said Max. He was hungry himself, though, and when he spied the chocolate cake, he picked up a fork and speared a big slice of it. He put his hand under his chin and brought his mouth down to the counter to eat. The cake crumbled all over.

"Right," Sidrah said, laughing. "Max, has anyone told you that you're a bit of a pig?"

He smiled, showing his teeth, knowing they were full of chocolate. He took another large bite of cake and then speared some more. He walked toward her, intending to feed it to her. "Come here," he mumbled.

"No." She dodged him, grabbed the champagne and glasses, and ran down the hall to a door near the entry. He and Bones followed as she slid the doors open and disappeared inside.

Max and Bones entered a library or office type room and watched while Sidrah flipped on a couple of lamps and then picked up a remote. A fire immediately crackled in the hearth, making the room homey.

"Another fireplace. How many have you got?"

"Four," she said as she poured more champagne into their glasses. They settled into the light-blue sofa and sipped their drinks as they stared into the fire. The fresh, relaxing atmosphere, along with the enormity of their circumstances, sobered him a bit, and a slight awkwardness set in.

"Hey, do you want me to get that delivery at the front door?" he asked.

"Sure," she said as Bones made her way over to her and crawled onto the sofa, replacing him.

"Save my place," Max grumbled to the dog and watched Sidrah embrace her. He went to the front door, slightly stunned that so much had happened since he'd last walked through it. While he couldn't be happier, it was all mind-blowing.

He stopped cold in the entry, hit with the thought that maybe his gift was leaving him. *Could it be?* First, he couldn't feel Bones, and now, Sidrah. He always thought he'd be grateful if his cursed ability left him. But would he?

When he opened the heavy door, he spied the big box. He picked it up and went inside, shutting the door behind him. Realizing that they hadn't locked it after he'd entered, he frowned and flipped the deadbolt.

In the library, Sidrah sat by the fire with a glass in her hand and the dog at her side. She looked like a picture. He suddenly felt powerfully protective of her. "We didn't lock the front door," he said.

She nodded. "I should have done that. But I was distracted. By you."

"Sorry, I should have thought of it when I came back with Bones."

He put the large package on the table in front of them and sat on the sofa as she got up and went to her desk. She returned with a sharp letter opener and began opening the package from Amazon. "I'm a little embarrassed here, Max, but I don't think we should keep secrets from each other." With the box open, she moved some packing material out of the way before lifting out another box for him to see.

"A mini panini press." He smiled. "You're right. I'm glad you didn't keep that from me."

"No. There's more," she said and sat next to him. "Umm, so I have a confession. There wasn't ever anyone to consult for. I made that up. I saw you in my *dreams*, Max. Several times in my dreams. And I saw you at the rally. I don't know why, but I followed the vision. I went there with one purpose: to meet you."

"So, you were playing me," Max deadpanned, teasing her.

"Screw you." She punched him playfully, but somewhat hard. She gave him a questioning look, apparently not sure of his sarcasm.

"Ow," he said, grabbing his arm and pretending she had really hurt him.

She dug through the box. "I *misled* you. For the cause. I ordered some stuff off Amazon, so I'd have artifacts for my cover story. So you could tell us the history of the pieces." She froze. "Oh my God. You *could* tell us the history. You can see the past. Is that why you teach it?"

As he sat back into the sofa, he nodded. "You could say I have an interest."

"Have you ever used the visions to instruct you or to write about them? Like your dissertation?"

He looked down and put his hand on Bones, who was lying next to him. He petted her while he thought about how to answer. Using his gift to advance his career wasn't something he was all that proud of. In a way, it felt like cheating. But then, not really. Who had better insight than he did? For brief moments, he saw the faces of people in history. At times, it could be amazing. He caught glimpses of battles, parties, dinners, travel, coronations, fear, pain, and joy. Every human emotion scattered over time. The visions did not always contain the particular insights he was searching for. They were often unfocused, sometimes giving him understanding as to who they were when they were alive. But the visions were always overwhelming and often painful. He'd learned to use his skill carefully. Why not impart what he knew to others? When he reflected on the positive side, he felt a bit less like a fraud. Then again,

Sidrah had used her gift to help the police. Maybe they were meant to work together.

He cocked his head. "Yes, I have. Sometimes."

She stared at him. "Well, I think that's good." She again busied herself with the box and pulled out some packages. He watched her unwrap them as she read off the boxes, "Coins . . ."

"Have you used your visions, your dreams of the future, for any special purpose, Sidrah? Other than helping the police? I admire that, by the way."

Package in hand, she put her head down and screwed up her mouth. "Umm. Yes."

He sat forward. "What have you done?"

She looked at him and shrugged. "I won the lottery."

He blinked. "You did what?"

She showed him all her teeth. "A couple of times."

His eyes grew, and he dropped back into the sofa. He looked around the room, seeing it all in a new light. "Holy fuck."

She put a hand on his arm but then yanked it back. "You know what, Max. Don't judge me. You don't know me—my life, what I've been through. The hell I've lived. If I used the dreams to help myself, who cares? I'm not hurting anyone. I've *helped* people too. Why are you judging me?"

"I'm not judging you," he said. But he was. He was jealous. And guilty. And excited. And . . . he didn't know what. Everything between them was happening incredibly fast.

"I can see it in your eyes," she said, bouncing up.

His thoughts froze as he looked up at her in wonder. He'd only met this goddess yesterday, and she'd already changed his world. The discussion surrounding their enormous issues practically vanished as she stood before him. Her face was flushed, her hair wild, her eyes like fury. She mesmerized him. He could have taken her on the oriental right that moment. "No. Really. Hey, settle down. You're right. I don't know anything about you."

She continued storming. "Just my most deepest, darkest secrets. The most profound and confusing part of my soul."

He smiled. "Well, yes, that. But I showed you mine, so I guess you had to show me yours."

Reading his eyes, searching for reassurance, she responded to his joke and sat back down. Still a bit cross, she looked at the package, then pulled out some stuff and held them up. "More coins."

He put his hand out, thinking a change of topic might be useful. "What have you got there?"

She gave them to him. He put his glass on the floor and looked at the coins under the lamp. His mouth went a bit dry; he knew exactly what he was looking at. "The Fates. The Moirai. Clotho, Lachesis, and Atropos. The three sisters."

What's happening here? His chest tightened as he turned to her. "Why did you choose these?"

Sidrah, her face a bit drawn, looked concerned also. "I don't know. I clicked on a bunch of stuff. I didn't overthink it."

Max sat up and laid the first coin on the table. "In Greek mythology, the Fates were sisters. They more powerful than the rest of the gods, except for maybe Zeus. Clotho here weaved the web of life if the sisters decided someone should live or die. She used her spindle, her distaff. She spun the *Book of Fate*."

He placed the next coin on the table. "This is Lachesis. She measured the threads to determine how long they would be. Calculating the lifespan."

He placed the next one down. "This is Atropos. She used her shears to snip the thread of life. Her name means *inevitable.* The three sisters knew the past, the present, and the future. They were oracles. They decided a man's destiny. They were fate *and* destiny. They knew what each man was put on earth to do, and when he'd done it, they turned into the Goddess of Death. You cannot change fate."

"What about destiny?" Sidrah asked solemnly.

Max shrugged. "Supposedly, you can change it through conscious decision. By taking responsibility for your life and growing. Destiny may be changeable. At this moment, with all that's happened between you and me, and with the literal Sisters of Fate staring at us, I honest to God don't know what to think."

They sat in silence, each lost in thought. She prodded, "So, if you zig right, you can change something, if . . ."

He grabbed her arm. "What did you say?" he demanded, his skin prickling.

She stared at him. "I . . ."

"Jenny," he said quietly. "She can zig. I understand."

"You understand what? Who's Jenny?"

He looked at her, almost afraid to voice the absurdity of his thoughts out loud. "She's the present. She's destiny. And my student."

Sidrah stood, and Bones jumped off the couch, barking at her. The dog turned to bark at him too.

"What is going on here?" she said.

He rubbed his temple, staring at them. "I do not know."

"What do you mean you know destiny?"

Max told her everything he knew about Jenny Gallagher—how they met, who she was, and what they'd discovered about one another. He told her about Jenny's words, *following up on a zig*, and how the portrait of the Cumaean Sybil—the prophetess—reminded him of her too.

Sidrah, who had poured more champagne, paced in front of him. "Just how many women have you told about your gift, Max?"

He shook his head, clearing the feed, feeling her go off track. "What?"

She shrugged and drank some more.

"You're jealous? That's what you're focusing on?" he said, surprised.

She looked off coyly and batted her lashes. "No."

He inhaled. "Look. I think we've got enough on our plate to deal with right now, so let me make this clear. There are no other women in my life. There is nothing to be jealous of. Does that make you feel better?"

She shrugged. "Maybe."

He ticked off people who knew on his fingers. "I've told my mom, my dad, you, Bones, Jenny a little bit, and a girl in college."

"And what was her name?" Sidrah asked.

He stared at her. "I'm not going to answer that. It's. Not. Relevant. Now pull yourself together."

She held up a hand and closed her eyes in surrender. "Okay, okay."

But then his gut tightened. He frowned as he realized he didn't know her circumstances. "Are . . . are you seeing anyone?" he stammered. "Who have you told?"

Both of them had had unpleasant reactions when they'd shared their abnormal capabilities, and Sidrah's list, too, was short. Those who suspected something unusual got spooked and didn't stick around. She told him a bit about her childhood, about growing up in foster care, and how she'd fled Florida and hid behind her money. There was so much to learn about her. He felt terrible for possibly making her feel guilty, but he also felt crazy relief that she, too, wasn't in a relationship.

"There's a reason for everything, Sidrah. If we didn't believe it before, I think it's time we embraced it."

She picked up the empty bottle of champagne as she and Bones walked out of the room. "Follow me," she called.

He watched her leave the room but then turned to the fire, his mind going in circles. It was getting late. He had class in the morning. Physical therapy in the afternoon. Jenny Gallagher to meet. He absolutely had to see her now. *Jenny, Sidrah, the coins.* His mind tugged at him to reach some conclusion. Something new and even freakier than he'd experienced so far in his life was happening.

He dropped his head and ran his hands through his hair. *Holy fuck.*

How was he going to get Jenny alone? Had she been *physically* scared of him? After what she'd been through, he should have thought of that.

For the next meeting, he had to make sure she felt protected. He also had to somehow see her without being fired from his job for seeming inappropriate. Wellesley College took the safety of their female student body seriously. He'd been through enough human resources training to believe the hard and fast consequences.

As he got up from the sofa, an idea came to him. Maybe Sidrah could talk to Jenny. Or they could do it together. He couldn't be accused of being alone with a student with Sidrah around. It could work.

He walked out of the library, then stopped to look at the oil paintings that lined the staircase. He hadn't given them a glance when he'd gone upstairs with Sidrah the first time, but he did now. They were of dogs—almost all of them. Landscapes, country scenes, and working dogs—gilt-framed in gold and individually lit like heroes.

"Have you ever had a dog?" he called toward the kitchen.

"What?" Her face appeared around the corner. She walked toward him.

He pointed to the collection. "Dogs. Have you ever had a dog?"

She shook her head. "No." Reaching down to pet Bones, who'd followed, she said, "I had this dog when I was twelve. Well, it wasn't really my dog. It was my foster family's. His name was Argo."

Her voice cracked a bit on the name, and she squatted to hug Bones fully. Max dropped down by them. "What happened?"

Sidrah looked reluctant but continued. "He came between me and a beating. He was an older dog, a lab, and he just threw himself between this guy and me." She pressed her lips together, blinking hard. "He took the hit. A lot of them."

She buried her face in Bones's fur. "I don't want to talk about it now. Not today, Max."

"Come here," he said, gathering her and helping her up. He held her close, not comprehending how anyone could be so cruel. Bones pressed her body against their legs.

"I've always wanted a dog," she said into his chest. "I love them, but the guilt . . . it's followed me."

"I always wanted a dog, too," he said. "But my hands held me back. I can feel animals' emotions. Then Bones appeared out of nowhere, and I couldn't feel her. And now, there's you."

Max released her. *Bones.* He looked down at the dog, who sat between them, staring up. *Where had she come from?* The dog looked over at the wall lined with pictures, then sat back on her haunches, her paws up in a begging position.

Sidrah perked up at the dog's silly face. "I think she's smiling."

"Yeah, I think you're right." Max tenderly stroked the dog's head until she dropped down and barked at them.

"Ahh." He exhaled loudly and grabbed Sidrah's hand, pulling her toward the kitchen. "I tell you what. You got anything other than champagne in this palace? I could use a real drink."

Chapter 28

Have you ever considered dusting?" Sidrah asked the next morning after they'd arrived together at Max's home. She wrinkled her nose with disgust at the state of his house and the way that he lived.

"I just did," he said, pouring dog food into Bones's bowl from a big twenty-pound bag.

She looked at her finger, covered in a thick coating of dust, and shook her head. The place definitely needed some help.

"I'm going to get dressed. Let her out when she's done eating," Max said, disappearing down the hall.

Sidrah walked through the living room, inhaling the rarified air, enjoying the experience despite the rustic and untidy surroundings. *Maximus Dyer lives here. This is his home.* Their day yesterday, their night together had been epic. She knew other couples casually threw that line around, but they didn't have a clue what they were talking about.

Bones finished eating and ran to the door. Sidrah pushed the metal blinds on the sliding patio door out of the way, searching for the cord to retract them, and batted at a load of dust molecules that rained down on her. "What the . . ." she said, discovering that the cords were held together with duct tape. "Whyyy, Max?"

She let the dog outside and followed her into the yard. Bones bounded off into an overgrown corner to take care of her business. The yard was another shamble, but she cautioned herself not to insult him with her observations. She also didn't want to feel like a snob. She'd been raised with nothing. If not for her gift, she'd still be living in Florida in God knew what type of circumstances. It wasn't such a distant memory. Life could be cruel without money.

She left the sliding glass door open and walked back inside. The house was on the small side, but with a little money, it could be cute. *Super cute* was a stretch. Not unless they threw a ton of money at it. She walked to a bookcase and almost cried. There he was—her Max. Pictures of him were everywhere. Someone, probably not Max, had stocked the case with pictures of him at every age.

She picked up a photo and smiled as she looked into the loving eyes of what had to be Max's parents, one on each side of his face, in a closeup. The happy family. Max made three. He'd told her he was close to them.

She was glad that he'd had a strong family and had been loved. It was probably what made him normal . . . ish. Spying a dirty sock lying randomly on a chair, she picked it up with her fingertips. She dropped it with a *yuck* and turned her attention to the kitchen. She opened the old refrigerator door and bent to look inside. Beer. Beef jerky. A rotting avocado. A huge bag of apples. A dozen bottles of protein shakes.

He came up beside her and slapped her ass. She straightened as she shut the fridge door. "Are you making applesauce sometime soon?"

"Maybe. My mom got them from Costco. She's big on that place. It makes her happy to stock me up." He went to the pantry door and opened it to reveal economy size boxes of granola bars, chips, enough rice to feed a small army, and a case of baked beans.

"No wonder my cooking was so incredibly good."

He guffawed. "Your cooking. Right. Like you made all that food."

About to protest, she gave up the charade and ran her hands through her hair. It was parted in the middle today, and she smoothed it and flipped the ends into place as it hit her shoulders. She felt pretty in her long-sleeved black and white silk Dolce blouse with large red and pink roses. Initially, Max had seemed interested in her morning dance through her closet as she sorted through her options, but he eventually grew annoyed and suggested she throw on some jeans. As a concession to hit the "proper campus" look, she chose some skinny ones. But she couldn't resist wearing the red Dolce heels with the sweet tie-ups.

Max, once again in cargo shorts and a T-shirt, moved around the house, grabbing papers and stuffing them into his backpack. She smiled at him as he boyishly shook his damp hair off his face.

"I'm so excited to watch you teach. Will you make me stay after class for some *special* counseling?" she teased.

"One class. Try to hold it together." He walked over to kiss her.

Their passion escalated quickly. Reluctantly, she pushed him away. "I will if you will."

Max inhaled and nodded his thanks. He clipped the leash on Bones as they walked out the front door. "Right.

So, after class, we go to my office and text Jenny. I pulled up her schedule. She doesn't have classes today. She should be on campus, but I don't know."

The three of them got inside his Jeep Cherokee. They'd driven to his place together, taking his car since Max thought he should get it off the street outside her home. Sidrah got comfortable for the short ride to campus. She fixed her lipstick in the visor mirror and then opened his glove box.

"What are you doing?" he asked.

She pulled out wads of paper, receipts, and dog poop bags. "Nothing, just snooping," she said as she shoved the stuff back in. She went for the center console and stopped before opening it. "Don't tell me." She waved her hand theatrically over the leather box. "I see more paper. Mints. Cigarettes. Money, and . . . pens."

She popped it open. They both peered inside. "Pretty close," she said, pulling out a big utility knife.

"My dad gave me that. With one swipe, you can cut yourself free of your seat belt if you should find yourself in a jam."

She put it back next to a flashlight and some other tools and glanced back at Bones, who was sitting smartly in the back, her head out the window. Sidrah reached back to pet her. "God, she's great. It's a miracle she found you, isn't it?"

Max squeezed her knee. "That's the right word for it. We've got a lot to be thankful for, but now we need to find out why. For the first time in my life, things seem to be falling into place. There's momentum in the air, and we need to follow it."

Chapter 29

MONDAY MORNING

Jenny lay in bed, she and her beautiful laptop practically one as they worked together on a research paper. She found the work interesting and challenging, and the time flew. She couldn't believe that it was already Monday. Between the work and the breaks for meals and socializing in the dorm, she hadn't moved much since she and Lisa woke late Saturday afternoon.

Her phone, as ever lying next to her, buzzed. She sat up and read the text from Professor Dyer.

Are you available? I have a research opportunity, and Bones could use some exercise

Her face flushed. She'd been avoiding Professor Dyer. She should have texted him back, but something other than maybe saving Lisa's life made her uneasy about doing it. Almost frightened. The things she'd told him about herself and what he'd shared with her was overwhelming. A feeling of foreboding lingered. Not a true premonition, but something. *Why can't I just be normal?*

She inhaled and counseled herself to face him. "Come on, Jenny."

She texted back:

Sure! 😊 *I can run the dog. Should I pick her up at your office? When?*

She watched the little dots move, indicating he was typing a response. They stopped without a message. She knit her brow, wondering what was up and waited. Several minutes later:

No. She's at my house. Key under mat. Can you feed her lunch? Food, cup, leash, bags in pantry. I should be there at 1.

Jenny looked at the time. Ten thirty. She could go over there now, get the dog, and be back by one for them to meet.

Ok! 😊

After closing her laptop, she put on a pair of leggings with a pocket on the side, zipped in her phone, key, and student ID, and left the room. She said hi to a couple of nice girls as she made her way downstairs and outside to the bike rack. It was still gorgeous out but quite a bit cooler. She hadn't seen the sun for a while, and her spirit lifted now at the sight of it. It would feel good to go for a run.

As she pedaled the roughly six blocks, she admired the houses with expansive front lawns. Then she came to Professor Dyer's house. It was a bit of an eyesore, and a Jeep was parked on the cracked and crumbling driveway. She puzzled over the car as she pushed her bike up to the front door, then propped it on the sidewalk near a bunch of dying hedges and piles of leaves. She lifted the front door mat and found the key. When she touched it, she had a flash. It was a quick one, which showed a pretty woman smiling at her. In the vision, Jenny's eyes were slightly clouded as if teared up, but then the woman hugged her. She was the same woman she'd seen before when she'd been with Professor Dyer. *Who was she?*

Jenny inhaled with patience as she put the key in the lock, turned it, and pushed open the door. The house was quiet, and Bones did not run up to greet her. The smell of cigarettes and garlic lingered. Jenny stopped short and gasped when she entered the living room. The woman from the vision was there, Professor Dyer standing next to her. Bones sat obediently between them.

"Oh!" said Jenny. She blushed, this time with shock and surprise.

Max held a hand up. "I'm sorry, Jenny. There's been a change in plans. This is Sidrah Keeling, and of course, you know Bones."

At the dog's name, Bones whimpered her way toward Jenny, then stopped to stare at her, her tail wagging furiously for attention. Jenny petted her as the woman spoke.

"It's so nice to meet you, Jenny. You probably think we're crazy for calling you over like this, but I can assure you that you will be even more astonished later. That said, I want to apologize for the state of Max's house. It's a pigsty."

Max turned to her. "Hey."

Sidrah put up her hands. "No need to pretend. We're all friends here. The smell alone, Max. I mean really. You've got to quit smoking."

Sidrah walked, smiling, toward Jenny with her hand outstretched. "Jenny Gallagher, thank you for coming. We didn't mean to frighten you, but the fact is, Max is a bit overdramatic about the human resources department and their rules about him not seeing a student alone. And in his home, to boot. It wouldn't do. The poor boy could get in trouble."

Jenny shook Sidrah's hand, amazed by the softness of the woman's skin. She was gorgeous. Her skin and makeup were flawless, and she had a huge emerald ring on her finger. Her red shoes were totally cute too.

Jenny said, "Oh, it's okay." She let go of Sidrah's hand and continued to pet Bones, but the fact was, it wasn't okay at all. She did feel a tiny bit frightened, not to mention ambushed. Professor Dyer had lied to her.

As if on cue, Sidrah said, "I realize Max lied to you, and we're sorry, but we had the right intentions. How about we all settle in for a quick chat. Bones really does need a run, but if we could have a few minutes of your time first, that would be great."

Sidrah walked toward the lone sofa and swatted it, pushing off some dog hair and crumbs. "I don't recommend the couch. Max can take that. You and I can pull up those two awful kitchen chairs made of God knows what—woodette?—for our chat. I didn't have a chance to brew any tea or coffee, and Max only has water and beer. *Tap* water." Sidrah rolled her eyes as she carried two chairs into the living area and placed them a bit apart. "The cups, naturally, are filthy too," Sidrah said as she sat.

Max scowled at her and dropped onto the couch. Dust shot up around him, illuminated from the rays of sunshine that came in through the sliding glass door. "Ignore her, Jenny," Max said. He swatted at some dust too. "It's drywall."

Jenny looked at their smiling faces and took her seat, a bit more relaxed now. They were obviously friends and just teasing one another. Bones sat by her side with her head in Jenny's lap. Jenny stroked the dog as Max cleared his throat and began.

"So. Jenny. You and I had an interesting conversation on Friday, and we need to ask you a few questions."

Jenny darted her eyes to Sidrah, feeling as though her chest was caving in as she moved her arms around the dog. Was Sidrah a shrink? With the school? Was she going to get kicked out for not telling them about the attack? Had he told Sidrah *everything* they'd talked about and lied to her again? Her throat constricted as he continued.

Max gestured to Sidrah. "Sidrah and I are friends. Close friends. She has no relationship with the university. But. She does share a bit of the same personal phenomenon."

Sidrah craned her neck and smiled like she didn't have a care in the world. "I can see the future. Bits of it. In my dreams."

Jenny's eyes popped. "I . . . I don't know what to say," she stammered, her breath catching. Three people with visions in the same room were two more than she'd ever experienced in her life. She'd always been alone with her gift, worried that she was a freak. No one understood what it was like. But now this.

Max said, "Yes. Nice blurting, Sidrah. I thought we were going to ease our way into it?"

Sidrah smiled and sat up straight. "Whatever for? Jenny knows what's what. She's been experiencing it for . . . well, most likely forever. So have I. So have you, Max, my dear sweet man. I think we should begin there. What a *relief* it is to *finally* be able to speak of it around other people who share similar predicaments. Am I right, Jenny?"

Jenny took in a deep breath, trying to process. A small tremble of anxiety worked its way through her. Bones jumped up, her front paws on her lap, and rested her head on Jenny's shoulder. Jenny put her arms around the dog.

"Get down, Bones," said Max, standing to shoo her.

Jenny laughed, feeling better as the dog complied. Bones looked at Max and let out a small bark.

"Don't bark at me," Max scolded.

Jenny could tell the admonition was also good-natured, and that helped her too. "It's okay," she said. "I think she was trying to comfort me."

Bones nodded at her—there was no mistaking it. Jenny's jaw dropped.

Max sat back into the couch and rolled his eyes.

"Yes," Sidrah said. "Well, that's another thing. We *think*, we think Bones may be in on this too. She may be a little, what shall we call it, advanced for her station."

Bones lay on the ground and put a paw over her eyes. "Oh, now," said Sidrah. "Max, you comfort her. You've known her the longest. I think I hurt her feelings."

"Oh, for God's sake," Max grumbled and waved at the dog. "She's fine. It's a theatrical gesture."

Bones got up and turned away from Max, then narrowed her eyes as she looked back over her shoulder. She shot him a stifled bark. Max raised his voice. "You're not helping. You're probably scaring her."

Jenny had covered her mouth in amazement. Processing the wonder of the dog and all that was happening, her throat tightened with the threat of tears. She reached out for Bones, "Come here, baby."

To Jenny's surprise, Bones jumped fully into her lap, nearly toppling her as the adults got up, shouting, "Bones!"

The dog jumped off her as Sidrah neared, holding her arms out to Jenny, precisely as she'd seen it in her vision on the front porch. With tears beginning to run down her face, Jenny got up and walked into Sidrah's welcome embrace.

Not long after that, but definitely after a bit of quarreling, Sidrah convinced them to leave Max's house and go to hers for what she emphasized would be a better place for a proper lunch with a tolerable atmosphere.

Jenny, now in the back seat of the Jeep with Bones, felt comfortable and not at all concerned about leaving with them. The circumstances felt right, and her visions had been utterly calm since her last flash on the front porch. Once she got over all the shock, it almost felt like she could breathe easier around them. The four of them fit.

There was no doubt that whatever was to come needed to happen. She might finally get some answers to her lifelong questions. *No way* would she turn her back on that now. She laid her hand on her backseat companion, marveling at the dog's beauty and the comfort she gave. With Bones's head out the window, her ears flapping in the wind, Jenny felt like the kid of the family.

Jenny gazed fondly at Sidrah in the front seat, who was issuing instructions to someone named Marta on the phone as they drove the roughly fifteen miles into Boston. When the four of them stepped out of the car, Jenny thought she'd never walked a more idyllic, safer looking street in her life. The fall colors of the mature trees that edged the long line of stately townhomes sheltered them with their cave-like canopies. Sidrah's mini castle was made of old-looking but pretty brick. The house was five or six stories tall with

Victorian gables, and the impossibly large front door loomed as they walked up the stairs. A tall, sturdy woman greeted them at the front door. She did a double-take at Bones, who sat respectfully near Jenny's side.

Polite introductions to Marta were made all around. Sidrah instructed her to assemble the luncheon in the kitchen and to take the rest of the day off.

"Text me right before you leave," said Sidrah, walking toward the stairs. "We'll be in the living room. Max," she said, turning to him and speaking as she ascended like a queen. "I don't believe you've seen the living room, have you? Or the other levels. We'll have to have a real tour after lunch."

Jenny looked around in awe at what she knew was a crazy expensive home. It felt like a palace, although the acoustics didn't echo. It was solid and comforting.

Marta suddenly called from the foot of the stairs. The four stopped walking and turned as one.

"Oh, my. I forgot. There was a flower delivery. I put them on the sofa table under the parlor arch."

Marta disappeared as they made their way to the second floor, which was different than the lower level. It was really one long room, split in two by an archway. In contrast to the hardwood on the lower level, this one was floored in a patterned marble. Just below the arch, a gargantuan flower arrangement sat on what must be the sofa table Marta had referred to.

Sidrah picked up the card. Before she had it opened, Max grumbled, "Who are they from?"

She gave him a tender smile and a quick kiss. "Jealous, are we? Remember that it's *not* just me having these difficulties."

Jenny smiled as she watched Max steam a bit. She wondered how long the two of them had been dating. They seemed to be having a good time, but as Sidrah read the card, Jenny saw her bright expression change.

"Oh, it's nothing," said Sidrah, walking through to the side of the room, which had a fireplace. She picked a remote off the mantel and pointed it at the hearth. A fire came to life.

Max wandered near her and sat on one of the couches. He put his booted foot on top of a book on the glass coffee table—hard.

"Max!" Sidrah rushed over to push his foot off and inspected the table.

"Who are they from?" he asked again.

Sidrah handed him the card. Max looked up at her, his expression confused. "The Oak Bar at the Fairmont at five? Who the hell is Turner Black?"

Chapter 30

MONDAY

Turner fumed as he got out of his float tank. "No!" he yelled, slamming the lid.

He whipped his earbuds at a wall. His eyes scanned the room, his peripheral vision returning, his heart thudding. Something was happening. Forces were gathering and moving. Like a general in battle, he saw the first glimmers of light bouncing off the armor of an overwhelming enemy force, cresting a ridge in front of him, the sun rising at their backs. They were coming for him and his empire.

Fifty-five years he'd lived doing his great work, and he knew this time, in his life as Turner Black, he'd accomplished much. Born out of the great darkness of chaos, each time he'd awake in a new life with another opportunity to leave a permanent mark of corruption on the planet. That bit of knowledge was always divinely given to him.

He moved to the shower and threw on the hot water, the red lights pulsing, and centered his mind on the problem.

Whoever they were, they wouldn't be able to catch up. The tentacles of his evil were too deeply embedded. Great leaders with many followers were already in place or ready to take the stage. His dark army had a foothold this time, and erasing the legacy wouldn't be possible.

But his opponent was finally here; this other destiny was no doubt gathering its own army.

"Who are you?" he screamed, smacking the dark granite, pain vibrating through his hand and into his body. When he found them, he'd transcend and watch them suffer as they died in agony, knowing that they had failed. Only he would be left behind, standing triumphant, for they would come in human form, after all. Just like him.

Oh, the sweetness! He placed his hands on the shower wall letting his body sag, his eyes closed in ecstasy as the hot water and the red glow of the ceiling lights pulsated on him. His mind roared with a vision of his strong hands crushing his enemy's throat, bones breaking, cartilage snapping, eyes bulging. He felt the sweet flow of the intoxicating deep-red blood oozing from the sockets, pulsing out their life force.

Turner reveled in the fantasy, letting the images feed him until his release. Spent from the rapturous vision, he turned off the taps and stepped out of the shower to get ready.

For, like a puff of smoke he couldn't yet reach, the maddening race was on.

He hurried through his grooming, cautioning himself to focus on the tasks he could immediately complete. Given the developments in the tank, he needed to reconsider his timeline against Jett Franklin's political opponent, Mary St. Clair. Initially, he'd wanted to see if she would naturally slip in the polls, leaving Jett clear of her, but no. Mary St. Clair had to get out of the race. Now.

The progenitor would be her husband, Mitch St. Clair. Turner might have been moving slowly, but he hadn't been idle. He'd been doing his homework and discovered that Mitch was having an affair with one of the many young and eager campaign volunteers, Esme Stevens.

There were many ways to use the information. A simple plan would involve leaking the affair to the press. The stress of that could make Mary quit. Possibly. The young woman involved—Esme Stevens—had a past. There'd been an assault during a previous relationship, but the charges had eventually been dropped. Esme had proven herself to be a wiggly worm and a bit of a pushover, but what was even more interesting was that she'd been an escort at the time of the alleged assault. Esme could be compelled to do something; he could turn her. Or worse.

Someone once said that he who is born to be hanged will never drown. But Turner knew he was a fate changer. He was one with the three sisters. Once he changed destiny, a new fate would follow. People liked to believe there was a natural order to things in the universe. And there was. He was a part of that—a part of the equation that scientists and theorists hadn't considered.

Though still tense, he felt better now that he'd decided how to move forward with one of the problems. And tonight, he would meet with Sidrah Keeling. Where did she fit into his life and plans? It had been a gamble to place a specific time for their meeting on the card, but he believed in a good call to action. People tended to respond when they were told what to do and when, rather than giving them the wiggle room to make their own decisions.

Naturally, they still thought of themselves as being in control, but Turner would lay a nice, soft carpeted path for them to choose his. Sidrah would be at the Fairmont tonight. Of that, he was sure.

Chapter 31

Jenny relished the camaraderie around the table as they ate lunch at Sidrah's. The four of them together—Bones included—most definitely had a lot to talk about. She couldn't believe only hours before she'd been nervous about meeting with her professor. But now her world had changed. Both Max and Sidrah had trusted her and quelled her unease by sharing amazing and sad stories about themselves first. Now it was her turn.

"Have you ever not followed up on a vision or ignored it?" Sidrah asked her.

Jenny played with what was left of her food. "For me, sometimes it's not even a vision. It's just something I feel I *need to do*. It's become like a part of my personality. It's just . . . me. If I get a real vision or a flash of déjà vu and I know what's going to happen, then I feel really compelled to act. Like for better or worse.

"In junior high, I saw a neighbor girl, kind of a friend back then, get the lead in the school musical. I told her it was going to happen. I mean, no big deal, people say encouraging things, or guess what's going to happen, all the time. But then she didn't get the role, and I was confused. Two days later, the girl who had gotten the part dropped out because something bad had happened in her family. I saw my neighbor whispering about me and heard her call me a freak. She was someone I'd talked to when I was younger, so she knew about me. She and her crowd steered away from me after that, and the gossip just grew. By high school, I'd developed a reputation. It wasn't always nice."

"You didn't have anything to do with the bad thing that happened to the family," Max said, trying to reassure her.

She smiled as Max reached for the salad, upending the entire contents onto his plate. Sidrah held a big serving spoon up to his face, but he ignored it.

Jenny continued. "When I was little, I used to tell everyone *everything.* Like, I could see a kid drop a scoop of ice cream off his cone, and I'd tell my friends before it happened. Then, we'd all watch. When it happened, they'd think it was funny, but then later, they'd be mean to me."

Sidrah nodded. "Kids can be mean. But you've learned when to speak and when not to?"

"I don't just come out and tell people about it anymore, that's for sure. But as for directing people, telling people what to do, like I said, now it's almost a part of my personality. Like, I'm compelled to do something without thinking, and then I stand back and wonder about what I did. What's my role here? Why did I do that? It's becoming reflexive for me to intervene. Lately, I've been questioning everything because the visions are really increasing."

Sidrah laid a hand near her. "I know it's confusing. But you're growing, and so is your gift. And it is a gift, Jenny, not a curse."

Max held up a gloved hand. "It can be."

Sidrah frowned. "Yes, I know. I'm not trying to minimize it. You've suffered some trauma too, Jenny. Will there be a trial?"

Jenny had been trying hard to forget about it, but the event was still fresh, always in reach. The memories would probably be there forever. She sighed loudly. "Yes. In November."

"So, it's coming up soon," Max said.

"I have to testify. The prosecutors think it will only be for one day, though."

"There's no chance he'll take a plea? From what I've read, the evidence and his DNA are pretty damning," said Max.

Jenny inwardly flinched, thinking about Max and Sidrah reading up on the gory details. She hadn't even told Lisa yet. She hadn't wanted her roommate to treat her differently or think of her as anything but normal. Pretty soon, though, she might find out. Jenny worried she'd be hurt if she didn't tell her first.

She looked over at Bones, who was sitting at the table like one of them. The dog looked at her like a friend. The preposterous wonder of the dog gave her the courage to continue. "When it happened, I didn't get any warning. My *gift* let me down. You'd think *that* would have been the time to kick into gear."

"You were meant to stop him, Jenny," Max said. "Your gift protected you from the foreknowledge so you wouldn't have dread and you wouldn't change things."

Jenny gave him a quizzical look. "You talk about it like it's a living thing."

Max said, "Maybe it is. It's alive. It's a part of us."

Jenny glanced out the window. "Once he had me, I had a flash. I saw the knife and somehow knew I'd been there before. The déjà vu was really, really strong. Do you believe in reincarnation?"

Sidrah looked over at Max, who communicated something to her and nodded. "Maybe," Sidrah said. "Have you lived before? Has any of us? I'm sure we've thought about it. But what we do know is that there's just too much coincidence for the three of us—" She stopped and smiled at Bones. "I'm sorry, the *four* of us, to be sitting here together at this table. All of us with gifts. So, if that's not a coincidence, then what is it?"

Max nodded. "We believe we found each other for a reason, Jenny. We don't know what it is, but each of us has a different ability. Taken as a whole, we can certainly see a lot of the big picture. We might consider testing our skills at some point. I mean, as much as I've complained about some of the aspects, they are remarkable."

Jenny couldn't disagree. "So, you can see the past when you touch things, and Sidrah can see the future in her dreams."

Sidrah smiled tenderly. "Yes. And you are the present."

Jenny considered that and realized it was true. Even though she caught glimpses of both past and future, it all led to what was happening in the now. "But the details aren't always clear. I often don't understand the visions or what I'm supposed to do."

"I don't think you're supposed to *do* anything, Jenny," Sidrah said. "Just be yourself. Be kind to yourself. We've . . . we've talked about it and think, maybe . . ." Sidrah looked reluctant to continue. She turned to Max for support.

His eyes softened, but he looked determined. "We believe that you, not us, might be forming destiny. In the present time, moving through it and meant to help others. Fate brought you to Wellesley, first to Bones's attention, then to mine. You might be the most special of all of us. Maybe as older adults who also share gifts, we are supposed to be your guides. Your friends. But we were meant to work together somehow."

Jenny sat with that. Was she comforted? Surprised? More frightened? Glad she had friends? Her head swam.

Sidrah gave her a doleful look. "You know, I haven't told you, but I saw part of your attack too."

Jenny pulled her head back in surprise as Sidrah continued. "I help the police from time to time. They were looking for that guy, the serial rapist, and one of his victims had grabbed a button off his shirt. The police found it near her bed, and she confirmed where it came from. My friend, who is a detective at the Boston PD, called me for help. They were desperate, so I agreed, and he gave me the button. I slept with it. I saw that man stalking the Pride Convenience. I saw the name Brian on his credit card. I saw his cap and a tattoo on his forearm. I saw . . ."

Sidrah swallowed hard, and her eyes became misty. "I saw his desperation too. I felt it. I'm so sorry for what he did to you, Jenny. I can't imagine the terror you lived through."

Jenny, her eyes forever clouding with tears at the memory, wiped her eyes. She tried to put on a brave face. "And now what? What's going to happen to us next? Does this mean I'm going to be attacked again?"

"No," Max said forcibly. "We'll protect you, Jenny, I promise. We're together now."

Sidrah frowned. "I wonder how many other people out there have similar abilities. Now that we know about each other, there could be more, right?"

"Do you think they'll find us?" Jenny worried about what that might mean.

"If they're meant to," Sidrah said, "I suppose they will. Max was given to me in a dream, and I searched for him."

Max interjected and looked at Jenny. "Bones stared you down in class. Then you met us."

"And where did Bones come from?" Sidrah asked.

Each of them looked at the dog, who gave them a blank stare. A lump formed in Jenny's throat as her mind raced through the implications of a world beyond her control.

Max pushed back from the table. "Come on. We can't figure it all out today. Let's focus on something positive. For one, we can finally talk about our abilities with people who believe us and understand. None of us has had that before. It feels good, doesn't it?"

Jenny inhaled and tried to smile. "Yes, it does. It makes me finally feel a bit more normal."

Max nodded. "Good. Then let that be enough for now." He turned to Sidrah. "Speaking of normal, we need to make plans. I've got work to do and PT this afternoon. I'm sure Jenny needs to get back to her life too."

"I don't have class until tomorrow. I'm pretty caught up," Jenny said.

"Okay," Max said. "Why don't you take Bones for a quick run, and then we'll head back to Wellesley." He suddenly grimaced. "I don't think Jenny should be alone in the car with me. What if someone sees us?"

"Oh, for goodness' sake, Max," said Sidrah. "I'll drive her back. You and Bones can take your car."

Bones jumped down and turned in circles. Jenny smiled. "I think she knows about the run."

"I think you're right," Max said, getting up.

———————

Sidrah cleared the plates from the table and put a few things away as Max watched her. Their moods had sobered now that Jenny had left the house with Bones.

"How do you think Jenny felt about the conversation?" Sidrah said.

"I think she was glad for the honesty of it. I know I am." He got up and deposited a few plates near the sink.

"What do you think is happening, Max? Really. Tell me your thoughts."

Max crossed his arms and leaned against a counter. "We all agree there's a reason we're together. Going forward, I think we just need to carry on with our lives. Maybe I'm supposed to help you with the police. Maybe we all are. Now that I know there is someone on the force you trust, I'm more open to it."

Sidrah gave him a supportive smile, but her anxiety had been ratcheting up since they'd spoken of Jenny's attack and the danger. She put away some food as he spoke.

"I've written some papers on historical coincidence. Jesus. Stop right there, and think about that. The butterfly effect, too. Pluck someone out of history and see how it changes the world. Some ripples are larger than others, but they're always there. I teach about Thelma, Lady Furness in class."

"Who?" she encouraged as she fussed around the kitchen. Max's strong voice soothed her.

"She was the mistress of the Prince of Wales, later King

Edward VIII, the king who abdicated to be with Wallis Simpson. Thelma had an identical twin sister named Gloria Morgan Vanderbilt. The two girls were educated in French convents and finishing schools, then made their society debut as the Morgan twins. Thelma was on her second husband when she fell into bed with the randy debauched prince. From all accounts, she had the relationship strapped down tight until her twin sister, Gloria, needed her help in New York. Gloria's only daughter—the poor little rich girl herself, Gloria Vanderbilt—had been taken by relatives who claimed her mother was unfit. So, Thelma went off to New York for her sister's trial, but before she left, she introduced her good friend Wallis Simpson to the prince and asked her to look after him. History took a turn at this juncture—a very sharp turn. World War II was looming, and the future king was easily influenced. He was very pro-Nazi, but he abdicated the throne for her."

"I went to an auction for some of her things," Sidrah interrupted. "I read somewhere that Wallis spent a long time in China, but the only Chinese she learned to speak was 'Boy, pass the champagne.'"

Max shrugged. "But for the Morgan twins and their own extraordinary personal drama, history might have turned out differently. If you plucked Lady Furness and her link to Wallis Simpson out of history, you get a Nazi king of England, who might have changed the course of the war, and humanity."

"Pluck Jenny out of history and that rapist would have gone on," Sidrah added. "Those ripples are never-ending."

"That's where I was going. It's something like that," he said.

Sidrah wrinkled her brow. "She's so sweet, Max. You can see how worried she is about everything too. I feel very protective of her."

Max put his arms around her and leaned down for a soft kiss. "We'll look after her. We're heads and tails with time, but Jenny's in the now, and she's an immediate game changer for destiny. She's important."

Sidrah nuzzled her face into his large, warm chest, a wave of comfort washing over her. Their connection was complete. It had only been days, and yet her entire world had changed.

Max took off a glove, then lovingly ran his hand over her face. "We'll look after each other too. We're not seeing anyone else. Have I got that straight? No Mr. Over-the-Top-Flower-Arrangement guy upstairs. Right?"

Sidrah smiled. "I love that you're jealous."

"It's not something I'm proud of," he said, kissing her again.

Sidrah pushed him away, breaking the connection. Jenny would be coming back soon, and she didn't want to begin something they couldn't finish. "I'll miss you tonight in my bed."

Max raised his brow. "You can crawl into my bed later. Say around midnight? I really do have a lot of work piled up. Although God knows how I'll focus."

She smiled. "We'll see."

Chapter 32

After dropping Jenny back at her dorm, Sidrah drove home. She came in through the kitchen and tossed her purse on the kitchen table. "Hellooo. Anyone home?" she said to her empty house.

Now that Max and Bones had left and Jenny was safely back at school, Sidrah felt lost. How could she have lived for so long without them?

She walked down the hall and into the library filled with books—her best friends. Worlds and knowledge she'd explored while emotionally sequestering herself from others. It seemed absurd now to have lived that way, but then again, perhaps she'd only been waiting for her real family to arrive. For being such a short period of time, that thought, too, seemed absurd. But also, it didn't.

"Aaah," she said, confused, as she walked to her desk. She knew there was work waiting, but she no longer had the desire to do her research. Her portfolio was enormous; there was no reason to amass more of a fortune, other than out of habit. But it was how she'd spent her days before Max had come into it.

She half-heartedly opened her e-mail and sorted through the messages. How could she focus on anything now? What was her purpose? What was *their* purpose? Max thought they'd been brought together to protect Jenny. That was a good thought. She could help with that.

She perked to the idea and shot off an e-mail to Detective Bodine at Boston PD, asking for references for a personal security service. She marked the e-mail as urgent and sent it along. Jenny and Max might not think it was necessary, but it never hurt to investigate the options.

Her eyes traveled to Turner Black's business card, which he'd given her at the rally. She picked it up and thought about the enormous flower arrangement upstairs. She smiled, not only pleased by the attention but by the jealousy it inspired in Max. The timing had been perfect. It made her girly heart flutter watching Max squirm as they Googled Turner and found his image on his firm's website. Max didn't seem impressed.

She looked at the time. Three-thirty. She'd have just enough time to change and get to the Fairmont for their five o'clock meeting. Should she go?

Fresh off hours of discussion about coincidence and their changed lives, she thought that maybe Turner Black and his timely flowers were a part of it. It wasn't every day that the founding partner of a major law firm came courting. Not that it would be a romantic date. No. Her heart now wholly belonged to Maximus Dyer.

But Turner Black had power and influence. Not key characteristics she typically turned away from. One never knew when one might need a good lawyer, did one?

She put down the card, popped up from behind the desk, and started upstairs to change. Max was busy; Jenny was busy. She'd feel better if she were too. She'd meet Turner, then come home and pack a bag. A large one. She'd go over to Max's place later, but no way was she going without fresh sheets.

Her new life was exciting. She bounded up the stairs feeling blessed. And now, yay, she would get to dress up too!

Sidrah dropped her car at valet and sashayed into the Fairmont, a fine hotel that she'd been to many times. She felt very James Bond-like in her Ralph Lauren tuxedo jacket. Her tuxedo shirt was fashioned in a vivid, ultramarine blue, complete with a black bow tie that matched her black pants. Simple diamond studs sparkled in each ear, and she had donned a large multicolored cocktail ring. It felt girly and playful next to her mannish ensemble. Not wanting to exude too much femininity, and knowing the evening would not lead to romance, she still wanted to feel pretty.

She walked into the Oak Bar, a piano tinkling somewhere in the elegant Edwardian atmosphere, and looked around until she saw Turner. She put one hand in her pocket, feeling powerful as she walked toward him. She smiled, fully intending to enjoy herself and order a martini, shaken, not stirred, once she was seated.

Turner, looking handsome in a well-tailored suit, stood and pulled out a leather-studded chair at a solid four-top table. A cheese plate and olives waited. She took a seat.

"Thank you for joining me this evening, Sidrah Keeling," Turner said, smiling.

She returned the playful smile. "You're welcome." She'd not recalled him being quite so alluring when she'd met him at the rally. Maybe it was the difference between the sunlight and the bar's soft lighting. A waiter approached the table. She ordered her vodka martini and settled in.

"Thank you for the flowers," she began. "They were gorgeous. I'm not sure I've ever received anything that opulent before, especially from someone I don't really know."

He cocked his head. "We know each other, I think. From somewhere. Surely our paths have crossed."

She looked into his dark eyes. His full head of silver hair was neatly cut. There was a youthfulness to him. Something . . . she wasn't sure. Possibly familiar.

She shook her head. "I don't think so."

He put up a hand. "No matter. We know each other now, and I want to learn all about you."

No way was she going to share anything remotely close to the truth. She scolded herself for the thousandth time, wondering if she'd made a mistake for not changing her name after winning the Florida lottery. This guy could be a gold digger. But then again, he was a founding partner of a law firm. He had his own money.

"Why don't you tell me about you, instead." She smiled as her cocktail was delivered.

Turner acquiesced, but the details of his life lacked an element of depth or personal joy. It was like he was reading from a resume, which wasn't at all what she was interested in hearing about.

"It's your turn now," he said, taking a bite of an olive.

This whole thing had been a bad idea. She shouldn't have come, and Max would be furious. And although that thought thrilled her, it was strange, given that she and Max had only just met. In fact, it was the same day she'd met Turner Black.

"Look, Turner," she said, smiling apologetically. "I really was very flattered by the flowers, and I felt I needed to thank you in person, but I'm afraid I'm seeing someone."

Turner didn't blink. "And who is that? Someone I might know? Boston is a small town."

Sidrah was not going to give him Max's name. She shook her head. "I don't think so." She pushed back her chair and made a motion to rise. "I'd better be going."

Turner reached out and touched her hand. Somewhere inside her, an unpleasant feeling sparked, and her stomach did a flip of worry.

"Please don't leave yet. We haven't gotten to know one another," he said.

Sidrah stood. "I'm sorry. But thank you, Mr. Black. It was a pleasure meeting you."

As she walked out, she felt his eyes on her back. She sensed they were angry. She couldn't wait to get home and pack.

Chapter 33

Turner Black glared at the empty birdcage in the corner of his home office; the bird had not returned. "Fucking animals," he snarled.

He sat on the sofa and flipped through the political shows on television to give him comfort and encouragement. There was so much hate out there, so much conflict and rage. Things were really shaping up. He knew his counterpart was out there working against him somehow, but was it possible there were other fate-changers in the world? He couldn't know for certain, but he doubted the three sisters would allow many such as he. It didn't matter. Whatever was coming next, he'd be merciless and reign supreme.

He flipped off the TV. It was time to get to work. Since returning home from the hotel *without* Sidrah, a development that, although not unprecedented, had still surprised him, he'd gone into the zone. Women could be such bitches. Sidrah was beautiful, and there was most definitely something special about her, but he couldn't place it. He'd seen her in a vision. He'd done what he could to track her down and discover her purpose, but it eluded him. He wasn't done with her by any means; their dance would continue. Somehow, she fit into his life and plans, and he would eventually come to it. Perhaps the next session in the tank would enlighten him.

He didn't take her rejection too personally. He was disappointed, but women were women. The simple ones like Sidrah were mostly interchangeable, and he typically took very little interest in them outside the bedroom. The dark ones, though, they could be exceedingly twisted. Fascinating creatures. Some of them were more blood-thirsty than men. Those women could be extremely useful.

Tonight, his preemptive strike against Mary St. Clair would begin. Esme Stevens, the little piece who was currently bedding Mitch St. Clair, was, alas, a simple soul. Earlier today, he'd finally laid eyes on her. He realized she couldn't be counted on to become personally helpful in Mary and Mitch's downfall. For that, he'd need to bring in the professionals.

His bell rang, and Turner left the couch to answer it. Jorim Patrick stood in the doorway, all five feet six inches of sinewed evil. Turner had met him in the bowels of the justice department many years before when the man worked as a jailer. He'd known with one look that the intensely dark aura surrounding Jorim would make him a useful soldier in Turner's army.

Turner didn't greet him, he just walked back toward his office, knowing Jorim would follow. They each took a seat on the small sofas facing one another. "We've got a job," said Turner.

Jorim scratched the back of his hand and sniffed. "When?"

"This weekend. Saturday night."

"Who and where?"

"The *who* is a gentleman by the name of Mitch St. Clair," Turner said. "The *where* is at this address." Turner slid over a piece of paper with Esme Stevens's address on it.

"Allston," said Jorim. "Scofflaw landlords, students."

Turner nodded. He could see the excitement appear behind Jorim's normally dead eyes. "It's a bottom floor apartment in a rundown house. Nice enough neighborhood. Street parking. The renter is a woman named Esme Stevens. No known roommates, but she could have someone helping with the rent."

Jorim chewed the side of his thumbnail. His leg, which was resting on his knee, began to bounce. "How?"

"Mitch St. Clair will be compelled to visit Esme on Saturday evening at that address. You'll be waiting there. Leave the door unlocked. Make it look amateur. Hit him over the head with something in the apartment. Stage it like a crime of passion, a temper tantrum. I want a lot of blood and confusion—a slippery mess. Head wounds are best for that. So, hit him with something sharp-edged. Esme Stevens is about the same height as you."

Turner slid another piece of paper toward Jorim, this one inside a plastic bag. "Place this note in a pocket on the body and leave."

Jorim picked it up and read, "I'm begging you. Something terrible has happened. Please come over right away."

Jorim folded it neatly and stuffed it into his pocket. "How are you going to get Mitch St. Clair over there? What time do I need to be inside?"

"On Saturday night, Esme Stevens will be at a fundraiser for Mary St. Clair at the Hyatt Regency in Cambridge. Dinner. Dancing. I will be there too. Someone from the campaign will make sure Esme has a ticket. That night, Esme will get dressed, attend the function, and while she's there, she, too, will get a note. She needs to go home. Mitch is waiting, upset. When she arrives, Mitch will be there, hopefully, having just finished pumping his blood onto the floor, definitely unrecoverable. I think Esme should arrive home at about 10:00 p.m."

"Why won't Mitch St. Clair be at the fundraisa for his wife?" Jorim asked.

Turner broke into a full grin and pointed at his Boston-bred comrade. "An excellent question. Because another associate will distract him. Mitch St. Clair is most definitely not interested in attending another one of his wife's tiresome events. He works for a hearing aid company—Starkey. Some kind of engineer. Someone, a most attractive someone from out of town, a colleague of sorts, will have a short window to meet with him. He will agree to the meeting. She will delay him, tease him. Mitch is a bit of a drinker. Once inebriated, he will complain about leaving the important meeting to attend his wife's function. But then a waiter will bring him a note in a sealed envelope, very similar to the one you have."

"Why would Esme know where he was at?" Jorim interrupted. "How would she communicate with the waita?"

"She won't. But when Mitch receives the note, he'll ask himself those very questions and be quite puzzled. And worried. And my associate will have him horny. He won't question anyone. He'll just go to her place intending to fuck and question Esme after he arrives."

"You don't think the cops will figuh this out?" Jorim asked.

"You would think so, wouldn't you? But alas, once Esme's previous job as an escort becomes known, once the salacious, bloody scene and note are found and the affair discovered, the police won't want to search for other suspects. Esme can scream her innocence all the way to the gas chamber. But once she is home with that fresh corpse, she'll panic. The police will come. Her destiny will change."

"And if she doesn't panic, if she flees the scene and pretends she was never home?"

"Trust me. After she sees Mitch St. Clair bludgeoned and dead in her apartment, she will not be able to act her way out of it."

Jorim nodded and smirked. "All right. Nine thirty, Saturday night. Mitch St. Clair. I got this."

Turner nodded. "I know that you do. We'll enter into the usual arrangement for payment."

Chapter 34

Jenny lay in bed that night, her sleep troubled. Something disturbing woke her, and she sat up. Lisa was across the room in her own bed, her back to Jenny, but her laptop open.

"Lisa," she whispered.

Lisa rolled over and smiled. "Hey."

"What time is it?"

"Two. You okay?"

Jenny licked her lips, then wiped them off and grabbed a tube of Chapstick lying nearby. "Yeah. I just had a bad dream." She put on the balm and said, "What are you working on?"

"Poli-sci. We're supposed to pick a political race to follow. Like a lotto. I got the local race for Governor Jett Franklin of the Republican GOP versus Mary St. Clair, the Democrat. It's down to the two of them now."

"Oh my God, did you miss the rally?" Jenny knew they'd spent all day in bed on Saturday and that Jett Franklin had been on campus.

Lisa shrugged. "A friend from class videoed it. She met Jett Franklin too." She pointed to a picture of the governor and some materials piled on the floor next to her. "She brought me some stuff from the rally."

"That was nice of her."

Lisa smiled, then closed her laptop and rolled fully toward Jenny. She put her hands under her head and lay there, looking relaxed but reflective.

"Are you homesick? Do you miss Hong Kong a lot?" Jenny asked.

"Yeah. I do," Lisa said. "It's so different here. But in a good way, I suppose."

Jenny knew Lisa came from a small family. She was an only child, just like her. "It must be hard on your parents being so far away. I know I really miss my dad."

Lisa didn't answer right away. "They've always traveled a lot. I have too, but I guess I've gotten used to them not being around. I had a lot of nannies. My favorite one was a sweet woman from the Philippines named Esme. I haven't seen her since graduation, but she was with me for eight years."

"Where is she now? With another family?"

"No. She went back to her own country. Hong Kong was getting tricky. I think my parents took care of her."

"That's nice," said Jenny. "She came back to Hong Kong for your graduation?"

Lisa rubbed her face. "Yeah. Esme has a wonderful, sweet old soul. She always had a proverb or saying to help me through anything."

Jenny could see the emotional tug the woman still had on Lisa. She guessed she should feel lucky that her dad had always been there for her. She looked at her roommate, wondering if she should tell her more about herself. It had been another overwhelming day, and all her life, she'd dreamed of having a really close friend. Sidrah and Max and Bones were now her friends, but they felt different. Lisa was her age, right there in her room. *Was she another person placed in her life for a reason?*

Jenny closed her eyes and lay down, realizing that maybe she'd question everything for the rest of her life. Maybe she needed an Esme with wise sayings in her life too. The thought cheered her. She turned to look at Lisa. In all her kind ways, maybe Lisa was meant to be the friend she'd never had. In her heart, Jenny thought she could trust her.

"So, I have a story. About myself," Jenny began haltingly. She'd tell her about the attack and the upcoming trial. As crazy as it sounded, that part of her life was somewhat safe territory.

Lisa sat up, and Jenny began. It would be a long night.

Chapter 35

Sidrah lay in Max's bed, happy and horrified at the same time. She stared at the popcorn ceiling overhead and noticed a large dark stain coming down the wall. The roof was leaking. She put a hand on the dog's head, who had jumped into bed and taken Max's spot.

"What are we going to do with him?" she said. She could hear the shower going, could imagine Max naked and lathery inside. It was tempting to join him, but he was running late. She got up and reached into a bag for her robe. She put it on and picked up her purse, which was lying on the floor next to a pile of his dirty clothes. A wad of dog hair clung to the bottom of the red suede bag. She removed it with disgust. She put the purse on a nearby chair, it too covered with debris, and dug inside for her phone. She'd missed a text from Jenny.

She walked toward the bathroom door and got a pleasant eyeful as Max emerged from the shower. She smiled at him. "Jenny texted."

"What did she say?" he said, grabbing a towel off the rack.

Sidrah noticed the towel was not fresh but rather looked as if it had been used many times. "You know, it's a wonder why I ever let you touch me with your filthy paws. Your lifestyle needs a serious adjustment."

He flipped the towel in a circular motion, creating a long cylinder, and snapped her with it.

She jumped out of the way. "Stop. Jenny said she had a flash last night. She saw the three of us at a political fundraiser for Mary St. Clair. She said she was wearing a pretty dress she did not own."

Sidrah smiled. She now had two new missions to add to her life—shopping and a gala. Max continued his grooming routine, lathering up a shaving brush from an old cracked cup. He dolloped the foamy soap onto his neck and face and picked up a razor to shave. "Did she say when it was?"

"I'm Googling," she said, going to Mary St. Clair's homepage. "This is going to take some time."

"Well, if she saw us there, we'd better go. Don't you think?"

"I do," she said. "Why do you think we're going?"

"I don't know, but we might find out when we get there."

"I'll text her and let her know we're on it. By the way, I thought we might consider getting Jenny some legitimate protection."

Max threw some water on his face and picked a towel up off the dirty sink to dry himself. "Why?"

"Because her gift has put her in danger before. Because we know she's special, and we're her protectors. We can't be with her all the time, Max. Now that the four of us have come together, there might be a big reason looming out there. I've already contacted Detective Bodine. He'll let me know who to hire."

Max walked out of the bathroom, and she watched him search through a dresser drawer. Not finding what he was looking for, he then went over to the pile on the chair and pulled out a pair of underwear.

"Please tell me those are clean," she said as he put them on.

"Yeah, they're clean. You really need to lighten up."

She gave him her best showgirl smile. "Max, how would you feel if I took your home up like a little project? You know, just some basic things, fix a few things up here and there. Maybe do a little cleaning?"

"Knock yourself out," he said, pulling on some jeans. "God, it's nice to have the boot off."

"You look rather good in those jeans too," she said.

"Just don't do anything major. Like paint or something. My mom wants to be involved in those decisions."

"Speaking of your mom and dad, when am I going to meet them?"

He picked a T-shirt out of his closet and put it on. "You know, if this were a regular relationship, I'd say you were a stalker. We've only known each other for four days."

She put a hand on her hip. "This is not a regular relationship. We've discussed that. You told me . . ."

He interrupted her with a laugh, came over, and wrapped his arms around her. "I'm just kidding. I agree it's full steam ahead. Why don't I see if they can come to lunch this week? I've got Thursday open—at least, no class."

Sidrah brightened. Another huge something to look forward to! Her to-do list was growing by the hour. "Are you taking Bones to work with you today?"

He nodded. "She's used to the routine."

"Okay, but I'd like to have her with me sometimes too."

"We can do that," he said as he walked out of the room.

Sidrah raised her eyebrows at Bones. "You hear that, girl? You can hang with me sometimes too!"

Bones pulled her lips back and smiled.

Sidrah felt like a housewife, or the wife of a dirty house, as she kissed Max and the dog good-bye as they left for work. She turned around and looked at the scene, thrilled that Max had given her permission to do some work. Finally, she could give back and do something absolutely wonderful for her sweet baby, Max. "My God, where do I start?"

She texted Marta and told her to report for duty at Max's house. She did an inventory of supplies, food and otherwise, and got dressed. After starting a load of laundry, the bell rang, and she let Marta in. Never had she been so relieved to see her stalwart, no-nonsense housekeeper in her life. They walked through the home, made a list of to-dos, and got to work. Or, Marta got to work. Sidrah went shopping.

She hit Target hard, filling her cart with cleaning supplies and household items, rugs, and candles. After dropping that off, she went to the mall, filling her car with luxury bedding, towels, dishware, and then organizing same-day delivery of new furniture from an agreeable merchant. She tipped her way heavily through the process as she made the arrangements, determined to overhaul Max's home by that afternoon. She and Marta had been in constant communication, and Marta somehow found and hired a landscape company to begin work that same day too.

By the time Sidrah got home, and the deliveries began to arrive, she knew that despite her disorganized approach to decorating, it would be a vast improvement. She sent Marta out on her last errand of the day to purchase groceries. At the same time, she ordered delivery of an excellent stock of liquor, along with takeout from a local Thai restaurant through Door Dash, due to arrive at five-thirty that evening. Max would be home around six since he had a late class at four-thirty.

She and Max had texted all day too, and she was over the moon that he had followed up on their conversation and scheduled lunch with his parents. When she finally finished fussing with the house, but with loads of laundry and unpacking still left to do, she sat down and got to work on the fundraiser for Mary St. Clair. There was one scheduled for that Saturday at the Hyatt Regency in Cambridge. She officially became a Mary St. Clair supporter and contacted the organization directly to secure tickets to the Saturday event. It might not be the one Jenny had seen in her vision, but it was the closest one from today.

Near six o'clock, she jumped off the comfortable new sofa and opened the door for the restaurant delivery. She smiled at the front yard, pleased that the horrible dead shrubbery had been cut way back, and the yard, if not exactly pretty, was at least clean and ready for winter. She frowned at the large oak trees, wondering about the last time they'd been pruned. She put hiring a tree service on her mental to-do list.

A little after six, Max pulled up with Bones, and she ran out the front door to see him. "Surprise, I did a bit of gardening," she said.

Max kissed her hungrily as Bones ran around the front yard sniffing the freshly manicured lawn.

They released one another, and Max said, "Wow. The yard looks great. It must have taken you all day to do it."

She gave him a small shrug and smiled, linking her arm through his. "I'm a hard worker. I did a bit inside too."

She walked through the front door and spread her arms wide. "Ta-da!" she said, smiling triumphantly.

Bones ran past them, checking things out as Max stood frozen in the entry, his eyes scanning, his mouth hanging open. "Where is my stuff?"

Still smiling, Sidrah said, "I had them haul it away when they brought in the new furniture. And look." She ran over to the kitchen cupboards and threw them open. "New dishware. It's so cute. Not *too* cute, but just right. Kinda kitschy."

She stopped talking when she realized Max was still standing in the open doorway. "You don't like it?"

"No. It's . . . my stuff is gone. *My stuff.* Don't you understand? I could touch everything; it was safe to take my gloves off here."

Her hands flew to the sides of her face, which began to flush with embarrassment. "Oh, God, Max, I didn't think about all that. I just thought, oh my God, I don't know what I thought. I'm so sorry." She felt sickened by the enormity of her mistake and began to cry.

Max walked over to her. "Hey, now, don't cry. We can . . . we can get past this one."

"But I wanted everything to be nice. I wanted to make it clean and pretty for you. We all worked so hard," she said, drying her tears.

His eyes opened wider. "How many people have been in here?"

Her heart sank as she did a mental calculation. "I don't know. Maybe a half dozen. Marta was here all day. She brought in some help."

He walked past her and looked at all the new kitchen items, the candles, chairs, and food items stocked in his pantry. He opened the fridge.

"Okay," he said, straightening up. "I can see that you went to a lot of effort here, and I appreciate it. But in the future, it would be great if you'd ask me before you throw my stuff away and replace it with new stuff."

She saw a tightness in his mouth. She'd been foolish to turn his sanctuary into a hotbed of unfamiliar molecules and karmic debris from a hundred sources. She rubbed her hands over her face, wiping the tears, and then wiping them onto her jeans. She sniffed, hoping for forgiveness. "I'm really sorry, Max. Can we clean it a bit at a time to get it ready for you?"

He shook his head, worry now creasing his brow. "Of course, we can. Hey, listen, I'm sorry too. I know you just got carried away and wanted to make me happy."

She rushed over and held him tightly, lost in their world, safe in his arms. Grateful he understood.

Chapter 36

FRIDAY EVENING

It took days to clean, and Max felt terrible that he'd been so harsh with Sidrah initially. He should have told her about his concerns before he gave her the go-ahead, but he didn't know how far and fast she would take it. Sidrah's energy and enthusiasm for him and their relationship sometimes felt like a tsunami crashing toward him. He was completely blown back by the urgency of their relationship, but he felt it too. Thoughts of her consumed him whenever they were apart also.

She'd torn down any of his previously held beliefs about needing independence, and he relented almost helplessly to most of her plans. If he'd thought himself level-headed in romance before, he'd now changed. As a man with an admittedly large ego, the absurdity of love at first sight would occasionally bite him, but then he'd think about the miracle. Sidrah had that right. Everything about them—all four of them coming together—had been just that.

Sidrah had tweaked his plan and suggested they invite his parents to dine with them on Friday night and put them up in a Boston hotel. Dinner, in Sidrah's view, was much more intimate than lunch, and she'd impressed that they had a lot to discuss.

All parties agreed to the revised invitation, his mother teetering on the verge of a nervous breakdown for details, and they also agreed to the offer of free lodging in a suite at the Beacon Hill Hotel. Dinner that evening would be downstairs in the hotel's elegant, intimate bistro.

Earlier that week, Max had been horrified that his safe space had been virtually erased, but he had gotten over it. After the house debacle had cooled and things were put in order, Sidrah had gone to work on his finances and gave him a credit card. With cheerful instructions to pay off all his debt, she also told him to use the card for his parents' hotel and their evening together.

Max had hotly rebuffed her offer but then cooled a bit after she had begged. He drew the line at her offer to remodel his home. As part of a compromise, he let her off the leash to shop for him. The delight she took in her tasks astounded him, but Sidrah apparently needed to stay busy, and he had walked into her life, in her words, "a fully formed project."

Before Sidrah, he hadn't thought of himself as someone needing work. His home, sure. Anyone could see that. Things between them were moving fast, and at times, he thought it wise to slow down. But then, when he was around her, all sensibility would evaporate. They talked about him moving into her place so she wouldn't have to go back and forth but then split the difference on that front too.

Tonight, Friday, he and Bones would stay at her place in Boston, and over the coming weekend, Jenny would join them. Sidrah had filled a spare room in her house with personal items to make Jenny feel comfortable as well as designer clothes and accessories that would "fill a young girl's heart with glee." Sidrah's words.

Max stood now, as requested, at the bottom of the stairs, dressed in a nice sports coat and pants, watching Sidrah walk down the stairs toward him. She looked ravishing in a tight pink dress and strappy black heels.

"Do you like it?" She posed on the landing above him. "I wanted to look conservative for your parents, but the off-the-shoulder brings in a bit of fun. The simple bows on the shoulders, too, don't you think?"

"Are you coming down, or am I coming up? I'd like to skip dinner and order you instead." He placed his hand on the banister and made a move to walk up.

She held her hand up to stop him and laughed. "I'm not coming down until you promise to behave yourself," she scolded. "My makeup is perfect."

He smiled and held up three gloved fingers. "Scout's honor."

"Were you ever a Boy Scout, Max?" she said, striding toward him.

"No."

When she reached him, he inhaled her scent and tried to control himself. "Are you ready?" he asked in a deep voice.

"Yes," she mimicked him. "You drive."

They said good-bye to Bones and left Sidrah's house in her Mercedes. They argued about putting the top down, but she didn't want it to mess up her hair. They dropped the fine car at the valet, then walked into the Beacon Hill Hotel to meet his parents. He didn't have a clue how this evening was going to go. So much of what was happening to all of them was borderline ridiculous.

Without preamble, Max spotted his parents in the lobby.

They looked good, all dressed up, and his mom's face creased in a jubilant grin. He went to her with his arms wide.

"Mom," he said, kissing her on the cheek, then hugging his dad. It felt great to see them. Turning to Sidrah, he smiled. "And this is Sidrah Keeling. Sidrah, my parents, Scott and Tracey."

Tracey began to giggle. "Oh, my gosh, I don't know what to do here. Do we hug? Can I hug you?" she asked, already holding Sidrah.

Max beamed as the two came together. "She's very pretty, Max," his father said near his ear.

Sidrah put out her arms and hugged Scott. "It's so nice to meet you, Mr. Dyer. Thank you for driving up to see us."

General introductions made, Sidrah and his mom began to go through some girl ritual, admiring and talking about one another's clothes. "Nice suit," his dad said, eyeballing him. Max shrugged with amusement and nodded his thanks. When they had eventually disentangled the women, they made their way into the restaurant and to an elegant corner table near a window. Max knew that Sidrah had requested the particular seating location. She'd researched the place and spoken with someone who was now another recipient of her generosity.

After some initial chitchat over beverages and appetizers, Max said, "So, Mom, Dad, we wanted to meet with you because something extraordinary has happened between Sidrah and me."

Tracey put a hand on her heart. "What is it?"

Max took off a glove, and Sidrah placed her hand inside his. They held it up for a moment of display, then dropped the embrace into his lap. "I can touch her. Freely. Without intrusion, without thoughts."

Tracey and Scott glanced at one another. "But you've only just met," his dad said. "Six days ago? And you've told her?"

Max nodded and reached down, lifting Sidrah's hand to kiss it. He couldn't help himself, and he reached for her lips too. Reluctantly, he dragged his attention back to his parents. "She knows everything."

Sidrah jumped in at his mother's startled expression. "It's perfectly okay, Tracey, because there's a big coincidence in front of us. I, too, have a gift, similar, in fact, to your son's."

Tracey leaned forward and whispered, "You can see the past?"

Sidrah leaned over the table. "The future."

His parents pulled their heads back. It was just as well that their entrees arrived at that moment. Each of them sitting with the momentous knowledge, they waited until the waiter left before launching a million questions. Sidrah, to her credit, was forthright and answered them all. It took a huge leap of faith for her to trust more strangers with her secrets, but she even told them about the money.

Absorbing that information was one thing, but over dessert, Max and Sidrah spoke about Jenny and their belief that they were her protectors. Maybe it was the wine or the brandy, but at that point, Tracey burst into tears.

"I knew there was a reason. There had to be a reason. You're so special, Maximus." Tracey wept.

Scott put his arms around his wife and comforted her. They were all quite full and unable to absorb any more food or knowledge, so they made a hasty retreat from the restaurant. Once in the lobby, Sidrah said, "Max is staying with me now. I'll be with him during the week when he has classes, but over the weekend, he and Bones will move in with me. Would you like to see my home? There's plenty of room if you ever want to stay."

They made arrangements for his parents to come for breakfast the next morning. Driving home that evening, Max grumbled while holding Sidrah's hand with his glove on. He'd had to re-cover it because the valet had driven. They decided from that moment forward, they'd carry wipes in the car, so they'd be prepared. Sidrah had had Marta clean all week; Marta's hands were gloved while wiping down every surface so Max could relax. She'd told Marta some convoluted story about a rare skin condition, and Marta had bought it.

Eager to take his gloves off and hold her once more, he looked at Sidrah, her head resting against the cream-colored seat. She looked dreamy and beautiful. Focusing on anything other than the magic that had brought them together, on their newfound love, was difficult. In less than a week, she'd utterly upended his world, and he was okay with it. "You were wonderful tonight. I was so proud to be with you. You're fearless."

She smiled at him. "Thank you, Max. Your parents are awesome. Aren't you grateful there won't be a my-side-of-the-family to deal with?"

His brows came together with worry. "No. Not at all. I'm sorry you don't have parents or a family that I could meet."

"But I do now, Max. And their names are Tracey and Scott. And Jenny and Bones."

The side of his mouth went up. "And me."

She gently touched the smile with her fingertip. "And most especially you."

Chapter 37

Jenny stood in Sidrah's room-like closet and looked at herself in the three-way mirror. She picked up the hem of the black chiffon skirt and let it fall. "It's beyond weird that you bought this for me. I saw it in my vision, and now poof, here it is. I didn't even tell you what it looked like."

Sidrah stood behind her, pretty in her own conservative long-sleeved little black dress, a big gold and ruby pin affixed near her shoulder. She zipped up the back of Jenny's dress. The top was a delicate floral embroidery that overlaid a strapless sweetheart bodice.

"I understand," said Sidrah. "But focus on how wonderful you look, and don't worry about how it got here."

Sidrah patted her arm in a supportive manner, then presented the shoes. Another awesome and perfectly coincidental accessory. "Well, these are next level." Jenny smiled as she sat on a stool and adjusted the crisscross straps on the Louboutins, not at all used to the feeling of such delicate and expensive designer footwear.

"Wow." She wobbled a bit with the extreme height of the heels as she stood next to Sidrah. "We're both so tall now."

Sidrah smiled and clapped with glee. "Gorgeous."

Jenny walked around a bit and got her balance. "What am I supposed to do when we get there?"

Sidrah didn't seem nervous at all as she fussed with the bag selection. "I don't know. I think we just let nature take its course, Jenny. I'm beyond questioning everything that's happened in the last week. All I know is that you were meant to be here, and me and Max and Bones too. We're a family now, at least that's what I think. Let's listen to the visions and take you out for a spin."

Jenny smiled at Sidrah. The woman was not only beautiful and generous, she was also somehow funny and maternal too. Jenny had to admit that having the three of them in her life did make her feel more secure, accepted, and safe. *Calm,* too. Almost as soon as they'd met, Jenny had felt serenity in their presence. It was a merciful respite from the noise in her head, from trying to continually evaluate and censor her inner turmoil.

She'd been in constant contact with Sidrah since the day they'd met. Sidrah had even come to her dorm with a care package. The memory of that sweet and awkward visit flooded her with happiness. She'd hardly spoken with her mom for weeks.

Counting Lisa, Jenny felt like she now had two new best girlfriends. And while she had to compartmentalize the things they could discuss, the fact that they *were* being discussed felt tremendous. Things were definitely changing. If she were reluctant to bond with strangers and venture out before, Sidrah's buoyant acceptance of the situation made it easier to believe that there was a grand and good purpose, that everything would be okay. Those were Sidrah's words, but Jenny wanted to believe them too.

Even with the fear she'd felt during and following her attack, Jenny agreed that her gift had to have some kind of useful purpose. Months ago, she'd been introduced to one of her attacker's other victims. Jenny had seen the fear in the poor girl's eyes. But she'd also seen the gratitude that Jenny had stopped him. That was the only good part of it. The rest was still a nightmare.

Once again, working to shake off the memory, she couldn't help but feel happy when Bones came into the closet to get them. The dog was a solid ball of comfort. Jenny corrected her math from before. Three. She had three new best friends. Four, really, with Max.

"Be careful. Don't shed on us," Sidrah said, and Bones backed up. "Aww." Sidrah reached over to pet her. "We'll tumble around later when we get home. I promise."

Bones seemed satisfied, and with the bonding complete, the three of them went downstairs to the waiting Max.

Jenny had never been to a political fundraiser before. Lisa had been curious about who she was going with and why, but Jenny had lied to her, saying it was her wealthy cousin Sidrah, who'd come to the dorm. She hated lying to Lisa, especially since they'd avowed friendship, but she'd concocted the cover story and now had to stick to it. She hadn't told Lisa the enormity of her secret life. Maybe she would, maybe she wouldn't. But one thing was sure, Sidrah, Max, and Bones were a part of her life now. She felt that truth all through her bones.

Chapter 38

Max stood in the large reception area outside the Hyatt ballroom, watching cargos of people riding the glass elevators in the center of the tall, open atrium. The evening had gone long but had been interesting on many levels.

With the dinner and Mary St. Clair's passionate speech now over, the three of them, along with a tablemate, Esme Stevens, had entered the reception line to have their pictures taken with the candidate. They'd enjoyed some friendly conversation with Esme over dinner, and now she and Jenny were off in a corner along with a passel of what could only be students from Harvard or MIT since both universities were nearby. Once, while Esme was away from the table, Jenny had told him and Sidrah about her roommate's nanny, whose name was also Esme, and how wonderful she was. Jenny said she'd felt drawn to this new one and made it her mission to stay by her side.

Max watched now as Sidrah maneuvered her way around people, walking toward him with a couple more glasses of wine. As anxious as Max was to hurry home and be alone with her, he knew they needed to stay as long as Jenny wanted. It was the reason they had come.

When Jenny was not with them, they watched her. She bumped into a few people and, despite her nerves, she was quite social and positively engaging. For someone so young, she could work a crowd. They wondered what it was she was doing as she spoke to people. Was she nudging them, influencing them one way or another? Sidrah and Max believed she was a catalyst for good, and it was fascinating to observe her interactions with that lens.

Sidrah, at last, reached him. "Here you go," she said, handing him the glass.

Max reached for it, his hands abysmally gloved. Frustrated, he said, "I realize we need to keep an eye on Jenny, but I haven't had a smoke all evening. Can we please step outside?"

Sidrah gave him a dirty look, and he could feel an argument brewing. They'd discovered that they were both as fast to temper as to passion, but the heated exchange was delayed when a gray-haired man interrupted them. Max stood tall, heat gathering under his collar when he recognized him as the flower guy, Turner Black.

"Good evening, Sidrah. It's nice to see you again. I enjoyed our rendezvous at the Fairmont." Turner smiled and winked.

Max's hackles rose. He looked at Sidrah; her face was pinking up.

"Hello, Turner. Uh, may I introduce Max Dyer? Max, this is Turner Black."

Max, one hand holding his glass, shoved the other into his pocket and nodded. *What the fuck? She'd met him at the Fairmont?*

Turner smiled at him, his lips closed, appearing amused. He turned to Sidrah. "It's so good to see you. Are you a supporter of Mary St. Clair? But we met at the governor's rally."

Sidrah nodded. "Yes. Well, I'm just keeping my options open. How about you?"

"Engaging with both parties is very rare. I'm here to keep my eye on the competition. Tell me, did you meet Mary? How was she tonight?"

"Great! She's very passionate. I like her."

"I see," Turner said, then looked up at Max. "And you, Mr. Dyer. What do you do for a living?"

Max was momentarily thrilled that the putz had had to look up. His height sometimes gave him a subtle advantage. He hated this guy. "I teach," he said grudgingly.

Turner glanced again at Sidrah, this time with an eyebrow raised, clearly questioning her about why Max wasn't more forthcoming or polite. Sidrah filled in the blanks. "Yes. He's a professor at Wellesley. Isn't that wonderful?"

"And what do you teach, Mr. Dyer?"

Max stared into the guy's dark, beady eyes. "History."

Turner kept the stare going. Then, finally giving up, he said to Sidrah, "I'm keeping you. You look wonderful tonight." He put his hand on Sidrah's arm and leaned over to give her a quick kiss on the cheek. "Nice to see you."

Turner walked away. Max kept himself composed, feeling Sidrah's statue-like posture next to him. When he was sure Turner was nowhere within range to either watch or listen, he turned to her. "What. The fuck. Sidrah. What did he mean he was glad to see you at the Fairmont?"

Sidrah, her face scarlet, smiled with all of her teeth. "I was going to tell you. I just haven't had a chance. Really, I'd appreciate it if you'd stop glaring at me."

Max inhaled. He had to get a grip on his jealousy. What was happening to him? He'd never felt so out of control in his life. "I'm perfectly calm. Did you go out with him after the flowers?"

"I didn't go *out* with him, out with him. I met him. Once. For about fifteen minutes for a cocktail. You were busy, and I just thought it would be polite to thank him in person for the flowers. I mean, they were a lot. It's not every day a girl receives an arrangement like that. Besides, he's a powerful lawyer in the city. I've found it useful to have many contacts."

Max's pride was stung. "I know I haven't sent you flowers, but I've expressed my intentions in other ways."

Sidrah put a hand on his arm, her eyes soft. "Baby. Please. Even though I secretly love the jealousy vibe you're putting out, please don't worry. You're my guy. I'm your girl. There will be no other men in my life as long as we're together. I promise you that. I'm sorry I didn't tell you about him, really. But I don't give a crap about Turner Black. I only have eyes for you."

Max felt a bit relieved but also foolish for his reaction. Even though he wasn't into PDA, he couldn't stop himself from kissing her again. "I'm sorry," he said.

Chapter 39

SATURDAY EVENING

Turner walked away from Sidrah and her surly, immature date. He'd seen the man kiss her from across the room. He was most likely the guy she was seeing. It hadn't made him truly angry—only more curious. After all, Sidrah and her relevance in his life was still a mystery. The fact that she was once more on his path was the important item to consider.

He glanced at his watch and saw that it was nearly time. In the hallway, he looked for a dark soul. It wasn't difficult; the world was crawling with them. What he needed was waitstaff. He spied his person, a young man in an apron, and approached him. He gave the man a small blank envelope and a ten-dollar bill and asked him to deliver the envelope to Esme. He didn't use her name, only gave the waiter her description and whereabouts. He'd seen her in the reception area with a group of young people congregating near a dessert buffet. Esme, wearing a sparkling purple dress, would be easy to spot.

Turner moved to a nearby bar and ordered his typical sparkling water with lime and sipped it as he stood back to watch the game unfold. He adored being a spectator at his orchestrated events.

Nearing nine o'clock, he felt the burner phone in his pocket vibrate. Jorim was in place. Mitch St. Clair should arrive soon. The other scenario, conducted by another dark soul, was also in progress. Mitch would hopefully be dead in the next thirty minutes.

He watched his new associate, the waiter, approach the group and hand the envelope to Esme Stevens. She looked down, confused, but then smiled and gave her apologies to the group as she walked a few steps away to open it.

Turner reached a hand into a bowl of mints near the bar and popped one into his mouth. He sucked on it with amusement as Esme, clearly not much of an actress, looked around frantically, scanning faces and acting as if she'd been caught with her hand in the cookie jar.

A young girl with long blond hair, her aura quite bright, came over to inquire about her state. They spoke for a moment, then Esme peeled off. The young girl with the swirly black skirt and blond hair followed her.

Turner, not wanting to appear conspicuous, also followed and stopped when the two of them entered a ladies' room. All was still going to plan since Esme lived roughly three miles from the hotel. But then things went off track when she didn't reappear for about fifteen minutes. Turner milled about, speaking casually with a few people, wondering what was going on. He watched Sidrah enter the restroom as well.

He blinked, wondering, and took a small sip of his drink to hide his inner turmoil. He checked himself, not overly worried. It was only 9:15. Even if she was running late, she could still make it in thirty minutes by the time she got her car from the garage or valet. Taxis were available out front too. If she hopped in one of those, she could be home even earlier.

But then Sidrah came out, her head down, and went back to Max. They spoke, then annoyingly touched and kissed one another again. There was still no sign of Esme or the blond girl. It wasn't until some twenty minutes later that the two women reemerged, arm-in-arm, and walked back to the group of guys. They laughed and carried on for a while, Esme smiling coquettishly at one particular guy. The young people, forever with their phones at the ready, took a group selfie and then walked as one toward the elevators.

Turner watched them from a distance. Esme and the blond girl took a moment to hug, and then Esme continued her journey with the pack of guys and a couple of other females, who had joined them.

Turner watched the elevator descend to the lobby, realizing that there was a good chance Esme was not going directly home. He continued to follow the group with his eyes. Simple souls surrounded Esme, all of them glowing ludicrously pale. He walked toward a railing to observe them in the hotel lobby below, but then turned away, confused when he noticed Sidrah hugging the blond girl.

It was a fascinating occurrence, and one definitely worth consideration. Turner grabbed the next elevator down and made it out to the street level just in time to overhear some of the young group's conversation while they waited for valet. There were no misconceptions. There was a party, and Esme was going with them.

While he waited in valet, he considered the ramifications of Esme's tardy arrival at her home. If she stayed away all night, surrounded by people, simple souls who would vouch for her, she would have an alibi. It was not ideal.

However, she'd eventually have to go home, and when she did, she'd find Mitch St. Clair dead in her apartment. She'd call the police. They would come. They would dig and dig and dig. Their affair would be uncovered. A scandal, a funeral, and an investigation would ensue. Esme, assuming she was stupid, might even incriminate herself with the police, making their job easy. They might not even waste time on further investigation and just nail her for the crime. Maybe.

Turner sighed deeply as he got into his car and drove home. Despite the plan going awry, Mary St. Clair was now a widow of a murdered philanderer. Hopefully, she'd be too upset and tainted to continue the race. It had been a night of good work.

Chapter 40

S idrah kicked off her stilettos as Jenny and Bones left to go to bed. "Goodnight, kids!" she called after them, smiling at Maximus as they sat across from one another in her library.

The fire going, Max lounged on the couch and shook his head at her. "She's not a kid. Bones maybe, but not Jenny."

"I'm only teasing," she said as she walked over, hitched up her skirt, and straddled his lap. With his gloves now off, his entire body responded, and he moved in for the kill. She hopped off, realizing her mistake. No way were they going to go at it anywhere except her bedroom—behind a locked door.

"Heyyy . . ." he said, stretching his arms out for her to return.

She went over to her desk and sat behind it, primly folding her hands. "Sorry about that." His half-lidded eyes held a look of annoyed desperation. But now that they were alone, she wanted to make sure he was okay about the Turner thing.

He scowled at her question. "Yeah. I'm okay. I might have gotten a bit more worked up than I should have. I didn't mean to come across like a jealous asshole."

"I understand. If the roles were reversed, I might have done worse. Both of us seem to be pretty emotionally heated about each other. Not that I'm really complaining." She smiled, then looked down, her eyes landing on Turner's business card from the rally. She picked it up. "Here's his card. Maybe I'll just rip it up and throw it away."

"Don't," he said, jumping up. "Here, give me that."

She pulled the card away from his outstretched hand. "What are you going to do?"

"I want to touch it, Sidrah," he said in a serious tone. "Give it to me."

Recognizing his sincerity and control, she slowly gave it to him, wondering what, if anything, he might see. She knew Marta would not have cleaned the card.

As Max held the card, his body jerked as if a spark had shot through him. He squeezed his eyes tight, his face contorted with what looked like pain.

Sidrah jumped up. "Max!"

He opened his eyes and dropped the card on her desk.

"Oh my God, what did you see?" she asked.

"I saw . . ." He took a step away from the desk. "Jesus. He's evil. Sick."

"What?" she said, running around the desk to grip his arms.

Max dropped into a chair, shaking his head. "I saw him in the dark, floating. His eyes were red. I saw him strangling a cat. There was blood on his teeth. *Jesus.* I can't believe this guy . . ."

Max grabbed her. "Promise me you'll never let him near you again."

"I won't, I won't," she said, her own heart beginning to pound.

"This is fucking bad." He got up. "You met Turner on the same day you met me, right? Something's really wrong here. You said you have the name of a protection guy from your detective friend?"

She nodded, her hands now clenched.

"Call him. Call him *now.* See if he can come over. We need someone on the job tonight."

Sidrah watched Max with irritation as he smoked on her back patio but secretly wished she too had an outlet for her anxiety. The television played in the kitchen so Max could catch up on some sports and calm down, but they both jumped at the sound of the bell.

"He's here," Sidrah said.

Max threw his cigarette into a coffee can filled with wet grounds that she'd placed outside. He shut the door, deadbolting it, and the two of them walked toward the front door, Sidrah holding the phone in front of Max's face so he could see the man on her security monitor.

Bones walked down the stairs without barking, her ears perked and tail up. "It's okay, girl," Sidrah said as Max opened the door.

"Hey there," Max said.

"I'm Leon Baird," the man said.

Max held the door wide. "Come on in. Getting cold out there."

Leon Baird stood about five feet ten inches and looked very fit. He wore small earrings in both ears, his skin a creamy black. He broke into a bright white smile as he stuck his hand out toward Max. "Nice to meet you."

Sidrah stepped forward and shook Leon's hand since Max wasn't wearing his gloves. "It's nice to meet you, too. Sorry, he's got a thing with his hands." She pointed to Max. "I'm Sidrah Keeling. This is Max Dyer, and this is Bones." The dog sat primly, her head cocked, studying him.

"Bones, this is our new friend, Leon Baird," Sidrah said. "We called him because we think we might need protection. He was kind enough to come over, even though it was midnight."

A side of Leon's mouth went up, and he appeared amused. "That was a thorough introduction. May I?" he asked before touching the dog.

"She's friendly," Max said.

Bones sat calmly, allowing Leon to scratch behind her ear before sniffing his shoe. She walked into the library and hopped up on a chair, sitting at attention, waiting for them.

Sidrah followed. "We're just in here. Can I get you anything to drink?"

"I'm thinking about a brandy," Max said. "Will you join me?"

"Sure," Leon said as they walked inside.

There was a small bar on one side of the fireplace. Max poured out three drinks, then put his fingers inside the crystal glasses before walking toward Leon.

"For goodness' sakes, Max. You put your fingers inside the glass. Your germs are all over it," she scolded.

Max stopped. "Are you kidding? The alcohol will kill the germs. Am I right?" He handed the glass to Leon, who nodded with his lower lip pushed out.

Sidrah rolled her eyes as she sat beside Leon on the sofa. Max sat in a chair across from them, Bones on her own seat next to him. Max took a sip of his drink and began. "So, we have a problem. There's a dangerous guy out there, who may or may not be a threat to us, and we have a vulnerable girl, age nineteen, sleeping upstairs. She may also need protection."

Sidrah leaned forward and pointed around Leon to the open door. "We should shut that."

Max turned to Bones and asked, "Is she sleeping?"

Bones nodded.

Leon's eyes widened, and Sidrah threw up her hands in exasperation. "Guys. Stop it."

She got up and slid the door closed. With her hands clasped, she began to pace in front of them. "Now then, Leon. Can we conduct a short interview? Where are you from? How long have you known Detective Bodine? Do you carry a gun? Can you be discreet? Are you available? And are you open to the ideas of the paranormal, premonitions, and extreme déjà vu?"

"You're grilling him, Sidrah," Max said.

"I am not. They're pertinent questions." She looked at Leon for support.

"Uh, hey," Leon said. "All right. I'm from Boston. After 911, I did a stint in the army, but I got hurt. After rehab, I went to school, thought about being a cop. I've known Detective Bodine for the last five years. Yes, I carry a gun. I have a permit. I'm wayyyy discreet. I'm available, but it depends on what you need. And to the other stuff. I have no idea. Although, that dog is making me nervous."

Sidrah gave him a level stare. "You're the nervous type?"

Leon shook his head. "Noo, but I don't usually talk to my dogs the way you do. She looks like she's following the conversation."

Sidrah continued to pace in front of him. "So, you have dogs then. Tell me about that."

"Leon. What do we need to do to get you started?" Max interrupted.

Sidrah stopped pacing and nodded at Leon, who'd checked in with her first before responding. She liked that in a man. He didn't ignore her.

Leon glanced at Max and Bones. "Sidrah and I e-mailed, but I hadn't spoken with Detective Bodine yet, so I called him on the way over here. He wasn't jazzed about the hour, but he told me to treat you right. He told me you were good people. I think he was talking about you, Sidrah. He didn't mention these other two."

Sidrah resumed her seat and smiled. "Wasn't that sweet of Detective Bodine? He and I go back for many years too. Do you know, he's never told me about his family? I've always wondered . . ."

Max cleared his throat. "I think we need to tell him about Turner Black."

Sidrah exhaled, wanting to pretend otherwise. "Go ahead. Bones hasn't heard this yet either."

Leon gave Max and Bones a slow, tolerant nod. "Okay, tell us everything."

Max recapped as much as he could without giving away their secrets. So, in fact, it wasn't much at all. It came across like they feared a guy named Turner Black and worried in general about Jenny's safety when they couldn't be around her.

"I'm happy to help, but I don't think I'm going to fit in too well on the Wellesley Campus. Also, it might be a good idea if I meet Jenny, so she isn't afraid of me."

"I agree," said Sidrah. "Gosh, though, I hate to wake her. Would you come back in the morning? Marta made an egg bake that should be hot and ready about nine."

Leon rubbed his glass in his hands. "Sure. But like I said, I might need to bring someone else in. I can't be everywhere, especially if all three of you need protection."

"Four," said Sidrah, nodding at Bones.

Bones pulled back her lips and smiled.

Leon drained his glass and put it on the coffee table in front of him. "Okay. So how long do you think you're going to need me? Is there some kind of window here that I'm not seeing? A period of time when Jenny, or any of you, might be most vulnerable? You're not giving me much to go on."

"Jenny might be vulnerable for the rest of her life, Leon," Sidrah said. "In fact, I think it would be a good idea for me and Max to take some defense courses too."

Leon looked confused. "The rest of her life?"

"Are you busy?" Sidrah asked.

Bones got off the chair and came over to Leon. She laid her head in his lap and whimpered.

"Forever may be stretching it," Max said. "How about we take it one day at a time?"

Chapter 41

SUNDAY MORNING

Jenny playfully rubbed her stockinged feet on Bones, who was lying under Sidrah's kitchen table. She put her coffee cup on the table next to Max and reached down to scratch the dog's head. Last night, Bones had been her companion in the smallish, fifth-floor dormer room of Sidrah's heavenly home. She'd felt like a princess sleeping in a tower with her faithful companion lying next to her, Sidrah utterly cool with the dog being on the queen-sized bed. When bad dreams had woken her, she'd been grateful for the dog's warm company.

She looked over at the television as Max rapidly flicked the channels, not settling on anything. As she readjusted her new robe, replete with her initials on the breast pocket, she relished the soft feel of it, along with the silk pj's Sidrah had bought her. They made her feel rather elegant. Watching Sidrah fuss around the kitchen, Jenny marveled that she hadn't even known the woman a week ago, and now Sidrah was treating her like a daughter.

"Do you want fresh-squeezed orange juice, Jenny? I've got an orange press somewhere, I think." Sidrah held an orange in her hand but looked confused as she stared at her cabinets.

"No, thanks. I'm good." She sensed an inkling of anxiety coming from the adults. Sidrah, in particular, seemed a bit nervous, but Jenny wasn't sure what was troubling them. Last evening had gone okay, but she still wasn't clear about what their attendance at the fundraiser had accomplished.

Max changed the station. "Patriots play at noon," he grumbled. "I don't know. I've got to get home and get some work done. Jenny, I'm sure you have work too."

Jenny nodded and looked at the screen, her interest suddenly piqued at a news report. "Stop," she said before Max could change the channel again.

Shock rushed through her as the chief of police spoke about the murder of Mitch St. Clair, whose body was discovered in an Allston apartment early that morning.

"Oh my God," Sidrah said, walking over. "Mary St. Clair's husband?"

A reporter was practically screaming a question at the cop:

"Who found the body?"

Cop: "The homeowna. We've taken her in for questioning."

More reporters screamed until the police pointed to someone: *"How was he murdered?"*

The cop scowled at the reporter. *"We're running an investigation. We have no further statements at this time."*

The cop walked away, and the cameras turned to the station reporter. *"I'm sure the police will have more for us today. Here is what we know: At approximately four this morning, the police were called to this first-floor apartment behind me in Allston. The body of Mitch St. Clair, husband of Mary St. Clair, political candidate for governor for the state of Massachusetts was discovered inside, dead, apparently murdered. The person renting the apartment made the call to 9-1-1. We have her name as Esme Stevens. She's been taken in for questioning. We'll have updates and further developments throughout the day."*

Jenny jumped up, blood rushing to her face. "No! She didn't kill him! Esme wouldn't have done that! She left with Blake and his friends. There was a party back at Harvard."

Sidrah's hands were pressed to either side of her face. "Could it be a different Esme Stevens?"

Max shook his head, his mouth a firm line. "No. I seriously doubt that."

Looking at the screen, Jenny was frantic as she recalled the lovely dinner and long heart-to-heart she'd had with the older girl in the ladies' lounge. They had talked about Esme's insecurities around the Harvard crowd. Jenny had adamantly convinced her not to put herself down, knowing with certainty that Esme was a good person. "I know she went to the party with them. We talked about it, remember? I saw her leave with Blake!"

Sidrah put a comforting hand on her back. "I remember. We believe you, Jenny. But what time was he killed? Why would Mitch St. Clair be in her apartment?"

At that moment, the doorbell rang.

"Who is that?" Jenny said, her pulse quickening with all the chaos.

Bones bolted toward the front door, whimpering. Max reached out and gave her arm a reassuring squeeze. "I got this," he said as he left.

Sidrah firmly clapped her hands. "It's a man—a very nice man named Leon Baird. We met him last night and asked him to come over for some egg bake. Don't worry, Jenny. He's really, really safe. I promise we'll explain."

Jenny watched as Bones returned to the kitchen, walking with a little prance next to a handsome black man in a leather coat. He had a kind of hipster vibe with his skinny jeans and graphic T-shirt.

Max waved an introduction. "Jenny, this is Leon Baird."

Leon extended his hand to her. She took it.

"Nice to meet you, Jenny." He smiled. His teeth were perfectly arranged, and some of his gum line showed. He had a kind, kind of cute, pleasant face.

Sidrah clapped her hands. "The egg bake will be ready in about five minutes. Leon, would you care for coffee? Or juice? I could squeeze something for you?" She picked up another orange.

Leon nodded. "Coffee would be great. Black."

Sidrah went to get him a cup as Max invited him to take a seat at the kitchen table. Jenny took a chair and sat on her hands, nervous.

"Did you hear the news?" Max asked Leon.

"You mean Mitch St. Clair?"

Max nodded. "We've got some information about that too." Max explained what they knew about Esme Stevens and how they'd spent the evening with her the night before.

Jenny's leg bounced. "She didn't do it. We *know* that. All of us. Me especially. I think we need to go to the police."

Max put up his hands. "Whoa. Whoa. Whoa. Let's just wait and see what they have to say about the time of death. If Esme wasn't there when he was killed, then we don't need to get involved."

Sidrah placed a cup of coffee in front of Leon. "I agree."

Jenny still wasn't sure who this Leon was or why he was there, but she felt unable to control herself from gushing some more of the truth. "I didn't see this happening. Why didn't I see it?"

Max's eyes widened, and he gave her a discouraging look, gesturing with his chin toward Leon. "So, let's focus for a moment on our guest. We brought Leon in for protection. We thought that maybe, you know, another set of eyes around us, around you, might not be a terrible idea."

Jenny tipped her head to the side. She'd heard Max trying to soften the delivery. "Wait. What? Why do I need protection?"

Sidrah came back to the table and placed a large casserole pan of eggs in front of her. "It's really hot. I think we should let it sit for a few minutes before dishing up."

Jenny, not completely distracted, suddenly felt herself sink, her breath catching as her mind rolled through what she knew. "What's going on here? Does this have something to do with a man with gray hair? An older guy with nice clothes? I saw you talking to him."

Everyone in the room, including Bones, stared at her. "What did you see, Jenny?" Max said with a serious, fatalistic tone.

Oh, God, no. Is it true? She put her hands on her face as hot tears sprung to her eyes, vivid flashbacks of the dream she'd had last night pulsing at her. She thought it'd been a bad dream! The evilness of it had scared the shit out of her. She remembered crying out and Bones prying her awake with her nose and paw.

Jenny wiped angrily at the tears. "I saw him with you last

night. I had a bad dream," she said, trying to pull herself together.

Sidrah shook her head. "It was the flower guy. Remember we looked him up? His name is Turner Black."

Jenny brushed her nose with the back of her hand. Max picked up his napkin and gave it to her. His face looked as drawn and worried as Sidrah's.

"Turner Black." She nodded. "Yes. That's him. In my dreams. He's . . . there's something wrong with him. He's dark. Evil, maybe." She grimaced. "Do you think we should be afraid of him?"

Leon gave her quizzical look. "You saw him in a dream?"

She tore her eyes to Max and then to Sidrah, who gave her a level stare. "He's here to help, Jenny. Just . . . just stick to the dream for now. Tell us what you saw."

Jenny looked at Leon, assessing whether he could be trusted, until Bones let out a short yip and nodded. Understanding the go-ahead, she bit her bottom lip and launched into her story. She did the best she could without revealing the entire truth. Leon listened intently, without prejudice, and remained calm. He was a reassuring kind of guy, but it didn't alleviate her fear.

Chapter 42

SUNDAY MORNING

Turner watched the news report from his kitchen television as he ate a small banana. He was pleased that events were going as predicted. As a bonus, on the way home last evening, he'd witnessed a simple pedestrian being hit by a car. Not his car, but still, it had been sweet.

He finished the banana and walked down the staircase to his basement spa, where his float tank was waiting. It was a technological piece of wonder and a game changer. The value of the tank could not be overstated; it had enormously facilitated his ability to receive messages from the beyond. He prepared the water, the salt, and the temperature, completely undressed, then picked up a jar of Vaseline and put a dollop on his hand where he'd been scratched. The moisture block would prevent the cut from stinging and distracting his mind while he floated in the salted water.

With his earbuds in place, he set the timer and wake-up music for one hour, then crawled inside and lowered the lid like a coffin. He lay in the near zero-gravity state, buoyed by the salt, in complete silence and darkness. The lack of signals to his central nervous system gave him a nurturing environment to allow him access to his thoughts, his deepest, innermost, and insightful visions.

He worked the tank and focused on Sidrah, the blond girl, and lastly, Sidrah's boyfriend, Max Dyer. History teacher. Sidrah had said the three of them had been photographed with Mary St. Clair. He could have his mole inside the organization send him the pictures. An aide would have taken the names and e-mail addresses for their distribution list too. From Turner's description, the mole would be able to locate the trio.

And Turner got that they were a trio. They were the three amigos. He saw that. He focused hard on the blond girl, and puzzled, he observed her aura glowing vividly brighter than the other two. *Wait.* It did not stop. It grew brighter, rounder, and shimmered with electric intensity. *Who is she? Why is her aura . . . could she be . . .*

His head jerked in the dark as if a bolt of pain had shot through him. His eyes popped open, his fists clenched, and his back arched. It was her. *His counterpart.* They'd always been cloaked from him. He'd long suspected that they had crossed paths during their lives, but their instincts protected them, zigging away from him to remain unseen from his vision. But no longer! The technology of the tank had helped him break through. He'd seen her! He knew who she was. Her youth confirmed what he'd seen in his vision, that he now led their dance for dominance.

He tossed in the tank as rapturous visions of blood, sweet and delicious, poured from the girl's eyes and ears. He dragged his nails up the side of his legs and onto this chest, scratching deeply, feeling the sting of the saltwater and his body contorting with the blessed release from the beautiful vision.

He smiled in the dark. Sidrah Keeling and Max Dyer. They were destiny's protectors, a part of the young woman's gathering forces. He'd found them too.

He giggled. "And what brings thee to me?" he whispered in the black echo of the tank. "'Tis she. 'Tis she. 'Tis she. Thank you, sisters."

Sitting in his home office, Turner felt revitalized as he waited for his mole's report from Mary St. Clair's campaign headquarters. Although impatient, he nevertheless felt wonderful, acutely alive now that he'd found his antithesis. In this lifetime, it was a young, vulnerable blond girl.

He got up and went to the wall safe, which was hidden behind a sizeable picture of no consequence. He spun the old dial and opened the safe, revealing a large, flat-bottom pyxis he'd purchased at auction. He reached inside, placed his hands on the wooden vessel's ancient concave sides, and brought it to his desk. The circular box depicted drawings of the Moirai, the Sisters of Fate.

As usual, he flashed on the words from Homer's *Iliad*:

On the floor of Jove's palace, there stand two urns, the one filled with evil gifts, and the other with good ones.

"If only you once belonged to Pandora," he sighed as he plucked the lid off the box. He pulled the box to him, salivating as he looked inside at the bones of a dead cat. Flecks of dried flesh still clung in places since he had not perfectly cleaned the bones. He lifted the box under his nose and inhaled what odor was left, bringing with it the intoxicating memories of their time together and the cat's fight to its death.

The thrill he got from killing and his constant pent-up desire to inflict pain was always near the surface. Repressing the eternal bloodlust and his intense desire to kill humans, he'd instead killed many, many animals. This one represented them all.

The creature's eyes remained vivid in his mind, and in fact, he often saw them looking at him when he was in the tank. The two of them would forever be one in the timeless battle for life and death.

"I'll see you again, my friend, in the next life. And then, heed my words, dead cat. Run."

Feeling stronger by the moment, the box and its victim energizing him further, he reluctantly replaced it inside his safe and returned to his desk. He smiled as he scanned his e-mail.

When the expected photo arrived, he double-clicked the image and saw them. He had them. Sidrah Keeling, Max Dyer, and the blond girl stood next to Mary St. Clair. He printed the image and then saved it to his computer. He did what he could to enlarge it and stared into the girl's grainy eyes. "Who are you, my sweet?"

He hungrily opened the second attachment, which contained the names and e-mails for the group. He had it.

Jenny Gallagher.

The name pulsed at him, alive. She was alive.

For now.

Chapter 43

"What did you discover?" Sidrah asked Leon as she and Max spoke with him over the phone. Not long after their first meeting, they'd all agreed to a cursory look into Turner Black's life. The night after Jenny's dream, Sidrah had slept with Turner's business card. Max hadn't wanted her to, but she did it anyway. She had to see for herself what they were up against.

They'd taken the card from her house, gently lifting it by the corners and placing it in a plastic bag. Since there was an upcoming week of school and work, they'd moved over to Max's house, as per their arrangement.

They'd eventually fallen asleep that night, Max lying beside her, and the card firmly in her hand. She'd seen evil, seen Turner staring at Jenny's face, raging into a blowup photo of her. He'd folded the picture over a chunk of clay lying on a flat surface. Then he raised a large knife high above his head, and drove it down on the mound, stabbing it over and over. She'd felt his rage with every stab. Her stomach had heaved when the mound began to bleed. Something red oozed out of the middle and ran down the sides, but parts of the thick red liquid shot up into his face. She'd felt his heat rising, rising, and then she screamed.

Max had been there, Bones too. They shook her awake and comforted her. Max used a towel to remove the card from her hand and placed it back into the baggie. He slipped the contents into an old textbook on the top shelf of his closet. They'd had a sleepless night, and from that moment forward, they both took the danger to Jenny seriously.

And now the report. Max had strongly cautioned Leon to keep the investigation quiet. No cops. No clandestine theatrics. Just find out what he could without alerting anyone.

"Given my limitations," Leon said, "you could have found out a lot of what I did. Turner graduated from New York University Law School and was on the law review there. After passing the bar, he landed a job at KBR in Houston. Kellogg, Brown & Root. Private contractors. Back in the Vietnam days, they were Brown and Root—or better known as Burn and Loot. It's a monster of a company and a former subsidiary of Haliburton. They built the Gulf War in Kuwait—providing security, building bases, procuring all goods and services, delivering fuel, you name it.

"Turner set out a shingle in 1993 and hasn't looked back. Black, Holt & Palmberg is a midsized, multinational law firm and doing really well. They have offices in downtown Boston and DC, and the profit margin is intense—about 60 percent. They make a lot of political contributions, but Turner himself has given no known interviews. No social media. There is nothing on him personally other than what I just told you, and that is strange. I dug through everything I could, but I didn't find a home address."

Sidrah glanced at Max, checking his reaction to this news. The tension in his face was evident. "He's secretive," he said.

"Yes," Leon said. "I could find out more. I could contact Bodine. I'm sure he'd help us."

"No!" Max said. "No cops. No hackers. If he's secretive, he could have firewalls and his own protection."

They'd had this conversation already. They knew Turner was evil, that he wanted Jenny dead. But why Jenny? What was wrong with him? How did he know her?

"Guys," Leon said, "you're tying my hands. I'm not saying we could get to his medical reports or find out if he's been locked up, but we could easily put a tail on him and find out more."

Sitting at her desk, Sidrah laid her head on her arms, her head aching.

"I understand your frustration, Leon," Max said. "But no. At least, not yet."

They suspected Turner was one of their ilk. Something had put him and Sidrah together first. And that something—whatever it was—had gone into overdrive lately, orchestrating their lives. It seemed to have a mind of its own. They didn't want Leon in on that bit and couldn't explain their suspicions. Whatever the case, Jenny had protection now, and they were on guard. But it wasn't enough.

"He could be a stalker. Has Jenny received any threatening mail? She's sharing stuff with you, right?" Leon pressed.

"She is," Max said as he rubbed Sidrah's back.

"I just don't understand why this powerful guy would be interested in Jenny. It doesn't make any sense."

"I agree, but you've just got to trust us on this," Max said. "She's the one who needs protection."

They wound up the call, all of them frustrated.

Sidrah sat up and frowned. "He met me first. I led him to Jenny at the fundraiser. If she hadn't gone, he might never have met her."

Max picked up her hand and stroked it. "Come on. We can't know that. We can't know everything."

Sidrah shivered. "He's tied to us though. We believe that?"

Max embraced her. "It'll be okay. We'll look out for her."

Sidrah breathed in Max's scent. Calming as it was to be in his arms, she knew he was worried too.

November

Chapter 44

Sidrah sat behind the desk in her library and listened to Fiona Croft's daily report.

"She's in class. I've got her all day. She won't veer off schedule. Max will pick her up outside her dorm at four this afternoon and bring her to your place. Leon has the night shift."

Sidrah inhaled. The day seemed tight. After her fateful vision of Turner Black several weeks ago, they'd hired more protection for Jenny. She now had a female agent on campus named Fiona Croft, who kept an eye on her. Jenny, to her credit, had been cooperative and never went anywhere without first alerting one of her team. They all felt that she was safe once she was inside her dorm, but they worried.

Max had also gone to human resources to explain that a student named Jenny Gallagher was his girlfriend's relative and that he would, with her permission, occasionally transport her and socialize. That she was a relative was a lie, but they didn't care. They'd also driven to Palmer, Jenny's hometown, and met with her father.

John Gallagher had initially been off-balance and wary of the situation. But over their time together, they'd gotten him to agree to their protection plan. Jenny had smoothed over the details and helped her dad through the various shocks about the circumstances. Bones closed the deal. The only wrinkle was when John Gallagher thought it wise to update Jenny's mom, Kate. They worked out the details of what to tell her, and John assured them he'd handle the woman; there was no need for a face-to-face.

After the group's trip to Palmer, John Gallagher met with the Wellesley dean of students. As Jenny's parent, he needed to present himself, along with Jenny and her protection team. Leon and Fiona expertly outlined the protective services plan with the dean and campus security. After the school had received Detective Bodine's reassurances of their credibility, they had passed the situation on to legal, who eventually green-lighted the unusual situation.

There had been quite a few headaches, but everyone was now in the loop. That was a good thing.

Sidrah ended the call with Fiona, brightening as the scent of fresh-baked bread wafted over to her. She walked down the hallway toward the kitchen. Tracey Dyer, holding a pan with oven mitts, smiled at her. "Doesn't it smell good?"

Sidrah adored Tracey. With Marta dismissed for a long weekend, the Dyers had arrived the night before. Now Friday, Tracey had woken early and immediately begun to cook. Sidrah came around the island and put her nose to the pan of bread, inhaling the intoxicating vapors. "Oh, I just want to rip off a hunk and spread some butter on it."

Tracey laughed. "Go ahead. I can always make some more. There's a tub of fresh-made honey butter over there."

Tracey pointed to a crock sitting near several dishes of homemade desserts, which she'd carted up from their home in Hartford. Max had been there to greet his parents the night before, and they'd made a significant dent in a chocolate cake.

"What can I do?" Sidrah asked, not wanting to get in the way of the big meal preparations.

"Absolutely nothing, I've got it all under control. That table should be featured in a magazine," Tracey said, referring to the layout in the formal dining room where they'd be eating that evening.

"Yes, well, a big thank you to Williams Sonoma, Marta, and the florist. I really did nothing."

Tracey walked over and placed her hands on each side of Sidrah's face. "You've done absolutely everything, angel. You've been a gift to all of us." She hugged Sidrah. When she released her, the two women gazed fondly at one another.

The doorbell rang, and Sidrah glanced at the monitor. "It's Scott," she said, turning to run down the hall.

Tracey yelled behind her, "He'd better not have forgotten the raspberry chipotle."

Sidrah yanked open her front door. "You don't have to ring the bell, just come in." She smiled at Max's father and grabbed a bag of groceries out of his arms.

"Of course, I need to ring. The deadbolt was engaged, was it not?"

Sidrah knew it had been, but she wished it wasn't necessary. "Okay, I'll get you a key."

The three assembled in the kitchen where they dropped the bags. "No snow yet. I hope it holds off until they get here," said Scott.

"They'll be fine," Sidrah said, trying to be reassuring. Just in case, she'd had new tires with deep treads put on Max's Jeep—without his permission. He'd claimed to be cool with it, but he'd been wary ever since the overhaul of his home. His aggravation surfaced when she reshuffled his life without asking.

Sidrah poured herself another cup of coffee and sat at the center island to watch. "So, I've been thinking about winter break, you know, after Christmas when school is out. I don't suppose you two would be interested in vacationing with us? I could rent a house somewhere warm; we could get away for a while."

Tracey smiled. "That would be wonderful!"

"Maybe we should stay back and let the two of them have some alone time," Scott said. "We could look after Bones."

"Oh, no. Bones goes with us wherever we go," Sidrah said. "I was planning to charter a plane so we could travel with her. Really, I'm happy to set the whole thing up. Once we're at our destination, you could babysit her sometimes if we want to split up."

"Oh, my goodness," Tracey gushed. "I can't imagine. I just can't believe how generous you are."

Sidrah ate it up. Nearly all of her life, she'd felt alone. She'd only dreamt of a mutually nourishing relationship with others. And now she had people in her life who she could be completely honest with about everything.

"Hey, I'm only glad that my ill-gotten gains are going to good use."

Tracey frowned, shaking her head. "You're always putting yourself down for using your gift to gain wealth. But we've all come to believe that there's a reason for everything, right? I've heard you preach it to Jenny. So, if you accept that premise as true, Sidrah, then maybe you should start putting your money where your mouth is—so to speak. Thank God, maybe, for your abilities and your deep resources. We might not have the answers to everything, but you're steadfast about helping in any way you can. I'm very proud of you."

Sidrah felt a little lightheaded with embarrassment. She'd never had a mother-type figure say such powerful words to her. Her throat tightened as she realized an absolution from someone she respected went straight to her heart. She hung her head. "Thanks for saying that, Tracey."

"Come now," Tracey said, walking over with her arms extended.

Sidrah held her, eating up the generous outpouring of love. When they eventually released one another, Tracey went back to burbling about food. Sidrah recognized Tracey's efforts to transition them to less weighty topics nicely.

Resuming their talk about vacations and the plan to lure Jenny to tag along, they rationalized that security would need to follow. They predicted that the hardworking Leon and Fiona might be amenable to a week or two near a beach as well.

"Sidrah, do you mind if I watch a little television?" Scott said as he carried a plate of cake to the kitchen table.

"Why are you asking me for permission? Tracey's in charge."

"Go ahead, Scott," Tracey said, waving a hand.

Sometime after he turned it on, they were drawn to the news, which was airing an update on the Mitch St. Clair murder.

The district attorney just announced that he will not be filing charges against Esme Stevens for murder. Her alibi for the night in question was confirmed after the autopsy concluded the time of death. While this is a blow to investigators, the search continues for the real killer. Gubernatorial candidate Mary St. Clair has officially pulled out of the race following her husband's death and his alleged infidelity before his murder. Ms. St. Clair's party has replaced her candidacy with Lane Ackerman, a well-known human rights activist and a much-loved figure in the Boston area, due to his time on the Red Sox winning . . .

Sidrah exhaled. "Well, that's a relief. For Esme."

Tracey shook her head. "Poor little thing. She's a victim too."

Sidrah nodded. Max's parents were in the loop on the Esme Stevens show and their role in her life. Sidrah decided to think about whether they should do something for the girl. If not for Jenny convincing Esme to follow her heart, Esme Stevens might be dead too. Attending the Harvard party had provided her with an alibi that had kept her out of court and possibly out of prison.

"Since you have everything under control in here, I'm just going to go upstairs to work out and then get ready. Is that okay?" Sidrah said, stepping away.

"Of course," Tracey said. "Don't worry about us."

Sidrah turned back to give Tracey a last hug before she left the room. "I'm so glad you're here. I'll have my cell. Call if you need me."

She walked upstairs to the third floor, the entire level devoted to her needs. She entered the small gym near her bedroom and looked over her options, finally deciding on the treadmill. She flipped on the flat-screen, intending to watch something while she worked out, but then decided against it. She had a lot to think about.

She did some fast stretches, then started the machine on a preprogrammed workout and hopped on. As she banded her hair with a ponytail holder lying near the handlebars, she thought about next week. The trial of Jenny's abductor—Brian-the-monster-Mosley—would begin. As if they needed another monster in their lives.

Sidrah picked up the pace. She closed her eyes and thought of the other monster, Turner Black, her skin crawling with the thought of him.

Sidrah pumped her legs, working the treadmill hard, and thought about how there was a psychopath loose who was bent on killing Jenny. If Leon and Fiona had seen the images, they'd feel differently, too. The import of the danger had been pressed into them, but it was one thing to be told about something evil, another to live it. Since neither Max nor Sidrah could share their visions, they alone knew the gravity of the danger. They didn't share the details with Jenny, but she listened to their counsel. She'd had her own dream of Turner. She understood the need to be careful, and thankfully, she cooperated with the awkward security arrangements.

Now, in November, there was another monster for poor Jenny to face. Brian, fuck-you-you-ballless-shit-rapist, Mosley.

The idiot was going to trial. No plea for him! Even with mountains of DNA now secured against him from other victims, he apparently wanted his day in court. It was unfathomable.

As previously discussed, Jenny would have to appear. Her testimony was vital. Sidrah had made reservations at the MGM Springfield, a hotel near the Hamden County Hall of Justice, where the trial would be held. She'd booked a fleet of connecting rooms for herself and Max, Jenny and Bones, and Leon. But then the plans changed. Max couldn't go. There were finals and a department meeting that he could not get out of.

She'd briefly considered asking him whether he should just quit his job, but she held her tongue. His position as a professor was a tremendous accomplishment, and Max was brilliant at it. The students and faculty loved him. When Max lectured, there was silence in the room. He brought history alive—not only the core subject but what it meant to all of them, the lessons history taught to the world in general. Max was needed at Wellesley just as much as Sidrah needed him at home. She couldn't be selfish. Max was her life, and if that meant working around his schedule, she shouldn't complain.

Sidrah ran hard, sweat dripping down her body, and reminded herself to be brave. She could manage the trip to Springfield next week. She could do it. She'd be there to support Jenny, and she would keep her safe. The travel would only be one day and one night. Jenny, too, had to get back to Wellesley for class.

Between Sidrah and Leon, not to mention Jenny's parents, Jenny would be well protected. Bones would not be able to enter the courthouse. Abandoning Bones at the hotel was not ideal either, so they'd agreed the dog would stay in Wellesley with Max.

Even one night apart from him now was hard on Sidrah. Tonight, he, Jenny, Leon, and Bones would be here. And along with Scott and Tracey, they'd have a wonderful meal and shake the cobwebs of lurking evil out of their minds. They had to stay positive. There was a tremendous amount of good in the world too.

Chapter 45

Leon pulled open the door to the Wellesley lecture hall, hoping to catch the tail end of Max's class. Having dropped Jenny safely at her dorm, he would swing by to pick her up after Max was ready, and the three of them would travel to Boston for the early Thanksgiving meal at Sidrah's house.

Next week was Jenny's big day in court testifying against the asshole rapist. What had begun as a job was now personal to Leon. He'd do whatever he could to protect them.

The hushed atmosphere in the room intensified what was happening at the front. His friend, the professor, gestured toward the projection screen as he read the words aloud. Leon stood at the back and listened.

> *From this day until the ending of the world,*
> *But we in it shall be remembered—*
> *We few, we happy few, we band of brothers;*
> *For he to-day who shares his blood with me*
> *Shall be my brother; be he ne'er so vile,*
> *This day shall gentle his condition;*

And gentlemen in England now a-bed
Shall think themselves accurs'd they were not here,
And hold their manhoods cheap whiles any speaks
That fought with us upon Saint Crispin's Day.

Max turned toward the room and immediately spotted him. Leon smiled and glanced at the ever-faithful Bones lying near Max's feet.

Max went on with the lecture. "Shakespeare's words, imagining the twenty-eight-year-old King Henry V rallying his troops before the infamous battle of Agincourt, were his own, but history tells us that Shakespeare got the sentiment correct. It's about glory and honor, but also brotherhood. The Plantagenet King, embroiled in the Hundred—actually 116—Year War against France, would be victorious in battle that day. The young king, war-hardened from an early age, faced overwhelming odds, and at the end, regardless of what other decisions Henry made after it was over, he wept bitterly over the body of his friend, Edward, the second Duke of York."

Max stopped and bowed his head before making eye contact with some students in the front row. In a softer voice, he said, "Brotherhood. Chivalry. Leadership. Loyalty. It was real then for Henry. An accurate personification of the king."

Leon hadn't known much about Shakespeare's play, but he'd heard the phrase *band of brothers*. His mind wandering with the sentiment, he knew he and Max had been flung together to guard Jenny, but he also knew there was much more to the story than the three of them—Sidrah, Max, and Jenny—were saying. But he went along because the more he saw, the more he believed they were good people somehow embroiled in danger with a higher purpose. The three weren't such great actors though. Bit by bit, some of the puzzle was leaking out. The dog, though. Leon never knew what to think of her.

On cue, Bones looked up and gave him a penetrating glare. Leon shook his head at the dog as Max wrapped up. Once done, a couple of female students walked past Leon, one of them saying, "I thought I'd literally die when he mentioned bare breasts on the effing maiden from that earlier work. My God, can you imagine..."

Leon snickered, his head down to fight his amusement over Max and his worshiping group of students. That bit, he had heard about. Leon made his way down the risers toward the brooding hunk of man now.

"Great speech," Leon said, leaning down to pet Bones.

Max fussed with his computer. "Yeah? Glad you liked it."

"I wasn't a-lone in that department," Leon joked, standing up.

Max shot him a hooded look. Leon pursed his mouth, trying to look serious. "Band of brothers, I liked that bit. Shakespeare, huh?"

"The man could write. I'm just shamelessly using him to make them understand how it may have felt actually being there."

Leon glanced at Max's uncovered hands, wondering for the umpteenth time why the hell he mostly wore gloves. He screwed up the courage to ask. "Is it a sensory thing?"

Their eyes met, Max understanding the question. Leon watched him glance down and turn over his palm, but he surprised Leon when he reached out and touched him. Max didn't just touch him though, he lingered, squeezing Leon's arm, his head dropping before releasing him.

Max turned his back to retrieve his gloves and put them on. "I tell you what. How about you and I have a few too many after dinner tonight? We can talk about your family. I'd like to get to know more about you too."

Leon's family. Only a mother really. His father, his beloved dad, was dead. No one knew how profound that loss had been to him. He didn't usually talk about himself with clients, but this job, these people, and especially Max, had become different. A real friendship had developed between them.

Not answering, Max filled the void. "Your dad. Was he your own liegeman?"

Leon startled as Max got right to the heart of what he was thinking. He crossed his arms and looked up at his tall friend, challenging him. "Maybe, Professor Budinski, we can *swap* a few stories. Maybe it's time you man up and tell me some of your shit too."

Max smiled and looked down at Bones. "He wants to know about our shit. Should we tell him?"

Bones looked up at Leon and cocked her head as if checking him out, uncertain.

Max reached down and scratched the dog behind her ear. "There are definitely mysteries my friend. Energy. The same souls circling one another. In one lifetime your friend, in another your father, in the next, your king."

Leon liked that. "Then who is she?" he asked, gesturing to Bones.

"I dunno. Maybe a goddess?"

Leon laughed, breaking the spell. Bones, however, pulled her head erect and did her high-steppin, hoity-toity walk toward the exit. Never in his life had a dog, and a family, mystified him more.

There was something reverential happening here. He loved being a part of it.

Chapter 46

Fuck!" Turner fumed as he cleaned up his mess. He'd filled a mounded ball of clay with dozens of fake blood capsules and butchered it with a knife. In place of a human or an animal, the simulation would have to appease his bloodlust and growing rage.

His patience was coming to an end with the failed attempts they'd made to lure Jenny Gallagher into a trap. It just wasn't working. Jorim was flummoxed, and his sidekick, Gary Daggett, was too. It turned out that it was hard to kidnap a young girl living on a college campus, especially since she was protected.

Gary, an older, unassuming guy with a nice, practiced smile, posed as part of the maintenance crew. He'd gone so far as to gain entry into her dorm. But he hadn't gotten much farther than the boiler room.

What he did observe during other various campus excursions, however, was that Jenny Gallagher had a bodyguard. A woman.

Jenny's instincts were also protecting her. She was turning right when he predicted she'd turn left. She was never alone, clearly being cautious. Both internal and external clouds surrounded her, keeping her safe like a foot soldier with the instincts of a jungle cat.

"Die! Die! Die, you bitch!" Turner screamed as he pushed the gooey red debris into a garbage bag. He'd placed a picture of Jenny's face over the mound and watched the blood shoot through the clay, blazing red onto her image. He shoved his fingernails through what was left of the mangled paper, clay, and blood. His rage had never been more out of control. He had to get a grip. Discipline was required now more than ever.

But the thing was, part of his rage was directed at himself because he realized he'd been an idiot. He'd focused singularly on getting Jenny and had gone about her abduction all wrong.

Jenny might not be able to be lured, but she could be persuaded. If Turner had the right bait, Jenny would come to him. He should have thought of that from the beginning, but no, he'd tried snatching her the old-fashioned way. They had planned to grab her, just shove her in a car or truck, and bam, she'd disappear. Not completely, of course, until Turner was personally done with her. But dead she would be. The pieces of her body would never be found.

He held up his bloody and dirty hands, fantasizing about the clay being a different kind of gray matter. When he was done with her body, he'd put one of her bones in his special box along with the cat.

Now though, he had a new plan. There was a trial coming up. Turner knew everything he needed to know about Jenny Gallagher, her history, and her family. She would be at the rapist's trial in Springfield next week, and so would Jorim and Gary.

But not to touch Jenny. No. This time they'd go for Sidrah. She was always around Jenny off-campus. It should be easy enough. They'd verified that Sidrah had no personal protection. All they needed was a moment, one moment when she wasn't paying attention, and Sidrah would be his.

And once they had Sidrah, Jenny Gallagher would come to him.

Chapter 47

Jenny's head began to pound as the lawyers badgered her with questions. Her throat was dry, and she felt lightheaded. Sitting in the high witness chair with so many eyes staring at her was torturous. There were reporters in the room too. She wanted to scream, to run and hide. Her stomach roiled, complaining it needed food, but it also would have to wait.

"Do you want me to repeat the question?" the lawyer asked.

Jenny opened her eyes, which she realized had been closed for too long. She shook herself free of the impulse to flee and focused. "No. He . . . he told me to get undressed, he, he wanted . . ."

"Objection!" a lawyer sitting near the man shouted. Jenny hadn't wanted to look at the monster, but she'd been forced to. He had given her a challenging stare. The rapist was punishing her by making her look at him. He'd gone to trial to force the women to look at his putrid face, so he could give them a last sick, triumphant smile. *Yes*, it said, *you got me, but I'll always have you.*

Between the lawyers, the judge, and the man, it had been a terrible day recalling the details of the attack, but Jenny had drawn strength from two other victims who'd come to support her. They were brave to endure the waves of pain that each step of the legal drama brought. That their suffering didn't equate to her own, didn't—or shouldn't have—mattered. But she had survivor's guilt that the other women had suffered more than she had.

Still, she had to live with the memories of being kidnapped, of what had happened in the barn, including her ability to stab a man viciously. She couldn't have imagined ever doing something like that. The impact of that moment, the blood, the scream, the feel of the knife in her hand, where she had landed it, was primal. She'd felt her teeth bared like an animal as she'd fought for her life. In a way, the man was right. They *were* forever shackled together.

She looked at the victims' faces now. They nodded and smiled encouragingly. Tears began to fall, and Jenny put her head down to wipe them.

You can do this, Jenny. You have the strength. You did the right thing that day, and now, again, today. See this through. Send him away so he'll never hurt another woman again.

She lifted her head and glared hotly at Brian Mosley. He had a name. Yes, he was human, but evil lived inside him. It had a beating heart. While he lived, it would live too. But because of her, his evil would beat in a cage.

She looked at Sidrah for strength too. They shared a mutual destiny, and this had been part of it.

The sterile halls of the Hampden County Hall of Justice were depressing. Sidrah was no stranger to utilitarian police stations, and in her youth, she'd seen her fair share of governmental setups. But this one reeked with the dripping remnants of Brian Mosley's evil. She wanted a shower, but it didn't look like any of her plans, let alone that one, were going to go off.

"It's ridiculous that you thought the MGM casino would be an appropriate place to stay," Jenny's mom practically hissed at John Gallagher.

"It was my idea, Kate," Sidrah interrupted. "I'm sorry, I just thought a hotel would be more convenient for all of us. I didn't want to put John out."

"This isn't about *John*," Kate said, tugging at the hem of her jacket. She lowered her voice. "Jenny should be with her parents, not in a hotel with some strangers. It doesn't look right."

Sidrah watched Kate readjust her expensive handbag and eyeball Leon, who stood to the side of the assembled group.

"We could go back to Boston. She's finished testifying." Sidrah offered.

Kate glared at her. "After the day she's had? You want her to go back to her dorm room?"

Sidrah hadn't meant the dorm at Wellesley, but she didn't argue. The weather was terrible, it was late, it was a two-hour drive to Boston, and Jenny wasn't her daughter. She reminded herself of that and held her lips tightly closed.

"Is Simon here?" Jenny said. "I didn't see him."

Kate shook her head. "I'm sorry. He wanted to come, but he's traveling for business. Something incredibly important.

Look, Jenny, you're exhausted. I made a casserole. It's in the car. We're going to Palmer. It's in my direction since I'm going home to Worcester."

John Gallagher gave his daughter an encouraging smile. "It's your home. You're all welcome." He looked at each of them in turn. His face, too, was drawn from the long day.

"It's settled, then," Kate said. "Jenny dear, would you like to ride with me? There's some bad weather, and Simon was sweet enough to give me the Hummer."

Jenny shook her head. "I'm going with Dad."

Kate, about to retort, was interrupted by a reporter and a cameraman, who were walking toward them. Sidrah put her head down and said to Jenny, "Don't talk to them. Let's get out of here."

Jenny didn't hesitate, nor did anyone else, and they began walking toward the bank of elevators. Kate smiled and gave a small wave to the newscaster, who beckoned them, but followed, nevertheless.

Sidrah let Leon drive her car as they caravanned to Palmer.

"Maybe I should get a Hummer," Sidrah said, looking at the wildly large vehicle in front of them leading the pack. Her Mercedes felt like it was being pulled in the slipstream.

"It feels a bit like a military convoy," Leon said.

She smiled at him. He'd proven to be steady and dependable, traits she liked in a man.

She got the MGM on the line. Having not yet checked in, she'd spend the forty-five-minute drive canceling their hotel reservations and checking out the options for a place to stay in Palmer. She was anxious to call Max too. He was waiting.

"Whatever happens, Leon, you stay with Jenny. John's house is small, but he's got a couch. Are you okay with that?"

"No problem. After what that kid went through today, I wouldn't want to be anywhere else."

Sidrah paused and put a finger under her nose, tears springing to her eyes as she looked out at the flakes of snow swirling in the night. It was only five-thirty but already pitch dark.

"She did good today," Sidrah said with a bit of a question, checking his thoughts.

Leon's hands tightened on the wheel. "Damn sure did. It took a lot of guts to sit there in front of that guy. He was challenging her. Smirking. Did you see that? Fucking asshole. It made her angry."

Sidrah nodded. "I saw it. She has enormous courage, doesn't she?"

"You better believe it."

"We've got to take good care of her, Leon."

"We will," he said.

She glanced again at his profile and felt a special closeness to him. Not just because of the proximity, and not just because of today. Over the last two months, they'd developed a bond. Max, she, and Jenny had shared plenty with him about their circumstances but not entirely about their gifts. Leon knew something was different, though. To his credit, he didn't back away from the strangeness of any of it.

"Do you go to church, Leon?" she asked. "Are you a religious man?"

He glanced at her, his face lit by the blue glow of the dashboard. "I've spent some time with that outfit. Every Sunday in my youth. I should probably get back."

"Do you believe then? In things greater than you. A god, forces, souls?"

"That's a lot of topics right there, but yeah. I believe. I know I'm not in charge, that's for damn sure."

Sidrah shook her head and worked her phone. "Neither am I."

They arrived at John's house, and Kate pulled the Hummer to the side to let John pass so he could park in the garage. She parked her rig in the driveway, which left Sidrah and Leon no option but to park in the street. Sidrah was glad that she'd worn tall boots instead of heels. Her conservative A-line skirt, which hung just below her knees, along with her crisp white shirt and long black cardigan, had kept her warm all day. As she got out of the car, she tugged her knee-length black jacket closed, then scurried to the back of the car to help Leon retrieve his and Jenny's gear from the trunk. "Leave my stuff. I don't think there's room for me here tonight."

They made their way inside the garage. Kate walked in front of them, she too carrying an armful of supplies.

"You get everything out of your car?" Leon asked Kate when they were in the garage.

"Yes. For the moment," Kate said over her shoulder as she walked through the garage door and into the mudroom and laundry room of the house.

Sidrah watched as Leon pressed the button to lower the garage door. He waited for her to pass before he followed her inside.

John Gallagher's residence was a small home on Bittersweet Drive. With two bedrooms and a shared bath upstairs, it was comfortable enough for a small family. Once through the mudroom/laundry room, they walked directly into a long kitchen. The dining room was straight ahead. To the left of the kitchen, the wall was cut out under the cabinets for a see-through to the front room. There, in addition to the living room setup, was another dinette table as well as a long counter with bar stools looking back into the kitchen.

"Sorry," Sidrah said to Kate as they fumbled near one another to remove their boots and jackets in the narrow kitchen.

Jenny reached out to Leon. "Let me take the bags."

He handed her the two bags, and she dropped one in the dining room, then disappeared up the stairs to her bedroom.

"You get out of those stinky court clothes and into something comfortable, Jenny," Kate hollered up the stairs after her. "I'm just going to put the casserole and rolls in the oven and whip up a salad. Dinner should be ready in about an hour."

Kate turned to Leon and Sidrah, her eyes on the soft-sided tote bag on the dining room floor. "You're staying?"

"Leon is," Sidrah said. "I've got a hotel booked down the street, about a mile from here. The Lofts on Main."

John, who had hung everyone's jacket in the nearby closet, said, "You can stay, Sidrah. You can have my room. I'll just need to change the sheets." He glanced worriedly toward the stairs.

Sidrah did not want to put him out. He was a nice man who had also suffered today. At the very least, he deserved to sleep in his own bed. "No, John. Thank you, but it's no trouble. It's just for the night. I'll be fine."

Kate was digging through the cabinets, looking for something in the kitchen. "I don't understand why either one of you needs to stay. John is here. He can look after her."

Sidrah didn't know what to say. She certainly didn't want to get into an argument with Jenny's mom. This woman, too, had been in pain today.

Before the trip, Jenny had shared her feelings about her strained relationship with her mostly absent mother. She'd also told Sidrah about the generous financial arrangement they'd entered into and that Kate and her husband, Simon, were funding her college education.

That impressed Sidrah, but she also knew that Jenny no longer had to worry about money. She'd told her as much, and while Jenny didn't wholly agree, they danced around the reality that somehow their fates were firmly intertwined.

John placed a soft but firm hand on the kitchen counter. "We talked about this, Kate. There's reason to believe that Jenny needs looking after. We all know she's special."

Kate's face flushed. "I don't know them, John. Who are these people? Why are they here? She's only known them for what, how many weeks?"

"Kate," Sidrah began.

"Don't you Kate me," she said. "I'm Jenny's mom. You got that? Does everyone here understand that? I may not have been around much, but she's . . . she's my daughter. I don't understand what you're doing here. My child needs rest."

Sidrah dropped her head, feeling terrible. Emotions were heated. She wished Max were here, but she supposed that would be one more person for Kate to contend with. And a gloved one too.

"I'm sorry," said Sidrah. "I didn't mean any disrespect. And you're absolutely, 100 percent right. We are virtually strangers. But tonight, I'm looking forward to getting to know you better. Leon is too. Jenny is very special to all of us. We're only here to help. I promise."

John walked into the dining room. There was a small bar in the corner, and he picked up a bottle of brandy. "How about a drink before dinner then," he said, walking back into the room, looking hopeful.

Sidrah watched Kate's jaw tense as she turned back to an insulated bag and pulled out some lettuce. "I didn't bring dressing, John," she said, her voice a bit trembly. "I hope you have some."

John put the bottle down on the counter and walked over to her. He put a hand on her back and said, "Katie."

Sidrah gave Leon a sidelong glance as Kate fell into John's arms and wept. Shocked by the emotional intimacy, she and Leon walked out of the room and took up positions on the chairs in the living room.

Leon folded his hands in his lap. His lips were pressed into a tight line. "It's going to be fine."

Sidrah gave him a soft smile. "I've got to call Max."

"Why don't you go upstairs to John's room. I'm sure he'd be okay with that."

She nodded and left the room. Max and Bones, her family too, were worried and waiting.

———

The five of them sat around the small table off the kitchen since a computer rebuild John was working on had cluttered the dining room table. The hamburger and egg-noodle casserole was almost gone as they lingered over the simple supper and attempted to make small talk.

Sidrah glanced at Jenny, who had eaten the least but appeared to be holding up.

"Tell us more about your roommate Lisa," Kate said. "She sounds fascinating."

Jenny shrugged. "She's really nice. We've gotten close. I think she's homesick, though. I hope she stays and doesn't go back to Hong Kong."

Kate shook her head. "Why would she leave America? We're everything they want to be and now can't have. They love us over there. Not like the many so-called liberals in this country."

Sidrah did not want to discuss politics, but it seemed like Kate often brought up the subject.

Jenny rolled her eyes. "Can we not?"

Kate put up her hands in surrender. She went to place one on Jenny but pulled it back abruptly. The incomplete gesture was not lost on Sidrah. Jenny had told her that her mother had an aversion to touching her. For some reason, the woman was nervous that Jenny might see something unwanted if she did.

Kate got up from the table. "Simon was crushed that he couldn't be there for you today, but he did send a present." She disappeared into the mudroom, then came back to the table with a hard-sided box. She placed it in front of Jenny with a big smile.

"Open it," Kate encouraged as she sat again at the table.

"Mom," Jenny slouched. She opened the box. Inside, there was a gun.

Kate reached over and picked it up. "Isn't it cute? It's a Tiffany-blue Walther .22. You didn't seem thrilled with my 9 mm Glock 43 idea, so I got this one."

Jenny's expression tightened as Kate gushed on. "There are some steps to get the conceal and carry, but I can walk you through them. You'll need to write up a little something to justify the CCG, but if *anyone* deserves one, you do. It's reliable, and the grip is wonderful. Our hands are about the same size, so I field-tested it for you. The shootability is fantastic. I've got another bag with some cleaning supplies because remember, a clean gun is a happy gun. I can teach you how to take care of it. There are fifty rounds of ammunition . . ."

"Mom," Jenny interrupted. "Stop. I get that you think this is super cool, but I just don't want to do this right now, okay?"

A tense silence settled over the table until Kate said, "Fine." Then she repacked the gear. Once done, she turned her head away from Jenny and sniffed.

"Jenny, I don't think it's a bad idea for you to learn to use a weapon," Sidrah said.

"Like I already did?" Jenny said forcefully. "It was awful—you have no idea how awful it felt to do that."

Sidrah's throat ached. "I know, Jenny. I felt him too. But he was an animal. He wasn't going to stop until someone stopped him."

Kate glared at her. "What do you mean you *felt* him too?"

Sidrah looked around the table. Leon and Kate had not been told about her special abilities, nor about how she'd had a vision of Brian Mosley stalking Jenny before the attack. She wasn't sure she was ready to open up to Kate. Leon, maybe. But something held her back from going down that path with Jenny's mom.

"I just meant, you know, you could tell," Sidrah said.

Jenny looked at her mom and made a face. "She's special too."

Kate visibly trembled before she grabbed the casserole pan off the table and walked into the kitchen. "I don't want to discuss that," she said.

"Why do you think they're here, Mom?" Jenny said, losing her patience. "Sidrah and Leon. What did Dad tell you?"

John scratched his head. "I told Kate that you met some people at a support group on campus and that they were watching out for you."

Jenny shook her head and squeezed her eyes shut. "I think we should tell Kate the truth. Maybe then she won't think I'm the only *freak* in the world."

Sidrah bit her lip, surprised by Jenny's behavior. It was clear that she was stressed and overwhelmed, but it wasn't like her to be so confrontational. But then, everyone had their breaking point, and Jenny was still practically a kid.

"If you think it's wise, Jenny, we can," Sidrah gave her a level stare.

Jenny's eyes filled with tears, drawn down in a look of regret. "No. I'm sorry. I shouldn't have said . . . it's not mine to tell."

Sidrah got up, ran around the table, and hugged her. "Don't worry, don't worry. It's fine."

"What's going on here?" Kate demanded as she came back into the room.

"Nothing, Mom!" Jenny shouted. "Nothing! Forget it! It's been a terrible day."

Sidrah stood up behind Jenny as Kate neared her daughter.

"Jenny, I think you're overwrought. You need to take a pill and go to bed," Kate said forcefully. "A good night's sleep will help, I promise."

John glared at Kate. "A pill? She doesn't need drugs." He looked at Jenny with concern as Kate marched out of the room to her purse. She dug around inside, then came back with a bottle. She put it on the table in front of Jenny.

"Prescription Ambien. I take one occasionally. The hospital gave you one to take after the attack too. Remember how it helped you sleep?"

Jenny looked at the bottle. "I was foggy and crabby the next day."

Kate opened the bottle and set a pill in front of her. "Just one. Take it. Go to bed."

Sidrah didn't know how to react to this advice. It seemed sound, but then she also knew it wasn't her place to chime in. Instead, she said, "You can sleep in tomorrow. We don't have to head back to Wellesley until you're ready."

Jenny picked up the pill and took it. She pushed back from the table. "I'm sorry, everyone. I guess I'm going to bed."

Sidrah watched her walk up the stairs. Everyone murmured goodnight to her departing back.

After that, the adults said very little to each other. Kate kept up the small talk while they all helped clean up dinner. After the dishes were done, John retrieved the bottle of brandy and offered a nightcap.

"We can sit down in the living room and talk," he said, getting out the glasses.

"None for me," Kate said. "I'm leaving. Simon should be home by the time I get there."

Kate's hasty departure felt a bit like a slight, but Sidrah let it go. They said their goodnights to her before she, John, and Leon took their drinks into the living room.

They were silent as they sipped the warm liquid, each lost in their thoughts.

"Dinner was good," Sidrah said.

"Real good," said Leon. "I love me a casserole."

John smiled. "Katie could always cook. She loved baking, being in the kitchen."

Sidrah saw the pain on John's face. It was obvious too that he still had feelings for Kate, even though she'd moved on.

"My Jenny and her sister, Cassie," John said, picking up a picture near his chair and looking at it.

She went to him. He handed her the picture, and she sat down next to Leon so they could look at it together. Jenny was little, maybe three, and she was gently kissing the infant's forehead. The tragic scene blew Sidrah away. How could someone suffer the loss of a baby and survive?

John looked wistful. "Both of them are angels. I wish Jenny had had a sister growing up. Of course, everything would have been different if the accident hadn't happened."

"I'm sorry, John," Sidrah said.

"How old was Cassie when she died?" Leon said.

"Almost a year. It wasn't Katie's fault. The seat belt or the car seat was faulty. Something didn't work."

John sipped his drink. "She's in good hands now, though. I don't understand the plan He has for us or why things happen. But then, it sounds a bit arrogant to think I'm important enough to be let in on it."

They sat looking out the picture window, watching the snow, which had begun coming down hard.

"I suppose I should go soon," Sidrah said.

"You can stay," John said. "I wasn't just being polite, you know."

The side of Sidrah's mouth turned up. "I know." She rose and put her glass on the kitchen counter, then pointed to the stairs. "Do you mind if I take a peek at her before I leave?"

John waved his permission, and Sidrah climbed the short set of stairs, stopping to admire Jenny's school pictures, which lined the passageway.

She knocked softly on the door. Receiving no answer, she opened it and looked inside. Jenny was lying on her side in bed, a nightstand lamp still on. Sidrah walked over and looked down at her unbelievably innocent and beautiful face. With all the evil in the world, all one needed to do was take a glimpse at this brave girl, and they'd know there was a God and goodness in the world. Sidrah leaned down and kissed her softly on the cheek.

"Good night, angel. I love you."

She closed the door behind her as she left and walked back downstairs, confident that Jenny would be safe tonight. She would sleep. The pill had been a good idea, after all.

Not wanting to linger, she said her good-byes, gathered her things, and went out to her car. It was time to get over to the hotel and call Max to say goodnight. He had an early morning class, but she'd be back in his bed tomorrow night. When she neared her car, she stopped and looked up at the beautiful sky. A streetlight at the head of the block illuminated the snowflakes, making the ordinary scene beautiful. Sidrah got inside her Mercedes. Life could be good too.

Chapter 48

WEDNESDAY

Turner watched with fascination as Sidrah left the house and hustled to her car, which was parked on the street. She stopped before getting inside and lifted her face to the sky. He could almost feel her smile and thought about how much fun he'd have removing it with a knife.

Excited at the thought of what was in store for her, he pressed a call to Jorim. "She's leaving."

"We're on it."

"Get her now," he whispered with urgency before hanging up.

So much of the plan had been remarkably easy—finding the date of the trial, finding the Gallaghers' house on Bittersweet Drive. Jenny had gone to school in Palmer. It had been her home before Wellesley.

Gary Daggett had sat in court every day watching the trial. And this morning in Wellesley, Jorim had seen Jenny being picked up by Sidrah and the black man. They all knew precisely where they were headed.

It was Jenny's day in court and Sidrah's day with destiny.

They'd placed a GPS tracking device on Sidrah's car while she was in court. No problem there. They could now track her movements, just in case.

Once the long trial day was over, and Sidrah and the black man had gotten in the car, they'd followed from a discreet distance. They were a small group of hunters and hunted, led by a huge Hummer. Jorim had reported that there was a woman at the Hummer's wheel, so Turner supposed that was Jenny's mom. Once they were on the road and headed east, everyone assumed they were going to John Gallagher's house in Palmer.

And they had. Turner sat in his family minivan, its windows deeply tinted, parked some distance down the street. He had been thrilled when they all predictably arrived. What he couldn't know was their plans for the rest of the evening. But then the mom and the Hummer left. And then, miraculously, so did Sidrah. Alone.

Turner watched the Mercedes's taillights disappear as it turned off the street. He smiled as the car containing Gary and Jorim eventually followed it. He looked back at John Gallagher's house. Jenny was inside. But so was the father and the black man—one of Jenny's guards. It was interesting that they'd hired protection for Jenny. He wasn't entirely sure how they knew that Jenny was being hunted, but they did.

He could take them all tonight. Once Sidrah was captured, he could even have Jorim come back to help him. But he hesitated, considering the vision he'd had in the tank. When he arrived, he parked down the street from the Gallaghers. He was thrilled that he'd seen the house before and that his vision had been undeniably accurate.

He'd seen the house clearly, but in his vision, there had

been snowbanks around it, the drive plowed. And most importantly, he'd seen Professor Max Dyer and the black man emerge from the house and leave in a Jeep. Which meant Jenny would still be inside with possibly only her father. Clickbait. Clickety click, click, clickbait for his semiautomatic, and later, the knife.

Turner realized that Max was not inside. There were no snowbanks yet—no plowed drive. No Jeep. The vision had to be for tomorrow. Max Dyer would come to Palmer in search of his lost love and, at some point, leave Jenny virtually unguarded, alone with her dad.

That would be Turner's best opportunity. He stowed his night-vision goggles and climbed quietly out of the minivan. A few lights shone behind the closed curtains on the quiet residential street, but he saw no potential for his presence to be spotted as he jogged across the street and down to the Gallaghers'.

He walked through the snow accumulating on the side of the house, confident his tracks would be covered by morning, and scouted access to the home. There was no fence in the yard, and around back, there was a sliding patio door and a door to the garage. No cameras were visible. He stopped and watched his breath fog the air for a few moments, listening to the silence, before he tried the handle of the back door to the garage. It was locked. He removed his gloves and pulled a couple of handy tools out of his pocket and got to work on the lock. Under a minute, and he had it. No trouble at all. He tried the door. He didn't think there would be an alarm, but it was time to find out.

The door opened beautifully, quiet on well-oiled hinges. Turner made out John Gallagher's car in the garage, but the door allowed him access to the house. He closed the door quietly, then used his tools to relock it. He left the backyard, retracing his steps to the van. After slipping into the driver's seat, he started the freezing car. He'd worn several layers of Under Armour, so he'd been perfectly comfortable during his stakeout. Tomorrow he'd be in position and prepared. He cruised into Palmer. Somewhere, Jorim and Gary were on the job.

He glanced at his phone when it rang and anxiously pressed the call to answer it.

"We have her. She was in the parking lot across from the diner."

Turner licked his lips. The setup was perfect. Because they'd previously scoped out the town, he knew there were very few cameras in the small, underfunded town of Palmer. The pickup site was especially excellent.

"Keep me posted," Turner said and hung up.

He drove toward the diner and past a small hotel on Main Street. Sidrah had probably been headed there. The street parking near the hotel was full, but there was a lot around the corner. He followed the path that Sidrah must have driven. Sure enough, he spotted her Mercedes in a half-full parking lot. The snow was gathering on all the cars.

He smiled as he parked the minivan some distance away from Sidrah's car and shut off the ignition. Train tracks ran behind Main Street, and he heard a train coming toward him as the neon lights of a closed diner across the street filled his vision.

He got out of the van and retrieved a duffle bag. The loud train rumbled past him as he walked to the corner and down Main Street. He'd try to get a room at the small hotel Sidrah had been headed to. Secure in the knowledge that things were proceeding entirely on schedule, he smiled as he entered the tiny lobby. The proprietor was there waiting and smiling back at him.

Chapter 49

In the morning, Jenny's eyes slowly came unglued from her sleepy state. It took her a moment to gain her sensibilities and recognize her surroundings, but once she did, her life came flooding back. And so did her dream. For a moment, it was still there, easy enough to grasp. But soon, it began to slip away. Sidrah had been there. She was sleeping poorly, tossing and turning on a carpeted floor, having a nightmare, her head lying on a towel, and a short, thin throw clutched under her chin.

Jenny felt a moment of amusement, thinking that Sidrah would never sleep on the floor. But then she closed her eyes. The vision came back more clearly, and she saw Sidrah still wearing yesterday's clothes, including her black boots and jacket.

She opened her eyes again, this time, uneasy. Her mouth felt terribly dry. Swallowing hard, she sat up, her head fuzzy with a hangover from the sleeping pill. *Argh.*

She grabbed her phone. Lisa had sent a few texts, sending her good wishes and inspirational emojis. She loved Lisa.

After sliding out of bed, she opened the door to her room and heard her dad and Leon talking downstairs. She went to the bathroom and then joined them.

Their faces looked anxious. "Jenny." Her dad's eyes softened, and he hugged her. "How did you sleep?"

Jenny rubbed her eyes. "Good. Hard though. That sleeping pill packs a punch."

"Glad you slept," Leon said. "Hey, Max texted. He can't get a hold of Sidrah. I can't either. It could be she hasn't woken up yet and has her phone off. Or maybe there's a signal issue."

"That sometimes happens in town," her dad said as he poured a cup of coffee.

Leon nodded. "Yeah, but I thought we might go over there and take a look. We could all grab some breakfast. John said there was a diner that serves some nice eggs nearby. You up for that?"

Her dad put a steaming cup on the table, and Jenny sat down in front of it. "Yeah. I guess." She blew on the hot beverage, then took a sip. "I gotta shower though."

Leon nodded fast. "All right. How about you get to that. John and I have some digging out to do. It snowed pretty hard last night."

Jenny looked out the front window, the bright morning light glistening off the snow. "Okay. What time is it?"

"Nine," said John. "I'm usually up early to get the plowing done, but I thought the blower might wake you."

"Nothing would have woken me," Jenny said, taking another sip. "Not even the trains."

"Well, you're used to those, I suppose," said her dad.

Leon walked to the front closet and got his jacket. "We're gonna get a start on that. Can you be ready quickly?

In like twenty minutes?"

Jenny squinted at him. "Do we really need to hurry? Couldn't she come over here for breakfast? We've got plenty of stuff."

Leon put on his gloves and hat. "No. No. I think we should head over there."

Jenny shook her head to clear it. "I had a dream about Sidrah last night. She was lying on the floor with a towel for a pillow. Can you imagine?" She gave Leon a faint smile. He didn't reciprocate.

"Hey," she said, her blood moving a bit faster. "It was only a dream. Right?"

Leon walked past her and patted her arm. "I'm sure it was. You about ready, John?"

Her dad glanced at Leon, then got his gear together.

"Be ready, okay?" Leon yelled before they went outside.

Jenny stood up, her legs a bit weak, but she recovered and ran up the stairs. She hopped in the shower, then blew her hair out in record time. Her anxiety increased as the plow whined outside.

She was downstairs, packed and ready in the twenty minutes they'd given her, and was putting on her jacket when her dad poked his head in from the garage door. "You ready?" he called.

She walked over to him with her bags. "Yeah," she said. "Let's go."

Her dad's car idled in the driveway, the exhaust fumes clouding the cold air. A gust of wind blew against her legs, and the snow swirled around her as she got into the front passenger seat. Leon was already in the back, texting.

Jenny turned to Leon as her dad backed out of the driveway. "You think she's okay, don't you?"

"Sure," said Leon. "Max is texting. He's worried. We gotta

check is all."

They drove slowly, a bit over a mile to Main Street, which had been plowed, but several people could be seen digging their cars out of the snowbanks that the plows had made in turn.

"It's right there." Jenny pointed to the two-story building with a painted window—Lofts on Main. She turned her head, scanning the street parking. "I don't see her car. Maybe she's parked in the lot around the corner."

Her dad pulled to the streetlight and turned left, going past a diner and toward the railroad tracks. A lot stood on the left, practically empty. "There it is," Jenny said, relieved as she recognized the sides of the bright-blue Mercedes.

"She's here," Leon said, his voice still pensive. "Lots of snow on it."

They parked in the lot and got out. Leon went to inspect Sidrah's car, brushing a wide swath of snow off the driver's side and peering inside. He shook his head, and the three of them dragged through the snowbanks until they made their way to the sidewalk and walked down Main to the small hotel's front door. Inside, they searched for a proprietor, but they had to ring a bell and wait. Eventually, a pleasant woman greeted them.

"She never checked in. She made a reservation and told me she'd be arriving late. I waited up for her, but after I didn't receive a callback at eleven, I closed up and went to bed."

Jenny's heart leaped. "But her car is out back!"

The woman shook her head. "I don't know what to say. She's not here. I'd know if she was."

Jenny turned to Leon, panicked. "Where is she?"

"Maybe she's in the diner," John added. "We could go over there."

"But where did she sleep? There's nowhere else around here," Jenny said, bouncing with tension.

The three of them hustled out of the hotel and began searching the streets for signs of Sidrah. They crossed at the light for the diner and slammed through the front door. Not seeing her, Jenny's heart thudded.

"I'll check the restroom." She ran through the familiar restaurant and burst into a small, cold tiled room. "Sidrah!" She caught her breath as she looked into the two empty stalls. Her body swayed slightly, her hand covering her mouth as she walked quickly back to group.

Jenny shook her head at her dad and Leon as she pulled out her phone. Her hand shook as she scrolled through for an image of Sidrah. Once she had it, she held it in front of the alarmed face of the hostess. "Have you seen her? Has she been in here? Last night, this morning?"

The girl peered closely at the shaking phone. "No. I think I'd remember her. I closed up yesterday at four and opened this morning. I haven't seen her."

"Her car is parked across the street," John said as he pointed out the window. Several other diners were following the conversation and looked in that direction too.

The woman shook her head slowly. "She wasn't in here."

Jenny's stomach lurched as she looked at Leon and her dad. Their faces held dread.

"I've got to call Max," Leon said. "But then I think we need to call the police."

Her dad paled. "I know them. I'll call."

Jenny dropped hard into a nearby booth. She put her face in her hands and stifled a scream. *No. No. No. Not Sidrah. Not Sidrah. No!*

Chapter 50

Turner had seen them. Sitting in a booth, he'd kept his eyes trained on the street. Jenny, her dad, and the black dude had pulled into the lot across from the diner and looked at Sidrah's car. He'd thrown some money onto the table for his breakfast and left the restaurant after the threesome walked down Main Street toward the hotel.

It was happening—they had finally been alerted and were searching for Sidrah. Turner went to his minivan and started it up. He grabbed a brush and scraper and did a quick cleanup so he could see out the windows. It didn't take too long, but as he pulled out of the lot, the threesome walked into the diner. He kept his face turned away from them as he drove past. The cops would be there soon, which was fine.

Turner drove back to John Gallagher's house and past it, casually noticing the plowed driveway and banks of snow. It was a similar scene to the one in his vision, but he couldn't be certain.

He headed west out of town toward Southwick and the

rental house on George Loomis Road, where Sidrah was being held. He thought carefully about the potential moves his adversaries would take but couldn't foresee any issues. They could have the day, scrambling, searching for Sidrah, but they wouldn't find her, and the cops wouldn't take her disappearance seriously until late tonight.

Once on the I-90 Turnpike, the windshield wipers went into overdrive as the snow picked up and began blizzarding. The weather complications were both good and bad. It wasn't really snowing so much as blowing. He hadn't heard reports of more accumulation, but weather reports were often inaccurate. If there were a snow emergency tonight, his minivan would be conspicuous and illegally parked on John Gallagher's street after one in the morning. He'd be inside the van, awake and ready to move it if he saw the plows coming, but the setup wasn't ideal.

He drove the twenty miles of interstate slowly along with other careful drivers, thinking about how to spend his day. He did not want to sit for hours in the rental house with Jorim and Gary waiting until dark. While his associates were always incredibly useful, he found them dull. He also didn't want them to mistake their relationship with him as personal. But the biggest drawback of being in the hostage house would be his proximity to Sidrah, where she could tempt him like bait. He wasn't ready for his special time with her yet. Nor Max Dyer. But his day, too, was coming.

He drove, considering where to hide until evening. He couldn't be in town to watch the cop show or hang too long in front of the Gallaghers'. Maybe he'd get a hotel room in Southwick where he could focus, relax, and catch some sleep.

He spotted a Hampton Inn as he got off I-90 and pulled into the parking lot. Once inside, he decided to stay, not go to the house. He made his way past a bar and restaurant to his room and went inside.

He flipped on the television, tuned it to the news, and called Jorim.

"How's it going?" he asked.

"No issues."

"Is she giving you any trouble?"

"I haven't checked on her. I thought you said no food. She's got a pissa in there."

Turner thought about his instructions. He'd wanted Sidrah as weak as possible, which was just plain hostage-holding 101. He wanted her fearful.

"No food. That stands," he said. "Go in. Check on her. Make her a little uncomfortable."

"How uncomfortable?"

With just a few words, he could have her raped, tortured, or killed. Even though he wouldn't be there to witness it, the visual was still satisfying.

He wouldn't share those upcoming treats with his men. Sidrah was his. After Jenny. "Nothing dastardly. Just hover. Smell her. Threaten. I don't want her physically harmed." He had confidence Jorim would think of something appropriate.

"You still want her to take the drugs?"

"Yes," Turner replied. Drugs were also in the textbook under hostage control.

"Okay. You coming out?"

"No. My work is elsewhere right now. But let me know if anything arises."

Turner hung up and looked around the room. He pulled back the curtains and stared into the swirling snow. "Professor Max Dyer. I'm waiting for you. Drive safely."

Chapter 51

Sidrah sat propped against a blank wall in the empty bedroom. There was an overhead light, but she hadn't wanted to use it last night and, instead, kept the bathroom light on. She put a hand on the white wall to push herself up and walked into the empty bathroom. There was nothing in there except a roll of toilet paper and working facilities. She'd checked the cabinets, the shower stall too—all were empty. There was nothing much to see anywhere. She wandered back into the bedroom, spying cracks of light at the edges of the boarded-up window.

Someone had prepared the room, even nailed plywood over the window. Sidrah walked over to it, examining the job. It was super secure. There was no way she was going to pry it off and get out the window, especially without letting them know. She walked to the doorway of an empty closet whose door had been removed. There were terrible carpet stains inside as if something had rusted on the floor.

The house was old and neglected. Now, it was her prison. She sat back down on the floor and pulled the picture of Max out of her jacket pocket. Her eyes immediately filled with tears. "Max," she whispered. Her lips burned and swelled. She gave the picture a tender kiss. Tracey had brought a boxful of albums over when she last visited, and Sidrah had hungrily devoured the images of her beloved man at every age. The picture she had now was taken on his graduation day. He smiled for the camera, wearing his doctoral gown with velvet trim and hood.

Max—the most precious thing in her life. Her lip trembled, thinking about all that happened yesterday. She feared what was going to happen now.

She'd been taken off guard when the men pulled their car up behind hers after she'd gotten out. Before she could react, one of them had her in a vise grip, and she'd dropped her phone. A hand covered her mouth, and she'd had no chance even to struggle as he shoved her inside the back seat of his car. He dove in after her, practically lying on top of her, as his accomplice at the wheel sped off. Sidrah lay face down, fighting for breath as the guy crushed her, mashing her face into the seat and threatening her with death if she tried anything.

She couldn't think as panic overtook her. He'd eventually let her sit up after she agreed to cooperate. She'd trembled and watched the roads change on their way to wherever they were going, sure that Turner Black was behind her abduction. She'd been foolish not to realize he would come after her too.

After the men got her inside the house, she feared the worst. But they shoved her inside the bedroom and forced her to take a pill while they watched. More than anything in the world, she didn't want to swallow that pill. The man who had grabbed her wasn't that tall, but he was strong. His muscles bulged through his tight shirt. He told her with dead eyes that it was a sleeping pill, that they'd leave her alone tonight if she'd take it.

She barely had time to process the consequences of taking the drug before staring down at the sharp blade in the guy's hand as he made his demand. He pointed at the pill on the bathroom counter, holding the knife to her face. Sidrah felt faint as she picked up the tablet. She turned on the faucet and made a move to bend down, but he shut off the water and slapped her. "No. On your tongue."

He turned the water back on and cupped his hand under the flow, producing a little puddle that he held out for her. "I wanna see it go down, and then you can lick this," he said.

She sickly complied and followed him back into the bedroom. The taller, thinner guy had poured the contents of her purse onto the floor and was digging through it. She watched while he pocketed about five hundred dollars in cash, took some pens and a nail file. He kicked at the rest and then told her to take off her jacket.

"I thought you were going to leave me alone," she said, her voice shaking as she backed away.

"Give him the coat," the short guy barked.

She reluctantly removed her jacket. The tall guy went through all the pockets while the short one pushed her up into a corner and ran his hands roughly over her body, frisking her. When he gave her privates a rough squeeze, she screamed and flailed, hitting him.

He laughed and looked at the tall guy, who threw her coat on the floor. Neither of them said anything further and left the room. Sidrah began to sob as she heard the lock click. Tears flowed, and she held to the walls in the corner, realizing that she was truly trapped.

Her adrenaline still on overdrive, her heart hammered as she lunged for her jacket. She scrambled into it, then fell to the ground and began digging through the contents of her purse spewed on the floor. She frantically searched for something, anything that might be helpful. But in the end, she came away with Max's picture, tucked into a side pocket. It stopped her cold. The thought of never seeing him again, or of being cruelly changed, ravaged her soul as she rocked and wept, holding tightly to the picture.

The pill, though, had its own mind. The adrenaline had begun to abate, and lethargy washed through her. She had gathered the towel for a pillow and lain down on the floor, tugging the small, nearly useless blanket over her, and drifted off.

Now awake, she realized she must have been out for hours, and she thought about her dreams. She'd slept with Max's picture; he'd been with her. At first, it was wonderful, but then it turned dark. The dreams had been incredibly strong. Vivid too. She didn't know if it was because of the intensity of her trauma, the pill, or the combination of the two, but she'd felt a solid communication with Max while she slept. The future, the dark glimpse that she'd seen, showed Max walking down the hallway of her shithole prison with a gun—a smallish turquoise gun that he held up like Dirty Harry but looked like a toy. The dream terrified her because she knew it was probably real.

What would happen to them? Had Jenny been kidnapped too? She closed her eyes and focused on the beautiful parts of the dream. Max's face had been filled with love as he kissed her mouth.

Her eyes popped open when she heard muffled voices close by. She looked at the door and wondered who was out there. What were they doing? And more than that, what did they intend to do? It was a bad sign that they hadn't blindfolded her because she'd seen their faces; she knew where she was too. She'd watched the route. They'd let her.

The logic of that made her tremble. She had to do something. Could she communicate with Max or Jenny? Could she focus on the address, where she was, the route they had taken, and somehow tell them how to find her? But if she did that and it worked, would Max show up with his toy gun?

Dickhead jailer had told her last night that he was giving her a sleeping pill. Sidrah had never had one before. If she could get one again, could she use her mind to reach out to Max and Jenny?

Uncertain if she should even try to reach them, she crawled over to the mess on the floor and searched through the items left out from her purse. She picked up and discarded her wallet, new and used wads of Kleenex, cosmetics, mints, sunglasses, hair bands, wet wipes, lotion, business cards. She picked up a hair band. It was Jenny's. She held it up to the light from the bathroom and saw a long blond hair wound around it. Her heart rate picked up as she grabbed the wad of tissues and Chapstick. Jenny had used them too, and Sidrah had just shoved the tissues into her purse for disposal later.

Hope surged through her. Could she do it? If she used her mind and really, really focused, could she communicate with Jenny in a dream?

But then she deflated. This all presumed she wouldn't be dead or worse in the next few minutes. Just as she had that thought, the door opened. The short jailer entered with a smile.

And a knife.

Chapter 52

Max woke that morning in a cold sweat. It startled him, and anxiety flooded his body. Bones, lying next to him, responded to his energy, jumped to attention, and stared down at him. He swallowed hard, trying to remember what it was from the dream that was bothering him, but it was gone before he could retrieve it.

He tried to shake it off as he went through their morning routine. He would arrive on campus for another seven a.m. meeting, conduct class at eight, and would be free to call Sidrah by nine thirty to check in. On the drive over, he decided he couldn't wait until after class and texted her when he got to his office.

"She's not answering," he said to Bones, who didn't take her eyes off him. The dog didn't flinch, only stared. "Maybe she's asleep," he said.

Bones stared at him as if focused on a squirrel.

He called Leon. The dependable guy answered, and Max expressed his concern. Leon told him not to worry, but Max couldn't help it. The worry persisted as he and Bones walked down the hall for the meeting. Everyone on campus now assumed that Bones was some type of therapy animal and no longer questioned her presence. His gloves, his dog—he was now just another eccentric academic on campus. He made it through the meeting and to class, texting Sidrah and Leon again on the way.

Still no answer from Sidrah, but he and Leon agreed that Leon would go over to the hotel and check on her after Jenny woke up.

Max stumbled distractedly through his lecture, but he managed to finish before returning Leon's call. As his students filed out of the room, he gathered his things and waited for privacy before he placed the call. "Are you at the hotel?" Max asked.

And then, his world stopped.

It spun around him until the walls felt like they were closing in. Bones barked at him, then propelled him to movement. They ran to his car and drove back home. Max threw random clothing and other items into a bag, utterly unsure about what he was doing. Then, he stopped and looked at the top shelf of his closet, where Turner Black's business card was held in a plastic bag. He grabbed the baggie and threw it on top of his clothes. He took a moment to get a blanket, a flashlight, and some survival gear together in case they got stranded. The weather reports had it blizzarding with road closures until late that afternoon.

At the last minute, he picked up a picture of Sidrah and him with Bones. He carried it out to the car, frame and all. Bones jumped into the front seat, and they started for Palmer, thankfully with a full tank of gas. But Max knew it would be slow going.

He alternately raged and worried as he white-knuckled the drive, receiving periodic updates from Leon. Jenny was frantic too. The cops had looked at Sidrah's car and then gone to the hotel, but they said they had their hands full with accidents and other assorted emergencies, brushing them off until Sidrah had been missing for twenty-four hours.

After that update, Max spent some of his drive visualizing himself ramming into the police station. He'd go through the glass front door, get out, and pound the shit out of all of them.

They needed help. They had to find Sidrah. Fiona had taken a few days off to travel to DC, and according to Leon, she was not getting out of Dulles. Flights were delayed across the board on the East Coast until the winter storm passed.

Bones was a comfort, and Max spoke with her through the entire ride. There wasn't a doubt in his mind that she understood everything that was happening.

Max stared at the road. "How are we going to find her?"

Bones whimpered a response.

His throat tightened. "We've got to. This isn't the end. It can't be," he whispered, blinking back tears.

He pounded on the wheel. "Goddammit! No! I should have seen this coming!"

The drive was maddening, but they made it to Palmer by early afternoon. Max drove directly through town and down Main Street. After getting the technical layout and reports from Leon, he felt as if he knew his way around. The street was mostly void of traffic when he saw the hotel on his left. He stopped at the streetlight, then saw the diner and turned left to the vacant lot. What had to be her car was practically snowed under, sitting by itself.

He slammed the selector into Park and threw open the door. Bones leaped over the center console and out the door after him. He slid his way over to her car and tried the door handle, but it was locked.

"Sidrah!" he screamed. He brushed the snow off the car and peered inside but couldn't see anything. Bones began to bark.

He looked down; she was frantically digging in the snow nearby, and Max dropped to his knees to join her.

They both stopped when they found a phone. It was Sidrah's. Max's eyes misted over, an ache in his heart building as he touched the phone with his ungloved hand. He closed his eyes. His body jolted as a vision of her struggle with a man came to him. But that was all. An image of her pained face was all he was left with.

Grief shot through him, the pain ripping him apart. He began to cry, his breath catching, until Bones barked again. She was back in the car, waiting for him in the passenger seat. Max hauled himself out of the snow and quickly walked to the car and got inside. He drove to John Gallagher's house, counseling himself to stay in control of his emotions when he arrived. Jenny needed him to be calm right now. So did Sidrah. He had to focus.

———

Max and Bones sat in the living room with Jenny, John, and Leon, everyone apparently working off the same set of blueprints and trying to stay calm. "She came to me in a dream last night too," Max said after hearing Jenny's tale about her dream of Sidrah lying fully clothed in an empty room.

"What happened?" Jenny asked.

Max shook his head. "I can't remember. I just know I woke up anxious."

"All this dream stuff aside, I think we need a plan," Leon said.

Max looked at Leon. He'd never fully answered the man's probing questions. "You know we have some special gifts that might help, don't you?"

Leon nodded. "I got that impression from the first interview, but the more I hung around, the more I believed it."

"So, if you *do* believe it, then we have to explore how to use them to help," Max said. "They're an asset. Don't you see that?"

"Yes," Leon said. "I just don't know where you're going with this. I thought maybe we could get the FBI on board. I can call Detective Bodine. He could grease the wheels and get on Turner Black too."

"It's a thought," Max said. "But I've got another one." He looked at Jenny in her fragile state and wondered if he should even ask her. He had to.

"Jenny. Would you be open to trying to communicate directly with Sidrah?"

She rubbed her arms through the blanket she was holding. "I've never done that."

Max nodded. "I understand, but it doesn't mean you can't try. It might work." He pointed to Sidrah's phone lying on the coffee table. "You could use that as a connection. I felt her. I saw her struggle when I touched it. I saw what had already happened. It's the past, which is all I can see. But you can see the past and the future. At times. And premonitions. You're the only one with that ability. I think you should try."

John Gallagher spoke up. "It might be asking too much. I don't want her to see, what if she sees . . ." He stumbled with his words.

Max knew what John was saying, but he didn't want to go there. Was it too much to ask Jenny to see something even he couldn't face? He rubbed his hands together and looked at Bones. The dog got up and went to the phone. She used her nose to push it in Jenny's direction.

"Damn," Leon said, covering his mouth. "I don't think the word *special* quite covers what's going on here."

Jenny stroked Bones's head, which the dog had laid in her lap. "I'll do it," she said. "But I think that pill last night made a difference. If we're going to try this, I think I'm going to need another one."

Max let out a breath. "John, have you got some?"

He shook his head. "It was Kate's."

Max searched the others' faces. Coming up empty, he said, "Then let's go get some. Can you call her and tell her we're coming by? Worcester's what, like thirty miles?"

John looked at Jenny. "Are you sure you want to do this, honey? We're drugging you to use your mind. I don't think it's right."

"It is right, Dad. I couldn't live with myself if I didn't try."

Chapter 53

Jenny was glad that Bones had decided to stay at her dad's house as they entered the lobby of her mom's high-rise building. They'd all been confused when she wouldn't budge from the house, but they'd granted her wish and left her behind. If she had come, they would have had to leave her in the car because Simon was a stupid neat freak and not a fan of pets.

Jenny led the way off the elevator toward the door. She'd rarely been to her mom and Simon's place. She looked back at her dad, Max, and Leon trailing her, all of them looking imposing yet vulnerable. Leon looked especially tough and was acting highly cautious. His typical smile was non-existent when he eyeballed some strangers in the elevator.

She rang the bell, and her mom opened the door with a smile. She dropped it when she looked at the three men. "Oh. I didn't expect so many of you. Come in," she said, opening the door wide enough to let them enter.

Jenny looked around her mom's tidy modern home. Free of any knickknacks, the place seemed cold. She could see it snowing outside through the bank of long windows overlooking a large, dark lake. So, the gloomy night, too, offered no relief from the somber lifelessness of the home.

Kate wore a cocktail dress with an apron. She gestured toward the dining room, formally set for four. "We're having a small dinner party tonight. I was just getting ready."

Jenny, annoyed as usual whenever she was around her mom, turned to Max. "Mom, this is Max Dyer. You haven't met."

Max extended a gloved hand, and Kate gave him a suspicious look, but then very briefly accepted it. Max pulled back his hand and said, "Sorry. Allergies."

Kate turned to John. "I'd ask you to stay, but . . ."

"When is Simon getting home?" Jenny interrupted, her temper building.

"In about an hour," Kate said.

"Hmm, never around when you need him. I don't think we'll stay," Jenny replied. "Could I get that pill now, Mom?"

Kate put her hands on her hips. "What exactly is going on here?"

Jenny shook her head. They'd talked about what to tell her mom on the way over. Jenny had decided that she wasn't going to lie to her. For some reason, she wanted to push her differences in her mom's face whenever they were together. Maybe because her mom never wanted to talk about it. Jenny had always resented the lack of support. And the labels.

"Do you *really* want to know?" Jenny said, not all that proud of the tone that came out.

Kate opened and closed her mouth like a fish, uncertain of what to say.

Jenny snapped. "Sidrah is missing. She's been kidnapped. But, hey, let's not keep you. I know you've got a party to prep for."

Her dad walked toward her. "Jenny, stop. There's no need for—"

"What!" Kate said. "What happened now?"

Jenny's face heated. "What happened *now*? Like it's all a big *inconvenience* to you?"

John stepped between the two of them. "Stop! Jenny. Enough. Your mom is entitled to know what's happening. I know you're upset, but let's try to remain calm."

Jenny steamed as her dad told Kate the details.

"So, the police are on it?" Kate said.

"Not yet!" Jenny said sarcastically.

"Technically, they won't be for twenty-four hours, but we have friends at Boston PD, and they've alerted the FBI," Leon said.

"My God," Kate said, taking a few steps back. She tucked her coiffured hair behind her ears. "So, Jenny is naturally upset, and she needs help sleeping, is that all?"

Jenny looked at her dad, who gave her a level stare. She turned to her mom. "Yeah. That's it. I just need some sleep, Mom. The four of us drove all the way over here to get a pill so I could have a good night's sleep."

Her mom did the fish mouth thing again but then smoothed her apron. "All right. I'll be right back."

Kate left the room. Her dad exhaled a frustrated breath.

"She doesn't want to know, Dad," Jenny said. "I'm not going to lay it out for her to criticize and judge us either. She doesn't want any part of my shit, and she doesn't care about Sidrah."

He was about to speak, but Max interrupted. "That's not true, Jenny. She loves you a great deal. She doesn't know how to cope with many things. I'm sorry. I think you should give her a break."

Jenny pulled back, a bit shocked, and began to tremble as Max softly chided her. She realized then that he'd seen something in her past, something she never wanted to talk about either. With all the family pictures in the house, Max could have seen what had happened to her sister. She closed her eyes and tried not to cry. Her dad held her as she covered her face, embarrassed and confused.

Kate came back into the room with the bottle. "I've removed all but two. They can be addicting, you know, and I don't want you to misuse them, Jenny. You have to be careful. I sincerely wanted to help when I gave them to you. You'd been through so much. I'm sorry about Sidrah. Really, I am."

Jenny sniffed up her tears and reached for the bottle. "Okay, Mom. I'm sorry. Thanks."

Kate nodded and looked softly at John. Her bottom lip quivered. "Take care of her, John," she whispered.

"I will," he said, hugging her.

Jenny clutched the bottle. It was time to go home and sleep.

Chapter 54

Turner sat on Bittersweet Drive, eyeing the Gallaghers' house. No cars were in the driveway, and more snow had accumulated on it. He frowned at the image, realizing that unless they plowed the driveway tonight and Max's Jeep was parked on it, the vision wasn't for Thursday.

Where were they? The house was mostly dark. Turner knew that the window of opportunity to plow the drive would be before 11:00 p.m. Most people didn't get out with their blowers after that. Of course, they could use shovels.

He closed his eyes and willed the vision back, checking the tread marks on the driveway. Were they made by plow or shovel? His eyes popped open as headlights approached. Turner smiled. It was the Jeep turning into the drive. He watched as four people got out and went in through the garage after John Gallagher keyed in a code on the side.

The garage door lowered, and Turner glanced at the time. Six o'clock. He'd wait. If they didn't come back out tonight, then his vision would happen tomorrow. He'd go back to his hotel to sleep so he'd be fresh for the final assault.

He tingled with excitement, knowing he was close. It was all coming together nicely.

Chapter 55

FRIDAY MORNING

Max ran a hand through his hair as he paced in the Gallaghers' living room, *willing* Jenny to wake up. "It's past eight," he said quietly to Leon and John, both sitting in the room drinking coffee. "Do you think we should wake her?"

Bones shook her head.

Leon grimaced. "It is so freaky when she does that."

"Right, right," Max spoke to Bones.

It had been a long, terrible night. Jenny had gone to bed directly after supper. John had made spaghetti when they got back, and Max had had several glasses of brandy trying to calm down. Having forgotten to pack Bones's food, they'd given her plain pasta and sausage. She hadn't complained. She'd gone outside with Max when he smoked, which was often, but when she needed to relieve herself, she walked on a path she'd made directly near the house. He wasn't at all sure what that meant. Maybe she didn't like the new snow.

Max and Leon had taken turns staying awake, each grabbing the couch for a few hours before giving it up at first light. John had scrambled some eggs for all of them. Now they waited.

"As soon as she's up, we're going over to those pukes at the police station and making the disappearance official," Max said to Leon. "I want to talk to that useless Detective Bodine that Sidrah has helped out too. What the hell is he doing?"

Leon nodded. "Yup. We said we'd give it until 9:00 a.m. Why don't you sit down?"

Max sat. Bones came over and put her head in his lap, and Max removed a glove to pet her. He'd had a long chat with John and Leon after Jenny went to sleep the night before. For the first time, Leon had heard all the gory details about each of their talents. To their credit, they both held up fine. Max realized John had more of a head start on the psychic phenomena happening in their midst, but still, he'd been pleased with both their questions and attitudes. As the night wore on, John had also shared his pain and loss, which gave Max a deeper appreciation for the entire Gallagher family. Not being a father, Max realized he couldn't fully appreciate the enormity of losing a child. Still, he understood that the explosion of their world after Cassie's death had radically changed them all.

His impatience built with the endless waiting. He pushed Bones away, put his glove back on, pulled a tin of gum out of his pants pocket, and popped a few. He chewed with vigor as his mind raced, wondering about Sidrah and what she must be going through. The thought of her *not alive* was unimaginable. He'd searched for her his entire life. Whatever it took, even if it meant his own death, he had to find her. His life was meaningless without her. He knew that now.

"Dammit," he raged. He got up and grabbed his cigarettes off the table. With his gloves back on, it was exasperating trying to extract one from the new pack. "Goddammit," he said, struggling.

"Send 'em here," Leon said, his hands up, ready for the pass. Max threw the pack at him, and Leon got up and handed him one. Max pulled his lighter out and was heading to the patio door when Jenny came down the stairs.

He wanted to pounce on her. Instead, he gave her a weirdly perky, "Good morning."

Jenny sat at the bottom of the steps. The men gathered around. She looked up at them. "It worked. She's alive. I saw her again."

Max sagged as he grabbed the banister for support. "My God. Thank you, Jenny."

"Are you okay?" John asked her.

Max lifted his head, realizing he should have thought to ask that.

Jenny put her hands over her mouth, her eyes filling, and Bones went to her. "I'm fine," she said in a shaky voice.

But she wasn't. Max felt a cold chill as the young girl began to cry. She hugged the dog, then paused to croak out, "I'm so sorry. I felt her pain. This can't be happening again. Why is this happening?" she wailed.

Max's stomach twisted as he rocked. "Is she . . . is she hurt?"

Jenny shook her head, her face contorted with grief as her tears fell. "I don't know. I tried hard. I kept trying . . ."

John went to her. "Enough. You need to eat. Something to drink. Come sit at the table, and I'll get you some coffee."

Max watched Jenny pass him; Bones's body was pressed next to her. They sat at the table, Bones in a chair too. John brought Jenny a cup of coffee, and he fussed over her for a few minutes. Leon had disappeared upstairs and now returned with a box of tissues, which he placed next to her.

Max sat at the table, swallowing back his impatience as he played with a finger on his glove. He chewed his gum rapidly and loudly, and Bones barked at him. Her annoyance was apparent.

"Right," Max said, taking a breath. He took out the gum and wrapped it in a napkin.

Jenny blew her nose. "I think she's okay. I mean, she must be. She was communicating the information to me somehow, right?"

"You slept with her phone and her picture," Max said. They'd printed a copy of the photo of him, Sidrah, and Bones, cut Sidrah out, and taped it to the back of her phone. It looked ridiculous, but it obviously worked.

"How's your head, Jenny?" her dad said from the kitchen. "Do you have a headache?"

She shook it, then stopped. "It's foggy. Like dizzy, but it doesn't hurt."

"Coffee should help," Leon said as he took a seat at the table.

John brought a piece of toast with peanut butter. "Eat," he said, placing it in front of her. Bones perked up and looked at John.

"Not *you*," Max said.

Jenny dropped her hand on the table. "Okay, everyone, stop worrying about me. I'm fine. We've got to focus on Sidrah. I think I know where she is, kind of."

Max's breath caught. "What do you mean?"

"I mean, she showed me the trip. Sort of. It was in glimpses and snatches, but I saw through her eyes that she went through Southwick. I went to a volleyball tournament there, so I recognized it. There's a Dunkin' Donuts that I saw too. But after that, the snatches were all dark, like in the country. Small roads. Narrow and twisty turny."

Max got the picture. If she were somewhere outside of Southwick, then she'd be about thirty miles south and west of Palmer. "We could drive it. Just drive around all the roads. Is she in a house? A trailer? What else?"

"A house," Jenny said. "There were lower power lines and a sharp turn and a red mailbox and a long driveway. It's set back in some trees."

Leon crossed his arms. "Okay, we go driving, but then we give the FBI the information and let them go in."

Max blinked. "What? No. The cops aren't going to buy this. The FBI hasn't even started investigating. And what, we're going to tell them about our shit? Then what?"

Leon narrowed his eyes. "Sidrah already works with the cops. They've kept her secret."

"That's Bodine. He's Boston PD. I don't trust the FBI. Not to mention that I doubt they'd follow up on it. Now that we know all this, we've got to go in and get her ourselves. You and me. We can move fast, and we won't fuck it up."

Leon looked at Max like he was crazy. "What are you talking about? These are motivated motherfuckers." He turned to Jenny and put a hand up. "Sorry, I didn't mean to say that."

Jenny rolled her eyes. "I think we should drive around and see if we can find her first. While it's still light out. All of us." She looked at Bones.

The dog barked and nodded. They had a plan—at least part of one.

The men instructed Jenny to take her time getting ready, to grab a shower while the three of them argued about the next steps.

"What the fuck, man? You want us to just show up and knock on the door? You think they'll send her out?" Leon said incredulously.

Max pointed at him. "You've got a gun."

Leon took the weapon out of a harness he'd strapped on before they'd left Boston. He placed it on the table. "All right, what kind of gun is that?"

Max looked at it and shrugged. "It's a gun."

"It's a Sig P226 9mm semiautomatic handgun." Leon pulled the gun apart. "Twenty-round magazine."

Leon snapped the magazine back with the ball of his hand, then laid it softly on the table again. "What you got?"

Max shook his head. "I don't have a gun."

"You don't have a gun?" Leon said. "What's your plan then? We back to knocking nicely on the front door?"

Max pounded his fist on the table. "I'm going to get her one way or another. I've got to."

Leon looked away from him. "John, do you have any guns?"

John shrugged, then said, "Jenny does."

Leon squished up his face. "The little blue gun? The .22 she got from Kate?"

Bones barked and nodded.

"Stop doing that, you're freaking me out," Leon said.

Bones put her paw on the table and inched her face closer to Leon's, challenging him.

Max pulled her by the collar until she was back in her chair.

"Have you ever used a gun, Max?" Leon said.

"No. But I could learn."

Leon stared at him and threw his hand in the air. "Helluva plan."

Max got up, aggressively pushed open the patio door, and stepped outside. He finally lit his cigarette in the freezing cold and inhaled, watching the snow fall around him.

He didn't know what to do. She was out there. Thirty, maybe forty miles away, and she needed help. He *couldn't* and didn't want to imagine the pain she was in or how frightened she must be. Jenny had felt it, though, and he knew from experience that the sensation was real. The visions weren't just images. They were real-life experiences with all the emotional drama attached.

Some visions were more intense than others, but there was a risk of overload if you were unprepared when the feelings rushed at you. He and Sidrah had had similar experiences when they had visions, but Jenny's were usually different. She had more premonitions about something that had yet to pass or a sense that she'd been somewhere or seen something before. Her thoughts and visions weren't quite as emotionally intense.

Until last night, when he'd put her through Sidrah's. He knew it had been a lot for Jenny to feel Sidrah's pain, but there'd been no choice. They just had to get on with it and do what they had to do.

He and Sidrah believed they'd been put together to protect Jenny. That she was a catalyst of good. They were supposed to be her guardian angels, but they'd screwed up.

And now, they might lose everything—each other and maybe their goddamned purpose. *No! That cannot happen.*

He tossed his cigarette into the snow and went inside. Jenny was back in the living room, looking vulnerable but determined. He was proud of her strength but felt guilty as hell for everything.

"I'm ready to go," she said with a forced smile.

Max shook his head. "I'm so sorry, Jenny."

Her eyes held the pain of an innocent child. He walked over and embraced her. He hadn't done that yet; it was his nature to avoid physical contact, but it felt good to hold her.

"I let you down. We're going to take care of this. We'll find her," he said before releasing her.

Jenny gave him a soft, tearful smile. "I know you will."

Max thought about the way she'd phrased that, but he didn't ask, and she didn't offer.

Chapter 56

———

It had taken hours, but they'd found the house, Jenny was sure of it. A wave of relief washed over her when it loomed into view. *Oh my God, it worked.* In real life, the one-story house looked small and neglected. Almost abandoned with one window boarded up from the outside.

"I'm positive that's it," she said, sucking in her breath.

They craned their necks as they drove past. Leon twisted in his seat to get a good look.

"That is a long driveway. Nobody's plowed yet either. Are you sure someone is home?"

Jenny felt her nose tingle with the threat of tears. There were things she couldn't tell them about her visions from the night before. Her instinct told her not to. But she said, "Sidrah's inside. I know that much. They drove her here."

Bones barked, jumping nervously in the back. Jenny took that as a sign that she was right.

Clear of the house and driving on a random road, Max said, "Maybe they have a plowing service coming later."

"Maybe," Leon said. "But if I were the kind of person who kidnapped someone, I might be more of the private type."

"Jenny said that in her vision, Sidrah was in the back seat with someone, so we know there are at least two guys in the house," Max said. "They've got to have access to the road eventually. Even if only to get away. There are three ways to do it. Shovel it, use a snowblower, or hire a service."

Jenny closed her eyes and leaned her head against the window. Her dad held her hand while Leon and Max argued. Feeling somewhat relieved about finding Sidrah, she was wiped out from the release of adrenaline.

Leon turned in his seat, fully staring at Max. "We've got to bring the police in."

Max pounded the wheel. "No! We've got to go back and get her. We can lure them outside somehow."

"And what, I'm just supposed to fucking kill some random strangers?" Leon said. "What if it's not even them? What if Jenny's got it wrong? I'm going to prison then, man. Forever. First-degree murder. Are you kidding me?"

"Bones!" Max yelled. "Was Sidrah inside that house?"

They all watched as Bones vigorously nodded her head. Jenny turned to pet her. The dog looked as upset as everyone else.

"Shit, man," Leon said, turning around.

"What if we could get our hands on a plow?" Max said. "A truck with a scoop. We go in there and make a loud mess, hit a tree or something. Then they gotta come outside to check it out. While you're arguing with them outside, I go in and kill any kidnappers inside and free Sidrah. We just take off and run. And you drive away."

"So, I'm driving the truck, and you're doing the killing? You're a history professor, man!" Leon argued.

"We can work that out, but yeah, I can definitely do the killing, no problem. John, do you know any people with a plow service we can borrow a truck from?"

Jenny looked at her dad, who had been focusing on her but following along. She worried about him too. Everyone was in danger, but it felt like a freight train was barreling toward them.

Her dad rubbed his forehead. "I know a guy. Sure. He lives a couple of blocks over. He does some landscaping in the summer months. He's done some tree work for me a few times over the years too. But he gets pretty busy when it snows. They work all night sometimes."

"Then we ask to borrow it at midnight. We need the cover of darkness anyway." Max said. "We give him a midnight deadline and offer him, say a thousand dollars cash to lend it to us. Do you think he'd go for it?"

Leon turned to Max. "You got a thousand bucks on you?"

"No," Max replied. "But we could hit some ATMs. Sidrah gave me a credit card. I'm sure there's a high limit on a cash advance. We could scramble together a thousand bucks between us, right?"

"I've got a card, too," John offered. "I can pitch in. He might go for it. But what would you tell him you need it for?"

"A plowing job for someone in the country," Leon said. "Tell him we'll return the truck by first light."

"I thought you were going to crash it into a tree?" Jenny said.

Leon turned to her. "It's called a lie."

"We can work out the details, but I like it," Max said. "John, when we get home, can you give him a call?"

"I can do that," John said.

Leon shook his head. "I don't know. I don't know."

They continued to argue over the plan throughout the drive, but they all agreed that Jenny wasn't to be a part of the raid and that her dad would stay with her until they got back. Jenny, almost passive to whatever fate had rolling at them now, gave in.

They picked up some fast food off the interstate, and Jenny handed Bones a couple of cheeseburgers, which the dog inhaled in only a couple of gulps. Bones was her touchstone now. She felt drawn to the dog more than any of the humans. Maybe it was because they both had unspoken thoughts. Bones, because she couldn't speak, and Jenny, because she shouldn't tell.

"I think we should get Bones a laptop with big buttons or something so she can talk to us," Jenny distractedly mused as she let the dog lap up the rest of her vanilla shake.

"That's a good idea," Max said from the driver's seat.

Leon turned to Max with an incredulous look. "I can't believe you haven't been doing that all along. If I had a dog like that, I'd want to know what she was thinking about. Imagine what that would be like?"

Jenny leaned forward. "Maybe the distraction will help while we wait. We could put something together."

"Like what? She can't read," her dad said, but then twisted to look at Bones. "Can you?"

Bones shook her head.

Her dad smiled. "Guess that's a no."

Jenny returned the tender smile, glad to have him so near.

Leon glared at the dog from the front seat. "She has got to stop doing that!"

Jenny stroked the dog's head when Bones laid it on her shoulder. "I'm serious. Let's at least get some picture flash cards together. There's got to be something lying around the house we can start with."

Max shrugged, veering back to the rescue plan. "Only if we don't bring in the useless Palmer cops and the fucking FBI and do it my way."

"That is not off the table," Leon said.

Jenny slumped back, resigned, and listened to them argue. She knew what they should do and wanted to chime in, but they needed to come to it themselves.

In the end, they drove through a bank, and Max got eight hundred dollars cash, the limit on Sidrah's card, and four hundred on his. Her dad popped his card in and retrieved another four hundred, and Leon did the same. They stopped at a Walmart and followed Max around as he loaded a cart with warm outerwear clothing, knives, and new boots for him and Leon. Jenny made them take a small detour to toys and got some communication cards and a play pad for teaching letters and numbers. She knew some of what was to come, and they had a long day ahead to keep their minds occupied. It would be difficult for all of them. But by this time tomorrow, they'd find out their fate.

When they arrived home, Jenny went up to her room to get a sweatshirt. She'd only worn a long-sleeved T-shirt under her jacket, but now that they were back, she wanted to be warm in the drafty living room. She reached into her closet and paused. By habit, she grabbed for her favorite hoodie with holes. She hadn't brought it to Wellesley with her, but it had always been her go-to comfy item when she'd been in high school. The pause now, though, came because she'd seen herself in the sweatshirt on this fateful night but hadn't remembered until this moment that she'd been wearing it.

She took the sweatshirt off its hanger and pulled it over her head. Even she had to abide by what was already written. She went downstairs and watched the men cut the tags off the new clothes and unpack the shopping bags.

"Where's Bones?" she said, looking around.

Max pointed with his new jackknife. "In the dining room."

Jenny found her lying in a corner. "What are you doing?" she asked, standing over the dog.

Bones stared up at her and yawned.

"You don't have to learn to read today, girl. Come on. I'm tired too," she said as she walked out and waved for the dog to follow. But Bones didn't follow, and Jenny lay on the living room sofa, wondering why. She grabbed a blanket and pulled it over her. The men were still arguing, but they had her new gun on the table, and Leon was taking it apart then seeing how it fit in Max's hand. Not very well, apparently.

Sleep pulled at her, and she closed her eyes in exhaustion. Her mind went directly to Sidrah. She could feel her fear but not as intensely as she had during the dream. The entire thing had been projected in fast clips. It was tough to put together, but she knew that nothing was going to happen until dark. With that thought, she tried to make her mind blank and go to sleep. Maybe something else would come to her if she did. It was all she had.

She woke with a start and sat up. The men were sitting around the table, quietly playing cards. It was nearly dark outside, and she realized she'd slept a long time. Her dad smiled at her, his brows raised, questioning her condition. She managed a small smile back. Leon and Max turned to look at her too.

"You all right?" Max asked.

"Yeah. Anything happen while I was out?"

Her dad got up from the table with his cup and walked into the kitchen. "I made some hot chocolate. You want a cup, Jenny?" He dipped his head and gave her an impish smile.

Her dad always thought hot chocolate solved everything. He'd tried every recipe and variation on it but usually went with his default of whole milk and chocolate syrup with marshmallows.

"Sure," she said, throwing off the blanket and getting up.

"Did you have any dreams?" Max asked, his face anxious.

She shook her head. "No. I was just out."

She sat at the table next to them, noticing that the scorecard next to Max was empty. It looked more like they were just going through the motions. "Where's Bones?" she said, looking around.

"Still in the dining room," Leon said. "She won't come out."

Jenny got up and peered around the corner. Bones was lying there, wagging her tail. She bent down to pet her. "Hey, girl, what are you doing? Why don't you sit with us?"

Bones shook her head. Jenny didn't understand, but she kissed her. "Okay."

She stood up and went to sit at the table. "So, what have you decided?" she asked.

"We're going later tonight," Max said. "At midnight."

Jenny bit her bottom lip and nodded. She'd known it was coming.

Her dad came in with the hot mug and placed it in front of her. "Now that you're up and the snow has stopped, I thought I'd get out there and plow again."

She looked out the window. For the first time, she noticed the distant sounds of someone else doing the same.

Max looked at her. "You and your dad will have to lock up tight after we leave. I'm leaving Bones here too. Your dad has a pellet gun. It looks kind of threatening and could do some damage."

Her dad pointed to the corner where the rifle stood. He'd had the gun since he was a boy. She'd seen it before, but she'd never seen him use it.

"Does it have any pellets in it?" she asked.

Her dad nodded. "We oiled it and cleaned it up a bit. It works. I tried it out in the backyard. I knocked some snow down from a tree."

He looked proud of himself, but she knew he must be scared too. Her strength wavered. "Why don't we call the police. They could send someone over to help, couldn't they?"

"I'll call them before we leave and ask them to keep an eye out over here, but I don't want to fast track their involvement," Max said. "Things have changed now that we know where Sidrah is. If we don't pressure the police, we can keep them and the FBI out of this for another day. I spoke with Detective Bodine too. He said it's not his juris-diction and that we'd have to work through the Palmer PD.

"I just need this one chance, Jenny," Max practically pleaded. "I've got to do this. We've got the plow truck set up. We gave him a $750 deposit. We can pick it up after midnight."

"I guess I've missed a lot," Jenny said.

"I don't want to walk the police through the psychic dreams and tell them we know she's inside that particular house," Max continued. "They won't believe you or me. They might mess it up or put the place under surveillance. Or worse, they might somehow believe us and turn it into a police circus with a hostage team lighting the place up. The element of surprise is on our side right now. With just the two of us, we can do it fast."

She pressed her lips together, her knees under the table too, trying to look calm. "You know you could get killed? That Leon could get killed? And Sidrah too."

Max inhaled. "Did you see that happening?"

She didn't answer. "Did Detective Bodine go to Turner's house? Did he question him? Boston is his jurisdiction."

"He tried," Max said. "Turner wasn't home. He's probably with Sidrah. The man needs dying, Jenny, but the cops might not see it that way."

Jenny looked out the front window. She closed her eyes and listened for any noise, any internal messages that she needed to respond to. She came up empty.

Max pressed on. "We're supposed to do this. Turner is a threat to you, to all of us. This has got to end. There's a reason we came together. Maybe this is it."

Jenny looked at him. He was so sure and being so incredibly brave. She needed to be brave, too, no matter what. He was right on all counts, and Sidrah, the love of his life and a wonderful person, was out there waiting for them, communicating as hard as she could. She needed to be saved. The end.

"Jenny," Max said softly. "You didn't answer my question. Did you see any of us getting killed?"

She hung her head. "No," she said softly.

She heard Max let out his breath. "Okay, then. It's settled."

Jenny got up from the table and went into the dining room to be with Bones. She didn't want to look at any of them because she didn't want to tell them about the blood. She didn't know whose it was. But it had been spread all over her favorite hoodie.

Chapter 57

Friday Morning

Turner watched, almost laughing, as Max and the black guy came out of the garage door and got into the Jeep parked on the newly plowed driveway. The garage door rolled back down as the car started up.

"It's like shooting fish." He smiled and inhaled with satisfaction as the idiots drove down the street. It most likely wouldn't matter where they were going. He'd be inside the house in a matter of minutes, and once he was inside, no one could stop him.

He slid out of the dark van. The interior light had been disengaged so that no one would be alerted to his presence. With his tools in one pocket, his Beretta and sound suppressor in the other, he jogged to the side of the Gallagher garage and tried the handle. Still locked. Using his tools, he opened the door quietly and entered the garage. After shutting the door, he made his way past the hood of the car to the house's interior door.

He retrieved the Beretta and twisted the silencer into place before releasing the safety. With one hand holding the gun at the ready, the other on the doorknob, he leaned in, listening for any sound on the other side. Nothing. He twisted the knob and pressed the door open.

The long, narrow kitchen beyond stood empty, lit only by a fluorescent light under one cabinet. Turner's eyes swept the length of the room and into another room beyond. He inhaled deeply, certain he could smell his prey and imminent victory over her. After padding softly through the kitchen, he turned to enter the living room and walked straight into the barrel of a rifle.

"Stop, or I'll shoot," the male voice said.

Turner looked at the weapon and nearly laughed. "With that?" Turner jerked his gun up and shot John Gallagher in the chest. He and the weapon fell to the floor.

"Dad!" Jenny screamed. She jumped to her father's aid.

Turner breathed in the smell of the fresh blood, savoring it, watching in fascination as Jenny's aura throbbed with white light. He'd never witnessed someone so strong, so vibrant, so simply good. Their energies together in the same room were like magnets—both repelling and attracting. The experience was powerfully invigorating. His senses burned.

"Jenny Gallagher. Tonight, I meet you. After all these years, all these lives we've lived—you and me! And finally, this time, I've gained a solid foothold. My work will live forever, growing and growing, because you won't be alive to stop it. Not this time."

His antithesis crouched before him, holding her bleeding father, her eyes growing wider by the moment. It was delicious watching her fear grow, it was . . .

From out of nowhere, a massive weight slammed Turner to the ground. Something, a beast, ripped at him, tearing at his face. He flailed and screamed, punching, pulling at fur, trying to push away from the penetrating teeth. He dropped his gun as his hands flew to the missing part of his face and throat. Hot blood poured out of it, spraying into his eyes. Red, red, red. And a red dog. The goddammed dog's teeth glistened with his blood, a part of his face hanging from its fangs.

A white aura stood before him, pulsing hot and brilliant. His own gun leveled at him.

No.

Chapter 58

FRIDAY NIGHT

Max and Leon drove separately, Max leading the way in the Jeep, Leon following behind in the Ford F250 with the snow blade. He got Leon on speaker once they started out.

"This rig is all right," Leon said. "The guy didn't seem all that enthused as he walked me through the controls, though."

"He got his money. I wrote a will before I left, instructing John to reimburse the guy for the truck if something happens."

"You wrote a will?" Leon said, his tone incredulous.

Max smiled as his headlights lit up the dark, empty freeway. He felt an indescribable sense of relief now that he was finally on the way to get her. "I left something in there for you too. Sidrah will take care of it."

Max listened to the silence for a bit until Leon said, "You know we're going to prison. Either way. If you kill someone or I kill or wound someone, vigilante justice is still a crime."

A side of his mouth went up, and he looked into his rearview mirror at the plow truck following him, driven by someone who had become his closest friend. Other than his father, Leon was the only man in the world who knew his secrets. "I've got a plan."

"You got a plan. You wanna tell me about it? Is now a good time?" Leon said sarcastically.

"We don't talk to anyone. No one. We get a lawyer. Sidrah will pay for a damn good one. Then we negotiate together, but only with the FBI."

Max could almost hear Leon's mind working, putting it together.

"You're going to offer up your services?" Leon asked.

Max looked at his hands, ungloved on the wheel of his car. He wouldn't be able to wear them when he used the gun either. His finger needed to feel the trigger. "Yup. The government might find our services useful."

"Did you check with Jenny before you decided to sell her out?"

"No."

There was silence again until Leon came back. "This is assuming we don't get killed."

"Right," said Max.

"Once the bullets start flying, the cat's out of the bag. And it's a dead cat. You gotta commit yourself to go the distance. We have to assume there are at least two guys in there, maybe three. You think more?" Leon asked.

Max smiled slyly. "Maybe the entire Bolivian army."

"Fuck you," Leon said.

They drove in silence for a while until they reached the Southwick exit. Once they had driven through the city, past the Dunkin' Donuts, and were in the country, he said, "Thanks for this, Leon. For everything."

"Yeah. You got a nice family, Max. Let's get that lady of yours home."

They arrived a block away from the house, and Max pulled to the side and cut the engine, leaving the keys behind in the ignition. He gave a final head jut to Leon as he pulled his black hat down over his head, then made off into the woods toward the back of the house. He worked hard, pumping his legs through the deep snow. His adrenaline was in high gear, and he felt like he could run forever. Leon said he'd give him ten minutes to get into place before he came up the road with the plow.

Max reached the edge of the property and stopped at the tree line, taking in the scene. The long driveway had not been plowed, but a section near the carport was clear behind a Subaru Forester. A shovel was propped near it. He went to the right-side passenger door, closed his eyes, and placed his hands on the cold metal. He saw a lot of activity, people and faces, but Sidrah's was there in the mix.

His heart thudding, he glared at the back of the small ranch house. There was no doubt at all that she was inside. He crept behind the carport, concealing himself, and pulled out his phone to text Leon.

Touched the car. We're at the right place. Drive not plowed. They tried shoveling. I'm in place out back. Glass door off patio.

Leon texted:

Shoot the glass once someone comes outside. I'm coming.

Max closed his eyes. He took a deep breath to control his shaking. *Please, God, if you're listening, let her be alive.* He waited behind the carport until he saw the lights of the plow, blade down, coming up the driveway like a beast from hell, straight at him. The bright lights nearly blinded him as he crept to the side of the house and peered around the corner, waiting for the action.

Leon put the truck in Reverse, then pushed some more snow up toward the tree line. He put it in Reverse again and then in Neutral, noisily revving the engine. Finally, he shifted to Drive and plowed forward past Max until he'd pushed a ton of snow into the back of the Subaru. The little shovel disappeared under the pile along with the back end of the car. The outdoor lights flipped on.

Leon put it in Reverse again and went all the way down the drive and back up with another load, heading for the carport. Then, he stopped. Someone stalked outside, waving his arms at the plow.

That was Max's signal. He went over to the sliding door and put a couple of bullets through it. It shattered, and glass rained down. He stepped through, adjusting his vision as someone ran toward him, his gun out. Max shot off as many rounds as he could until he was thrown backward, hit in the shoulder.

He bounced off the wall, hearing the loud pops of gunshots coming from outside. With his one good hand, he swung his gun out, frantically searching for more enemies. He stopped when he saw his guy lying sideways on the carpet. He was not getting up. Sweat poured down his back as he picked up the guy's gun. Violent images engulfed him, but he ignored them and kicked at the man. He didn't move.

He stowed the guy's weapon in his jacket pocket, and with his blue gun up, he peered around a hallway corner. Seeing no movement, he edged down the hall and stopped at a door with a deadbolt on the outside. He flipped the lock, again almost overcome with images, and went inside.

Sidrah was lying motionless on the floor. He dropped to

his knees, his breath ragged, and cupped her head. "Sidrah," he said.

She opened her eyes. "Max."

"Baby, baby," he said, kissing her face and pulling her up. "We've got to move. Are you hurt?"

Her eyes rolled a bit in her head—confused or maybe drugged. "Max, Bones," she said.

The pain from his shoulder hurt like a son of a bitch as he tried to move her, but he whipped his gun back toward the door when he saw movement.

"It's me." Leon pulled his weapon back.

Max let out a shaky breath as Leon entered, his gun out. "Thank God she's alive. Did you check the other rooms, the basement?" Leon asked.

"No," said Max, grabbing his shoulder.

"Can you get her to the truck?" Leon said. "How bad are you hurt?"

Max put his free hand on Sidrah and tried to yank her up. "I got her."

Leon nodded. "Stop bleeding all over the place. I'll meet you at the truck. Go out the front."

He disappeared as Max hoisted Sidrah with all his might. As she started to come around a bit, she tried to help, but like a bad drunk. She began to cry as she lurched forward with him. At last, they escaped into the night air, passing a guy lying in the snow on the way. A spreading pool of blood seeped into the snow around him as he groaned and curled into the fetal position.

Max pushed her into the truck, and she lay over the console while he got inside. It was a tight fit, so she rested on his lap, her arms around his neck. She kissed him again and again, killing him with pain until she straightened up.

"You're bleeding," she said.

For the first time, he saw a real light in her eyes. She was there. Fully awake. He looked past her to the house, worried about Leon. Sweat ran down his face, and he struggled not to pass out. The gun still in his hand, he wobbled, trying to get her to move so he could go back inside, but she pressed him down. "We've got to get to a hospital."

"Leon," he groaned.

"Max, Max!" his beloved's voice called his name. It grew faint until the darkness overcame him.

Leon used the towel, roughly wiping down every surface he could find in Sidrah's room. There was nothing he could do about the trail of blood Max had left on the carpet. He hadn't found anyone in the other bedroom, and other than the dead guy in the living room, there was only the basement. He'd pushed a table in front of the door and wiped his prints, then worked on the rest of the house. It was a longshot because he had no idea where Sidrah had been hanging out. But if he could get rid of her prints, the cops might never know she'd been inside.

He picked up her purse, the blanket, and towel, and cleaned the doorknob on the way out. After turning off the outdoor lights, he shut the front door and ran past the moaning guy in the yard.

When the guy had come out, livid, Leon had put up his hands and shrugged like an idiot before he grabbed his Sig P226 9mm and jumped out of the truck hot. He hadn't hesitated. He'd shot the guy in the balls. Once he went down, he'd searched him and found a gun. He'd stowed it in his pocket and then shot him in the kneecap with his own before running inside.

He'd been careful when he entered and taken a few steps into the living room. Cold air blew inside, and what looked a lot like a dead guy was on the floor, lying on his side. He'd backed out of the room, his gun at the ready when he'd heard Max's voice say, "Sidrah."

He'd walked down the hall and came upon them. Relief that they were both alive flooded through him, but neither of them was in good shape. After issuing instructions, he got back to work.

Now, he ran past the headlights of the truck and stopped to pull on a glove. He yanked fetal-position guy's gun out of his pocket and heaved it into the woods.

Sidrah yelled at him from the truck. "He's been shot, we've got to get him to the hospital."

Leon went over to the open passenger door and leaned inside. "Glad you're all right, Sidrah," he said, seeing that Max was passed out. No help for that. He ran his hands over Max's pockets, searching for any bad guys' guns. They'd talked about this. He found one, not the little blue one, and wiped it clean before he threw it too into the woods.

"Hurry," she said.

He slammed the passenger door and ran around to his side. He jumped in and tossed the items he was holding toward her, then threw the truck into Reverse. Trying hard to focus on his driving, he pointed to his phone lying in a cup near the console. "We've got to find a hospital."

Tears ran down Sidrah's face, and her hand shook as she reached for the phone. She was positioned on her side, smashed into the small space, practically on top of Max's body.

"Turner wasn't inside. He wasn't inside," he said as he

drove as fast as he could safely down the country road toward the interstate.

He glanced over at Max. He didn't look too good, still unconscious. "Can you put some pressure on the wound?"

She had the phone in her two hands, shaking. "Ah, ah, go to Springfield."

The calming voice of the navigation system from the phone said:

Take the exit. Turn left onto MA-57 East.

"How far is it?" Leon asked.

"Thirty minutes," Sidrah said.

Leon drove. Sidrah tried to rouse and help Max. "You can't die on me, Max. Stay with me. *Please*," she begged. She tore at his clothes and found the wound, then pushed the blanket on top of it.

"Hurry, Leon!"

"I need his gun. Find his gun, Sidrah. It's blue."

"It's on the floorboard."

He focused on the road—for now, that was his job. He tried to push his worry out of his mind.

When they arrived at the hospital, he rushed around to the passenger door and lifted Max down. Sidrah looked weak too, but she'd been gaining strength as they drove.

"They have a helicopter here," she said, stumbling forward. "We can get him to Boston."

He didn't know if Max would make it that far. Once through the automatic door, Sidrah began screaming for help. A guard standing at the entrance rushed over, and a nurse and other staff joined.

"He's been shot in the shoulder," Sidrah said to the nurse as she, Max, and Leon practically fell in a heap onto the floor.

The medical staff went into action, and Max was whisked away. Someone held Sidrah back as she begged to follow.

Leon grabbed her by the shoulders and pulled her to the side. "Listen to me, listen to me, Sidrah," he said. "You gotta cover our asses. Don't talk to anyone. It never happened. I'm going back out to the truck to get your purse. Then you stay here. I've got to get to Jenny."

Sidrah's eyes grew impossibly wide, and she swayed. He pushed her into a chair. "I'll be right back."

He ran past the security guard and said, "I'm going to bring in her purse, then I'm going to move the truck."

Leon dashed outside, stashed the blue gun which was lying on the floorboard into the center console, then got Sidrah's purse together. He slammed the passenger door and walked back inside. Sidrah was thoroughly shaking when he brought it to her.

Fuck, she's going into shock.

He ran to the triage desk. "She's in shock," he said, pointing to Sidrah. "She needs help, too. Right away."

The nurse signaled for someone, and they walked into the waiting area toward Sidrah. He backed up and out of the room. "I'm just going to move the car," he said.

He turned and left. He got back in the cab and headed for the interstate. He had to get to Palmer, fast.

Chapter 59

Leon drove the next twenty miles as fast as he could, but held himself in check, trying to keep the speedometer only five to ten miles over the limit. There were two weapons in the truck, both of which were likely murder weapons. Max's blood was all over his jacket. He looked like hell.

He didn't know what he was going to find in Palmer, but they'd been gone for hours, and it scared the shit out of him. Turner Black had not been at the house with Sidrah. If this was his show, then where the fuck was he, and what were his intentions?

He didn't think the man had been in the basement. From what he got from Sidrah and Max, the guy was walking evil. That scared the shit out of him too. The entire job had been crazy—not just tonight. But he'd reconciled the strangeness of it all and figured if this was his destiny, then it was a damn good one.

The miles to Palmer took about twenty minutes, his mind reeling with thoughts about how to cover their tracks as he drove. Sidrah would snap out of it, she'd come around and take charge of the scene. But she didn't have a phone. Max had his, but he'd been rushed out. Sidrah would cover for them. She'd get it together. She'd been through a lot, but the woman was smart, and she'd heard him. He hoped.

He thought about the guns too. They were screaming at him, but no way was he going to get rid of them until he had to.

Once in Palmer, he drove to Bittersweet Drive. "Shit," he yelled. Cop cars surrounded the house. He pulled over and removed his gun from his pocket, stowing it in the center console before getting out. A black man, covered in blood with a gun in his pocket, was a bad combination. He thanked God that his jacket was a dark color as he forced himself to walk in a nonthreatening manner toward the closest cop, who was standing near the front door. "I'm family," he said. "What's going on? Jenny and John Gallagher, are they all right?"

The cop looked him over. "Family?"

Leon did not want an altercation but said, voice raised, "Yeah. Practically."

The cop was pointing him away from the house, directing him to leave, when Leon heard a dog bark inside.

"Bones!" he yelled. Her face looked down at him from an upstairs bedroom window. Frantic now to get inside and find out what had happened, he yelled again to her. "Bones!"

Another cop came to the front door.

"What's going on here? Who are you?"

Leon shook his head. "Where are they? Tell me!"

Bones began to bark hard and fast. The cop turned his head and looked up toward the noise. "You know the family?"

"Yes! Yes. Are they hurt?" He craned his neck, trying to see inside as he took a step forward, but the cop put up his hand to stop him.

"You can't come in; this is a crime scene."

"For God's sake, please tell me what happened," he begged, stepping back.

Bones was going crazy, and the cop looked up again as if trying to make a decision. "John Gallagher was wounded. His daughter rode with him to the hospital."

His heart sank. "What? Jenny's okay?"

The cop nodded. "How do you know the family?"

Leon backed up further. "I gotta get to her. What hospital?"

Bones began howling, and he stopped. "Can I take the dog? She knows me. We're good friends."

"What's your name? We need to ask you some questions."

"All right, all right," he said. "The name's Leon Baird. I'm private security from Boston and was hired by the family to watch over Jenny Gallagher. You can talk to Detective Bodine, D-4 Station, Boston PD. He'll vouch for me. We had an emergency somewhere else, I, I had to leave," he stammered.

The cops looked at each other like they thought he was scum. "You know something about why Jenny Gallagher may have killed an intruder?"

Shit. Had to be Turner.

Leon did not want to get embroiled in any kind of interview. It was all about Jenny and John. "What? No, I don't know what happened. Just give me the dog. She's going crazy."

The cop yelled back to someone in the house. "You find a leash for the dog?"

"She doesn't need a leash," Leon said. "Just go to the door and tell her you'll open it if she behaves. Tell her that she's going with Leon."

The cop gave him an incredulous look but issued the instruction. He then eyeballed Leon, giving him the stink eye. "That dog was passive as can be when we got here. Just lying near John Gallagher, protecting him, but she was messing with the scene. We had to lock her upstairs. She cooperated well enough. I don't know what all this sudden barking is about now though."

"Like I said, she knows me. What hospital did you say they went to?"

"Baystate, near I-90, last I heard," the first cop offered. The second frowned at him.

Leon absorbed the information as the three of them watched Bones walk calmly down the stairs and to the front door. Her face was bloody. *Fuck.* Leon wiped his hand over his mouth and walked backward, then dropped to a knee in the snow. Extending his arms, he welcomed her. Bones sat calmly in front of him and whimpered. He hugged her. "It's okay. We got her," he whispered.

He stood up and started walking down the sidewalk with the dog, still trying to play it cool.

"I'll have an officer escort you to the hospital," the cop said. "We need to ask you some more questions."

"You got it!" Leon said as he smiled down at Bones. She gave him a bloody smile back. "Damn, you look creepy. Come here." He kneeled again. "We gotta clean you up." Bones calmly sat while Leon used some snow and his jacket to clean the blood off her face. It would be nice cover if someone saw the blood on his jacket in the harsh hospital lights.

Bones licked him.

He recoiled. "Don't do that! You're nasty."

She gave him a wink.

Leon stood up, his face a bit grim, and head-gestured the dog to follow him. They walked down the street toward the truck. He had to break the bad news. "Max was shot in the shoulder. Sidrah is with him at the hospital, but I don't have an update."

Bones stopped in the street, and Leon turned to look at her. If he knew what sorrow looked like on a dog, he might say that's what he saw. He swallowed hard, trying not to cry himself as he assessed all the damage.

"Come on," he said. He walked over to the truck and opened the door. Bones jumped inside and over the center console to make room for him. The cab smelled like blood. The owner was going to be pissed off when he got his rig back. But then again, if he didn't make a move soon, it might be impounded as evidence.

He closed the door and started the engine, watching a cop get into his own vehicle and look at him with suspicion. "They got a lot of questions, and I've got two hot guns here. I need to get rid of them fast. I don't know what to do."

He put the truck in gear and looked at Bones. "You did good. I don't know what happened, but I hope to God John makes it."

He drove down the dark road back to the interstate, and Bones gave him a soft growl and a yap, then put her paw on the button to lower the window. Cold air shot into the cab.

"What are you doing?" Leon asked.

Bones smiled at him, then looked straight ahead. Once they came to a stop at a streetlight, she head-gestured at him. Then, she jumped out of the window.

"What the hell!" Leon said as he threw the truck into Park. The cop rolled up behind him, and he watched Bones run into a field. He thought he knew what she was up to, so he grabbed the two guns from the center console and stuffed them into his pockets.

"This better fucking work," he mumbled, scared, as he got out of the cab and faced the headlights of the cop car. He shrugged and pointed to the field. He cupped his hands around his mouth and hollered, "I'll get her."

He ran into the field after Bones and found her digging a hole in the dark ground. She whimpered as he put the guns into the hole, and both of them worked to cover the mound. "Goddammit." He got up, shaking, and grabbed her by the collar. They walked back to the truck. "Look contrite, for God's sake."

Bones hung her head and put her tail between her legs as Leon dragged her back to the truck. She jumped back inside, and he waved to the cop, their journey outside done in less than two minutes.

He was breathing hard, his eyes stuck on wide, as he went through the intersection. Bones snickered in a doggy way. He gave her a sidelong glance and smiled. "Thanks, partner."

Chapter 60

It smells like a garden in here." Max waved his hand in front of his face as Sidrah came out of the hospital bathroom with another bouquet of fresh flowers.

"Heroes deserve flowers, Max." Sidrah smiled and winked at John Gallagher, propped up in his bed, looking for the first time as if he might survive his injuries. Jenny stood next to him, her sad countenance and fear only just beginning to abate from their ordeal.

"I didn't get any flowers," Max commented, readjusting his shoulder, still in a sling. Bones, now wearing her official service dog vest that Sidrah had purchased from Amazon, lay at Jenny's feet, shrugging her shoulders in laughter. Jenny's smile of approval as she reached down to pet the dog pleased Sidrah immensely.

Sidrah put the flowers down and kissed Max softly. "You got me," she whispered to the look of love gathered in his eyes.

She inhaled the bouquet, luxuriating in the fragrance and the feeling of contentment that her family surrounded her, alive and recovering. It was a miracle they'd all come out physically intact, but they were definitely still raw over the emotional damage.

The door opened, and Leon came into the room, his arms full of McDonald's. Bones, to her credit, restrained herself from mauling him, but she sat at attention.

"Okay, I bought out the place," Leon said as Jenny made room on her father's swing table for the food. "Maybe the grease will knock out the stink of the flowers," he said, glaring at the abundance of blooms and balloons cluttering the Boston hospital room.

Sidrah smiled, recalling John's and Jenny's reactions when they had entered the room for the first time. The helicopter ride to transfer John to Mass General had only been possible two days prior. John Gallagher had been officially declared stable, but he had a long way to go.

Max accepted the unwrapped burger from Jenny and ate with one gloved hand. He, too, would have months of therapy and recovery, but Sidrah was not daunted, knowing what a team of private therapists and proper facilities could accomplish. They could still travel; the entourage would just be larger.

Leon stood propped against the wall, eating fries out of his carton. "The cops aren't done with us, you know. I just got another call from Bodine. He told me a detective from Palmer called him, asking questions about my role. Specifically, why I left my client and was driving around Palmer in a snowplow. They're meeting this afternoon. Anyone care to be a representative and answer some questions?"

Sidrah stood straight and shook her head. "No. The lawyers can manage any requests. They don't get to question any of us without a court order."

The legal aspects had been tricky, and they'd discussed covering their tracks and all the issues many times. While Max had been in surgery, she'd received food, glucose, and coffee. As the drugs from her kidnapping began to wear off, she'd wrangled a cell phone from a kind nurse and got to work, getting her law firm out of bed and criminal attorneys to cover them all. One went to Palmer to help Leon, Jenny, and John, and another went to Springfield to cover her and Max.

The Springfield police had been alerted to Max as a shooting victim, and they had stopped in to her emergency room bay to ask her questions. But they had no idea about her kidnapping. She'd understood what Leon had been implying before he left, and she'd feigned illness, not answering the cops' questions until her lawyer arrived. Once there, she'd let the lawyer in on some of the details, saying that she had accidentally shot Max in the shoulder while playing with a gun. She claimed that overcome with confusion, she had thrown the gun into the Mill River on the way to the hospital. Her reported disappearance to the Palmer police had been painted as a misunderstanding as well.

The lawyer bought and sold it, and when Max came out of anesthesia after surgery, she'd whispered an update in his ear. He'd understood. Then he'd asked about the others. They were sick over John and Jenny and what happened at the house with Turner Black, and prayed for a good outcome. They were grateful that Jenny had Leon and a lawyer near her.

In various ways, it had been one step at a time on several fronts. The shooting of Turner Black had been questioned but accepted as self-defense. The police had found Turner's van with the surveillance equipment inside, and the gun, which had shot both him and John Gallagher, was registered in his name. They'd also discovered the locksmith tools in his pocket. Jenny and John, never without legal counsel, claimed no knowledge of the motives behind Turner's interest in them. Because Turner Black, a prominent Boston attorney, had been killed by a dog and young girl from Palmer after breaking into their home and shooting the girl's father, the story had made the news. The cops, stymied for the reasons why, were digging but getting nowhere.

The murders at the kidnapping house outside Southwick were being investigated, but there'd been a merciful delay. Snow had covered the body outside, and the scene hadn't been discovered for weeks because of its remote location and long driveway. This had allowed Leon and Sidrah to remove Max's car from the vicinity, away from the tracks leading directly from Max's car to the house. Leon had bitched loudly at this mistake as well as throwing the kidnappers' guns *toward* the snow tracks leading back to the car. He'd blamed "emotional distraction and undue pressure to implement a sloppy and bullshit plan."

After gathering information from the news, it appeared that the cops were convinced the shootings outside Southwick were some kind of drug crime gone wrong. Both the victims had long arrest records. The group of survivors guessed the cops would look at the guns found in the woods for evidence of additional crimes. They all assumed they would find something on them.

The group thanked God that the bullet that had hit Max had traveled through him and that no ballistics could be done that would tie his shooting to the weapons found outside Southwick. Max had left his blood and DNA at the crime scene, but unless they put his own shooting together with the corpses at the kidnapping house, it would lead nowhere. They all doubted the cops would dig too deep for explanations.

Their own guns, including the little blue one, had been recovered from the hole in the ground and also tossed in the unfrozen river.

Leon brushed the salt off his hands, then stopped, shaking his head at the group. "Am I the only one with a job here?"

Sidrah ignored him and walked over to Jenny. She gave her a side hug as they looked down at John. He managed a small smile.

"Thanks for the new sheets," he said to Sidrah. "They feel good."

She pursed her lips, feeling the tingle of emotions and tears trying to burst through, but feigned fortitude. She thought it her job to rally them all back to life and strength. "It's my pleasure, John." She gave him a tender smile, then turned brightly to Jenny. "So. I have an announcement. After your father has recovered, we're all going to Italy. We're leaving in three weeks. I've rented an entire floor in a lovely boutique hotel in Naples. Max's parents have agreed to come. Leon, of course. Bones. We're all going. The pool, the staff, the food, the view, the inner courtyard, the place is a dream. There'll be a full-time nurse for John and a physical therapist. We can travel the country a bit in small groups, and my darling Max can give you a private tutoring experience on the history of the area like no other. The two of you are on sabbatical from Wellesley. We'll take your education on the road."

Jenny's eyes grew large, and she placed a cautious hand on her dad. "Guys, no. Don't you think . . ."

Sidrah knew it was time to push Jenny back out into the world. It was waiting for her. "Jenny," she said, placing a soft finger under the girl's chin. "You've been very brave. We're all proud of you, but now it's time to recover and to be happy. There's work to do. Remember your strength, remember that you did a *good* thing and that there is definitely a higher purpose here for all of us. We'll be here for you, forever."

"Excuse me. Forever?" Leon said. "You might think to ask me about your plans this time before just assuming I'm available."

Bones nodded and smiled.

Leon narrowed his eyes at the dog. "She has got to stop doing that."

About the Author

Annabelle Lewis is a pseudonym for the author who lives in Minneapolis with her husband, children, and a wild thug of a dog who sleeps beside her. Get a glimpse behind the curtain and follow her feverish mind. Sign up for her fun, monthly newsletters and giveaways.

Thank you for your reviews and support!

https://www.theannabellelewis.com
https://www.twitter.com/alewisauthor
https://www.facebook.com/annabellelewisauthor
Annabellelewisauthor@gmail.com

Acknowledgements

I'd like to thank the writers of the Western Suburbs Writers Group for their wonderful help and counsel. This work was my brainchild formulated for the self-competition of NaNoWriMo. It was great fun knocking out the story in record time, so thanks to the organization for developing this writing contest to help authors push ourselves. To my editor, Erin Liles, who then helped me pull apart the fevered original and fix it, I thank you. Your professsionalism and support were priceless.

Made in the USA
Monee, IL
05 March 2021

61958019R00197